THE OTHER PRESIDENT

E.N.J. Carter

PublishAmerica
Baltimore

First printing

ISBN: 1-4137-1958-9
PUBLISHED BY PUBLISHAMERICA, LLLP
www.publishamerica.com
Baltimore

Printed in the United States of America

*This novel is dedicated
to the memory of*

Ron Bissell.

Special thanks to Debra Loven.

CHAPTER 1

What if I just walk away from being President of the United States? Maybe then the dreams will stop, thought Sam Wainwright. After all, in a recent survey only half the country knew who he was anyway.

Sam stood at the middle oval window of the White House Blue Room wearing bikini-style Jockey briefs, his skin still wet from the nightmare. He surveyed the darkness of the South Lawn, but couldn't help noticing the sweet-smelling aftershave lotion of the Secret Service agent.

"It was bad this time, wasn't it Luke?" Sam said without turning around.

"Yes, Mr. President it was."

"The White House was under attack again, Luke, just like the embassy in Saigon."

"You're a lot safer here, Mr. President."

Sam turned to look at Luke Parker, rocking back and forth on his heels, waiting for his President to go back upstairs and get some shuteye.

"That's what the CIA told me in Saigon, Luke."

"We'll make shredded wheat of anyone that comes over the fence, Mr. President. You know that."

Sam wasn't listening. He could still see the North Vietnamese sappers popping out of the ground like mechanical targets. He could still hear the screams of men and women wearing evening clothes begging for their lives, the dull thud of single-pistol shots, the rapid sound of AK-47 rounds. Phosphorous hand grenades exploding like a Fourth of July celebration gone amuck.

In Sam's nightmare it was the Saigon embassy one moment, and the White House the next. There was no real sense of place, just terror.

Sam, of course, was the first to acknowledge that he had other problems with being President than just his safety. He often wondered if he was the only politician to ever hate being President of the United States. He had never wanted the responsibility, or ever dreamed he would have it.

"Get some sleep," Sam said to Parker as he headed for the staircase. When he got to the top of the steps, Sam turned around. Parker was still there, watching him.

The next morning, Sam's doubts about the security of the White House grounds forced him to confide to Luke Parker that he didn't think it was just a bad-dream problem.

The response he got from Parker was predictable: Although terrorist attacks around the world had increased dramatically, particularly against symbols of American power like embassies, they could never get on the White House grounds. The attackers would be pulverized. It was that old *never could happen* — again.

The head of the Secret Service detail may have thought his explanation would suffice, but was told in no uncertain terms by Sam that he wanted a plan for his survival that was based on the White House being overrun by terrorists. Not being *attacked* by terrorists, mind you, but being *overrun* — meaning this President was still standing around when the attackers were coming through the door. Maybe even while he was taking a leak. Or talking politics at a State dinner. Whatever.

"What the hell would happen then?" Sam exclaimed to Parker. "And don't tell me the secret bunker in the East Wing is the answer."

Parker, by all appearances, was still incredulous, knowing full well that the White House grounds could never be overrun, and having stated that position a number of times. Nevertheless, the chief executive was promised a plan within five days. After all, with all their reassurances, no one in the Secret Service detail guarding the President could deny that four Presidents had been assassinated in office.

CHAPTER 2

Three days later, Sam Wainwright was just about to stick a spoon into a grapefruit when Luke Parker entered the small room next to the White House bedroom that Sam used for breakfast. Parker was carrying a black bag. The President smiled to himself. Parker, in hushed tones, made it clear to the President that the backup plan for the White House grounds being overrun by attackers was based on no one else knowing about the plan.

The Secret Service agent took out a fine-looking, mousy-brown hairpiece and explained that the idea was for the President to change his appearance in the unlikely event the White House was ever overrun. He explained that the Ambassador to Greece had done exactly that during a terrorist attack, creating lots of confusion, and giving the Marine guards enough time to regroup and take care of business.

"Sideburns too," asked Sam.

"Yes, sir."

"Ugly horn-rimmed glasses, of course?"

"Yes, sir."

"What about identification?"

Parker took out a wallet and handed it to the President.

Inside there were a number of credit cards and a White House pass. Sam studied the White House pass. It included a photograph of how the President would look with the disguise.

"My name is Eddie O'Hara?"

"Yes, sir. We even put it up on the computer."

"What do I do?"

"Maintenance man."

Sam smiled.

Parker looked concerned, "It's the best plan we could come up with, sir, everything else is already covered."

"No, it's perfect, Luke. Plain common sense, and I like that. Let me see if I look like the photo?" Sam, intrigued by the idea of being someone else, put the hairpiece on, then the sideburns.

"How did you know my head size?"

"Sir, there isn't much about your body we don't know."

"The clap in Danang?"

"Yes, sir that too."

"How do I look?"

"With a pair of jeans, you look very working class, Mr. President."

"You know, that's what they call me, Luke, the Blue Collar President. If it weren't for the Marines paying for most of my education, I'd be filling up gas tanks in Eastern Kentucky."

The look on Parker's face took a serious turn.

"What?"

"Would you allow the terrorists to shoot people if they demanded that you come forward, sir?"

"I don't think so."

"That's the problem with the plan, Mr. President."

Sam smiled. "Well, at least with this disguise I still could go to a few discos and meet some ladies who might not be interested in telling the gossip pages how lousy I am in bed. You know, I wouldn't even need you guys along."

"If that's what you have in mind, Mr. President. I wouldn't suggest it. Because if it is, we'll find a way to screw it up—remember, Mr. President, you're not the first bachelor that's ever been in the White House."

Sam put his spoon down.

"But I'm the first orphan."

Parker smiled.

Sam Wainwright could always get someone to smile, but this was serious. Despite his upward mobility, his first impressions of the world as an orphan stuck in his bones and never stopped reverberating.

Often those impressions were accompanied by instincts that saved him from being a victim of life's uglier moments. Whether it was a tight situation in a schoolyard full of bullies, or leading a patrol through a heavily mined rice paddy, Sam counted on his instincts to guide him through.

Sam went back to attacking his grape fruit. Without looking up he said, "The plan's got a lot of common sense, Luke. I like that."

"Let's hope we never have to use it, Mr. President. One of the agents will carry your alternate identity around in a black bag."

Sam looked up. "That's pretty funny, Luke. The Cold-War look all over again. The President followed by an aide holding a black bag."

Parker smiled, but Sam could see that it was forced. Parker, Sam suspected, believed, that a ground assault on the White House was impossible. But like any good agent guarding the chief executive he would go along with the program. That's what the Secret Service did with every President. Go along with any and all bullshit the President could heave in their direction.

Sam Wainwright took longer than usual to finish his meal. Even with a service staff of ninety-six, he felt alone. He dreaded the walk to the Oval Office and its pressures. He was well aware of the feeling inside the beltway that he had no passion for politics. Oddly, in the beginning, he had agreed to run for Congress with little hope of ever getting elected. It often amazed him how far he had come without planning it, beginning with a battlefield commission from the Marines.

As the President, Sam was secure in the knowledge that he'd been vaccinated against most deadly viruses, and a special ambulance stood by to handle any chemical attacks, but his doubts about the White House grounds persisted. He may have been the most protected human on earth, but he wasn't going to let that fact get in the way of his feelings. He didn't feel safe.

CHAPTER 3

Shelby Mannix was a throwback. The great-great grandson of a Confederate General, Shelby came from a long line of men who had long body trunks that made them look great on a horse. Unfortunately, the Mannix men seemed to have also inherited egos that fit perfectly with the idea of looking down on other people from a commanding height.

As chief coordinator for the Speaker of the House, Shelby wielded a considerable degree of power within the beltway. Particularly since the independent counsel's office had been given the heave ho. Not surprisingly, chief coordinator was not considered the position of a southern gentlemen. "They hire Jews from the North to do that kind of job, don't they, Shelby?" he had heard more than once from his former Citadel classmates.

Shelby, by inclination was a strategist, with a defense lawyer's penchant for investigation. He loved putting the Speaker's opponents in place. Sometimes with good old investigative work, sometimes with Machiavellian planning. In the back of Shelby's mind the concept of being noble was strong, but that's where it belonged— in the back of his mind. The politics of the new millennium didn't allow for such lofty ideals he had learned in the rough and tumble world of inside-the-beltway politics.

In his powerful role, Shelby had waited patiently to go after Sam Wainwright. Not only was Wainwright a member of the opposition, but the best target his party had encountered in a long time.

Shelby's boss, Luther Donald, Speaker of the House had done a good job of weakening the new President by preventing his nomination for Vice-President. It wasn't so much that Wainwright wasn't going to eventually get his way, but the longer the nomination was in doubt, the weaker Sam Wainwright appeared to his opponents and the American public.

Some would say Wainwright was already vulnerable. Foreign policy issues were in the sinkhole. The State Department was eating its young. The dramatic increase in terrorism on Wainwright's watch was now at the dinner-discussion level. Americans just didn't feel safe with Sam Wainwright in office no matter how well intentioned he was.

What's more, his leadership in office seemed static on just about every issue. He just didn't seem up to the job.

He had even been accused of bringing the baggage of low self-esteem to the Presidency, often appearing inadequate when holding discussions with world leaders. Often allowing them to hog the spotlight. Some psychologists attributed Wainwright's poor performance to his being an orphan.

Wainwright had admitted in interviews that the experience of being awakened from deep sleep, and suddenly placed with foster parents, had left emotional scars.

In his Capitol Hill office, five aides sat in front of Shelby, none older than 35. Shelby studied each one for a moment. Not one of them wouldn't turn his mother in for a promotion, he suspected. That was the plus side of this generation, he believed. Each one a product of a corrupt school system that encouraged political correctness to get somewhere instead of brains, but they were deliciously cynical, and he liked that a lot.

"So, what have you barracudas brought to me today?"

"Wainwright is a lousy lover."

"I'll pass on that."

"His support amongst women is dropping dramatically."

"Why is that?" asked Shelby as if he didn't know.

"Well, they all thought he was going to marry the girlfriend, not dump her."

"Who talked to the war buddies?" growled Shelby. Making his impatience known, but realizing that Wainwright had been an elusive subject from the beginning, coming out of nowhere really.

Even heavy digging by the press had turned up little on Sam, precisely because he was an orphan who had been moved around a lot in his youth.

"A few vets say they remember him. That's about it."

Shelby looked at his five young aides. "A man doesn't work his way up from Vietnam grunt to Vice President of the United States without screwing up."

"Maybe we should try and find out what the terrorists have got on him?" peeped a voice from the back of Shelby's office. It was Ruth Hoffman, the sixth and final member of Shelby's staff, and the most senior. She had just entered the room. Shelby didn't trust Ruth. He had inherited her from an influential Senator who had retired, and he couldn't turn her down without causing a lot of angst. She had an agenda, he was sure of it. Sometimes she was there just to spy on him, he suspected.

Of course, her comment was facetious as well. It was plain why terrorists took advantage of Sam Wainwright. He had no balls, concluded Shelby. On the other hand, Wainwright was an ethereal figure. He was hard to grasp, and always underestimated. He wasn't going to be an easy target to disgrace in office. But then again, Presidents never are—God, what he wouldn't do to get in the mind of a terrorist about to do Wainwright in. How would he do it? Shelby wondered in fascination.

CHAPTER 4

On most evenings at the White House there was always one official function or another going on. When he had the opportunity, Sam Wainwright liked to dance with the ladies. As President, however, he wasn't getting the kind of sex he had enjoyed as a flunky Vice-President. He couldn't even get close to his dance partner without it being in the papers the next day.

This evening he wasn't going to have much opportunity for sex, either. It was the State Department dinner for the new Israeli Prime Minister. Always a stiff occasion, he knew. He would have to be dressed and waiting at the North Portico at 7:30 to greet guests. And he could expect the women surreptitiously glancing around to see if he had anyone near his side.

He had long ago decided that there wasn't going to be a woman at his side unless he wanted her there. It seemed to Sam that at one time or another every branch in government had sent over a suggestion for a date, as if it were a *Ms. White House* contest or something, but he had finally put a stop to it. Not to mention turning down the daughters of dozens of Heads of State. But State dinners with Israel made him particularly nervous. Security had to be increased dramatically, which was more than okay with Sam, but then chaos always seemed to accompany State dinners for Israel. In many ways it was a free for all with beltway status seekers, media, and everyone at one time or another, it seemed, who had appeared on the Larry King show. Not to mention his own staff who always found a reason to attend. Israel, without question, had the most powerful lobby in Washington.

During previous functions for Israel, Sam, as Vice President, was well aware that guests seemed to wear their hearts on their sleeves. The President would get pats on the back for bombing terrorists, and remarks like 'Keep up the good work.'

Compliments like that had been very uncomfortable for the former President and now for Sam as well.

The new Israeli Prime Minister was a moderate. Sam had discovered a long time ago that moderates invited the most trouble. Terrorists feared moderates. They did everything they could to end the careers of moderates as early as they could. Possibly the worst thing one could do to someone at one of these State dinners was point to a representative from a Middle East country and say he or she was a moderate. Which meant they probably would never live to see their grandchildren

After the official toast at 8:30, dinner was served. It was Sam's favorite time. The State Dining Room was cozy, and the guests lively. He loved being surrounded by so many warm intelligent bodies. It was a validation of existence, really. Because underneath his sureness of demeanor, lurked a man-child that had grown into manhood with low self-esteem, and absolutely no interest in being the President of the United States.

As far as this evening was concerned it was perfect, Sam decided. He would sleep well tonight. Sometimes he felt a bit like Elvis. There was always a few females more than eager to chat with him before he went upstairs, but he always managed to discipline himself. He had gotten to the White House simply because the former President had died of a stroke and nothing more. That had been five-and-a-half months ago. There was little more than twenty four months left, and then he was out, and glad of it. *How can a man who doesn't even know himself, run the country?* he thought constantly.

Few would suspect what Sam was thinking, but for the first time in a long time he was feeling good as he readied himself for a toast to the new Prime Minister. He heard some shouts emanating from outside the White House, but that was not unusual. Israeli security and the Secret Service were always butting heads.

About to make his toast, Sam paused to look around the room. The bubbly evening seemed self-contained as if it were inside a paper weight ready to be shaken.

Raising a glass filled with California Chardonnay, Sam began to praise the new Prime Minister when the lights suddenly flickered out. There were a number of giggles amongst the guests, but Sam suspected it was more serious. Moments later a hand rested on his shoulder.

"Put this on, Mr. President," said the recognizable voice of Luke Parker. He handed Sam night-vision goggles, waited for the President to put them on, and then led him away from the dinner table. Sam Wainwright could hear the brash remarks, and confusion, emanating from the new Israeli Prime Minister's staff, but tried to stay focused.

"Tell me this is not happening, Luke?"

"The fuckers are over the fence, Mr. President. I can't believe it. They're all over the place. We think it's a decoy; they're going to blow this place. That's our best guess."

Sam couldn't speak. The unthinkable had happened. He had been right all along.

"Chopper One?"

"They've taken it down sir. I know you didn't hear a shot. They are a smooth bunch of bastards."

Jesus! thought Sam, *this is really happening. But why in God's name did the Secret Service think this couldn't happen?*

Now surrounded by a detail of Secret Service, Sam entered a small room just off the State Dining Room. He could hear the sobs of fear emanating from the glitzy diners in the next room. It was horrible. He felt responsible.

Luke Parker handed the President his Eddie-O'Hara kit. Taking off his jeans and sweatshirt, Parker then handed his clothes to the President. "We're going out, sir; this is the best way."

Most of the credit cards fell to the floor. Sam managed to stick the phony White House ID into the back pocket of Luke's jeans, but cut his finger taking off the night-vision goggles. The shirt he handed Parker was slightly bloody. He could hear the gunshots now. *Thank God for the Israelis*, he thought. If anyone could hold those terrorist bastards at bay, it would be them. There seemed to be chaos on the grounds — sweeping lights, rapid gunfire, trucks squealing on the dirt.

"You're going out cannonball, sir."

"Cannonball?"

"We got a souped-up Harley. We think things are going to blow."

There were screams now. Some terrorists had already reached the State Dining Room. The darkness however bought a little more time.

"Stick on the wig and sideburns, sir. It won't hurt. And don't forget this." Parker handed the President a flak jacket as he put on the President's clothes.

Unbelievable, thought Sam Wainwright, *just unbelievable*. But he did what he was told. Sam watched Parker cut an opening in the bulletproof glass with a hand saw, and then waved for the President to step outside. A motorcycle was waiting.

"You coming, Luke?"

"No sir, Mr. President. If they see me they'll know who you are."

Sam could hear the disappointment in Luke Parker's voice.

"It was the part I didn't tell you about, Mr. President. Your plan can only work without your being guarded by someone they can identify. We have to assume you're not going to get outside without being grabbed. Crazy isn't it. One of our new men will take you out."

Sam took one last look at this brave man standing in front of him. "See you later, Luke."

"Yes sir, Mr. President. See you later."

"Hold on goddamn tight, Mr. President," said the agent on the Harley. "Goddamn tight."

And they were off. The distinctive roar of the Harley momentarily drowning out the gunfire and explosions taking place on the South Lawn.

Thank God for the darkness, thought Sam. The Secret Service agent driving the Harley was sure footed and agile and kept screaming, "Cannonball," which Sam guessed was a code word of sorts, and which opened a path through the Marines now on the lawn.

Sam could see the flashes of gunfire popping off all around him like hundreds of flashbulbs going off at once, however the path for the Harley remained clear.

The plan is working, he thought, as they neared the front gate of the North Lawn.

Suddenly, the Harley slowed down and stopped. The agent made a grunting sound, and fell off the bike. As he lay face up in the darkness, the agent said, "Run sir." And stopped breathing.

As an ex-Marine it was distasteful for Sam to leave anyone behind, but as President he knew he had a responsibility to the people of the United States to remain alive.

Just as he bolted for the front gate of the North Lawn, there was a tremendous flash as the White House blew apart. The heat from the blast rushed at Sam like a crashing wave.

Sam Wainwright, alias Eddie O'Hara, flew in the air, his face on fire.

CHAPTER 5

The Speaker of the House was now President of the United States.

Iran, host country for the terrorists, was already being invaded by American and Israeli troops. The White House was a hole in the ground and 361 people were dead including the Israeli Prime Minister.

Using two World War Two British glider planes, thirty-seven terrorists, mostly from Yemen, had flown under radar to penetrate the White House grounds. Then creating a diversion, they quickly assembled a bomb, planted it in a nearby National Park Service truck, and drove it into the White House. The blast made the Oklahoma bombing look like a firecracker. In addition to the dead attending the dinner, including the entire Cabinet, White House staff, press corps, and Marine guards, 171 pedestrians—mostly tourists— were also injured, although many were more than two blocks away when the blast happened. The hospitals were doing their best, but barely coping.

Over fifteen bodies were assumed to have been vaporized by the near-nuclear blast including the body of the President of the United States.

Sam Wainwright was given a State funeral nevertheless.

CHAPTER 6

Reacting to the tragedy quickly, Congress passed an emergency health-relief bill for all innocent victims of the White House bombing. The bill included transportation of burn victims to a U.S. Army medical facility in San Antonio. No expense was to be spared. Some victims — all pedestrians — could not remember who they were. Some would wake up and not be able to recognize themselves. The blast had torn facial muscles and bones apart.

Saint Francis Hospital for Special Surgery in Washington, D.C., one of the best hospitals in the nation for reconstructive surgery, was backed up with victims. Eddie O'Hara, government maintenance man, however, was considered a priority. In addition to his shattered facial bones, most of his nose was gone, but surgeons were hopeful that they could still give Eddie a decent face job. His burns were secondary, but would have to be attended to as well.

Eddie was lucky, he was told, no one had survived within the confines of the White House gates. It was the one time not to be a beltway insider according to the current sick joke in Washington. The common folk were filling the wards. The power brokers were all dead.

The only identification that existed on Eddie was the White House pass with the computer-generated photo. Someone tried to call Eddie's next of kin but couldn't find a listing. The important thing was Congress had made it possible for every American hurt in the bombing to get the best care possible. And that's what was going to be done, was the thinking.

Eddie was in surgery for eight-and-a-half hours. He would not have a great face, but it wouldn't be a bad one either according to the Chief Surgeon. Not even the President, if he had survived, could have had a better job done, was the prevalent point of view. The next step was to treat Eddie's burns at Fort Sam Houston's burn center in San Antonio.

CHAPTER 7

His face covered with bandages like a mummy, Eddie O'Hara could not remember anything as he lay on a stretcher at Andrews Air Force base waiting to be airlifted to San Antonio for head trauma and follow-up treatment of his secondary burns. The constant flash of camera bulbs was numbing. *Who am I?* Eddie kept asking himself without an answer.

The separation of powers created a huge problem for the new President, Luther Donald. He preferred to work in the Capitol building until the White House was restored, but was told by constitutional scholars that his choice was out of the question. It was decided because of security reasons that the Vice President's quarters, located on the grounds of the Naval Observatory, would serve nicely while the White House was being rebuilt. The reception room, living room, sitting room, and sun porch of the three story 19th Century Queen Anne brick building were partitioned off for the new President. Living quarters were upstairs.

Shelby Mannix was given a tiny office less than seventy-five feet from the new President. It was generally understood, that until the official appointment of a Chief of Staff, Shelby Mannix was about as close as you could get to being one. Shelby, however, suspected the President would eventually call on him for help in the investigation of the White House bombing, and his role at the White House would no longer be the same. That's the way Luther Donald worked. But the fact that the attack was successful, was shameful, thought Shelby. *How in God's name did a bunch of terrorists coordinate such a brilliant attack?* Shelby seethed. Heads would roll in the Secret Service and the military, and he would watch them roll. They would goddamn wish they were dead, he thought, as he looked over the list of casualties. There were 361 dead, 171 civilians more or less outside the White House grounds, near dead, and just about hanging on. Bodies and faces mangled. A report to Shelby indicated that surgeons in the emergency wards, overcome with pressure, started referring to their patients as hamburge*r*, and in *triage,* burn classifications were broken down to rare, medium, and well done.

President Luther Donald, Shelby knew from past experience, would already be worried about the agenda of his political opponents. Everything was a fucking agenda with Luther Donald. A fart in the men's room was an agenda to the man. As Speaker of the House, he had brought back fear to first-time members of the House no matter what party they represented. Shelby didn't like Donald, but feared him like everyone else in Washington. Now that Donald was actually the President it was expected that he would be more paranoid than ever. It would be easy to get on his bad side, and Shelby Mannix had no intention of doing so. Shelby was also determined to get enough on the Secret Service to bury the bastards forever. They treated every President like another employee, but that would soon end. There would be no attempts on the new President's life as long as Shelby Mannix was part of the White House staff. Nevertheless, he anxiously awaited the President's instructions on the investigation of the bombing. He knew his role would be major.

Who is Eddie O'Hara? Eddie asked himself as he lay in his oxygen-tent environment. The nurses were nice. The physicians were nice. Everyone was so damn nice, but who was Eddie O'Hara?

A bearded man in a wrinkled doctor's coat peered down at Eddie.

"Mr. O'Hara."

"Yes?"

"I'm Dr. Sullivan. I understand you're having troubling recalling your past?"

"Yes sir."

"Don't worry it will come back slowly."

"I can't remember a thing, doctor."

"It's possible that you're attaching a form of guilt to the blast. You were a maintenance man I understand. Unfortunately, there are no survivors at the White House that can tell us about you. Your personal history is not on the computer either — not unusual for the White House staff, a security precaution really."

"The job description doesn't sound right," uttered Eddie, exhausted after speaking a few words. In addition to his facial injuries, his mouth was wired up, and sometimes his words got distorted.

Dr. Sullivan ignored Eddie's comment. "You've had very extensive reconstructive surgery, Mr. O'Hara. I'm afraid a look in the mirror is not going to help you either. However, in a few months you'll be good as new. I'm here just to reassure you that there's nothing to worry about. Your records are somewhere, and we'll find them. You'll be fixing government toilets, or whatever you do, in no time."

Eddie grimaced under the bandages. He would just have to ride this one out. *Maintenance man? Funny, I don't feel like a maintenance man.*

Luther Donald prowled back and forth in his spacious office. Thanks to Nelson Rockefeller who redid the official residence of the Vice President in the 1970's, it was an office one could pace in very well.

Seated in front of the new President, Shelby Mannix wondered what Donald would ask of him. Donald was still in shock over being the new President, but clearly relishing his new role, and already protective of it.

"We're sure the President is dead?"

"Yes, Mr. President, we are."

"DNA?"

"A shirt obviously blown off the President. Many of the bodies vaporized from the blast. The blood on the shirt matched the President's DNA."

"What's the odds of the President changing his shirt with someone, Shelby?"

"I would say impossible, sir. And hell, everyone at the dinner that night is dead, Mr. President."

Donald, walked to the west wall and looked at the recent portrait of Ronald Reagan that he'd requested. His eyes then rolled over to his prize dueling pistols. Exact replicas of the brass-finish flintlock pistols used in the duel between Aaron Burr and Alexander Hamilton, only these replicas, on closer examination, were capable of firing a .38 round in an emergency. Donald had told Shelby he was the only one who knew the replicas were lethal, and that's how he wanted it.

It was long rumored in the beltway that Donald had offered to duel with a young composer that had an affair with his wife who was President of the National Arts Council at the time. In fact, he had sent his *second* to the composer's residence in Brooklyn, New York, asking him to choose his weapon. When the composer broke down, Donald relented. It was also rumored the act had helped restore Luther Donald's libido.

Turning to Shelby, Donald said, "The FBI has nearly three dozen terrorist bodies on the lawn to keep them occupied with their investigation, but I want to make sure that every American citizen hurt in the blast gets personally spoken to from this office. Do you understand, Shelby?"

Shelby knew Donald, and his indirect, almost Asian way of expressing himself.

"Would you consider that public relations, Mr. President, or an investigation?"

The new President sighed. "It will look like the usual White House spin — we're making sure all the survivors are okay. This will keep the FBI from getting too nervous about us cleaning up the mess."

It was like Donald to end on the punch line. Shelby could see that the President was deciding whether to speak the next sentence. Donald's face grimaced slightly, "I *smell* something here Shelby."

"What would that be, Mr. President?"

"That's it. I just don't know, but something's not right." Donald was from Mississippi and one of the leaders of the new right that had come out of the Sun Belt with their American Roots Program — stop the multiracial buildup of the population, get religion back in schools, put Hollywood on the defensive, get the responsibility of education back to the local level. But above all, keep America *American*.

It was a platform that Shelby Mannix believed in as well, and with as much passion as anyone in the Republican Party.

Shelby said, "They're all gone, Mr. President. Wiped out. There are no loose ends."

Donald took out a sour ball, which he sucked excessively to keep from smoking, "Goddamn it Shelby. I'm sitting in this position because a President died of a stroke and another got blown up. Now that's destiny and I'm not going to let anyone take this moment from us, or the party. We have less than two years to get the steamroller rolling. And I want no screw ups."

"Sam Wainwright is dead, Mr. President. And every name on our injury list is accounted for."

Donald, straightened his bow tie. He looked like an older version of George Will. "This is the most wonderful thing that has ever happened to us, Shelby. A gift from our Founding Fathers. We must do everything we can to take advantage of it."

"I understand, Mr. President."

"We need more information, Shelby. I want to know exactly what happened that night, but make it look like we're just doing a little PR for ourselves."

"I understand, Mr. President."

"The FBI will eventually get around to interviewing the leftover human wrecks from the blast, but I want to be there first."

"I'll personally interview all survivors, Mr. President."

Donald relaxed. "We have to do things right, Shelby. The most votes I ever got were 131,000 as a Congressman."

"You were the most powerful man in the Congress, sir. We shouldn't forget that."

Donald peered at Shelby. "I'm now the President of the United States, Shelby. I'm humbled by it, do you understand?"

"I believe I do, Mr. President."

"I should be sending those terrorists flowers instead of blowing their asses out of Iran," he smiled.

"I believe I understand, Mr. President."

"We're going to change things Shelby. And this time no *Washington Post* liberals — or lefties in our party — are going to stand in our way. We have the government now, Shelby, and we're going to give it back to honest, hard-working Americans of American heritage. Now get your tail out in the field, and give me a report that makes me feel good about holding this office — Americans for America may sound a little corny, Shelby, but that's what we're about."

Shelby walked toward the door. "And there's one other thing, Shelby."

Shelby turned to face the President, "What's that, Mr. President?"

"This is a war. It isn't the North against the South. It's the left against the right, but it's the same thing. Do you understand? It's the goddamn liberals who want to give the money of hardworking Americans in this country to people who don't want to work or don't pay taxes. I won't have it. And I'm glad you're with me, Shelby. Because in a war, there's nobody better at your side than a Mannix, I'm told."

"Thanks, Mr. President," muttered Shelby, flattered but pragmatic. He left the President's office knowing exactly what the President wanted, and it wasn't just Americans for America. He wanted to make sure all the bases were covered on the former President's death.

CHAPTER 8

After three weeks at Fort Sam Houston, Eddie O'Hara finally saw his new face. He couldn't remember what the old one looked like so he didn't know what to think. His burns had healed nicely, but he was instructed to stay out of sunlight. The sun would interfere with healing, and he would have to be watched closely for pools of blood collecting under his skin.

The Army staff of physicians and nurses had treated Eddie O'Hara well, and he was grateful. San Antonio, he had heard more than one nurse remark, had the finest weather in America, and so it seemed. There was nothing to do really but sit out in his pajamas, and take in the beautiful weather — from a nice shady spot of course.

However, as much as he tried, he couldn't remember a thing about himself. Was he married? Did he have a family? Did he believe in God? And why just a maintenance man? That just didn't feel right. Hell, he hoped that Dr. Sullivan was right. He hoped it would all come back to him. Because if it didn't, he didn't know what he was going to do.

Shelby Mannix spent the next few days studying the terrorist assault. The damn fools at the White House had never figured on gliders. You couldn't see them on radar, or hit one with a heat seeking missile, because they didn't generate any heat. The sons-of-bitches had used two World War Two British assault gliders and floated right over the fence, then packed two National Park trucks with explosives, created a diversion, and set off the explosives. Oddly, Shelby discovered, whenever the White House was visited by the Israeli Prime Minister, part of the security system was shut down by the Secret Service because so many Israeli security people patrolled the grounds.

Damn fools, Shelby thought bitterly.

In the days ahead, getting statements from survivors proved to be more difficult than Shelby had expected. Many were not just up to it. There was no such thing as a survivor who wasn't injured. It got so he could tell how far away from the White House the victim had been just by the extent of their injuries. Just inside the White House gate there were no survivors. Just beyond the gate were the most serious injuries, usually internal, and usually including a loss of a limb, or at a minimum, a nose, or blindness. One block away was the zone for multiple broken bones, two blocks away, single broken bones, and so forth. Even from five blocks away a ten-year-old girl's ear drums were blown out.

Shelby liked investigative work, maybe loved it. The truth gave him goose bumps. When he heard it, he knew it, he believed. So far there had only been one embarrassing moment. A man who had been beaten badly by fellow drug dealers claimed to be a White House bomb-blast victim. Shelby looked into the man's eyes and knew immediately he was a fraud. But the interviews were tedious. The blast somehow had a life of its own. It seemed to have shaken the past out of its victims. They were like shell-shocked combat veterans crying, screaming, dazed and confused. Some even forgetting who they were.

Shelby's orderly mind resented the human mess the bomb had created, but the President wanted every piece in place, and it would have to be done, including the interviewing of all the victims who were at major medical centers outside of the Capital.

A preliminary check of the identity of the victims by Shelby's small task force turned up nine names that didn't seem to fit into a normal profile. Five names, it turned out were foreign visitors, three names homeless people, but one name was the most troubling for Shelby. It was a White House employee who seemed to really not exist. He had no Social Security number, no military record, no record at all but the White House pass that identified him. Shelby called the Secret Service, but they didn't have a clue. All their people were dead, he was curtly reminded. It was the first bump in the investigation.

Shelby's original plan was to interview the survivors in the Washington area first, and then fly to the various specialized medical centers that were treating the other victims. But the Eddie O'Hara name was a flare, an indication that things might not be as tidy as they first appeared. Much to Shelby's annoyance he would have to fly to San Antonio and interview Eddie O'Hara, White House maintenance man.

Eddie was told he could go out on pass for a few hours once a week if he wanted to. He was invited downtown to a Mexican restaurant by Captain Maura Scott, a nurse practitioner. She had made it obvious that she liked him.

She claimed she wasn't used to treating civilians, but there was a look in her eye from the first time they met. Her hands seemed to touch him a lot as well, and not only in modest areas, but she knew her stuff. Although civilians didn't realize it, you had to have a BSN to be an Army nurse. The Army was the first to make it a requirement in the late 1970's, and their health care system was the better for it. The treatment of the whole person not just the part that was sick, that was the idea.

As Eddie sat amongst the festive restaurant crowd with Captain Scott, he felt raw, unfinished. His jaw was still wired, and he discovered he could not speak as fast as he would have liked to. His voice, as well, sounded like it came from someone he didn't know.

Captain Scott just stared at him. She was in her early thirties, and Eddie thought, a real looker.

"What?" he finally said.

"You just look so familiar, Eddie, but I just can't place it. I feel I've known you for some time," she said in her deep West Texas drawl.

"Is that what you say to all your older patients?" he joked.

"Honest Eddie, I just don't know what it is. There's something so familiar about you. I feel so comfortable around you. But it's true, I do have a thing for older men."

He tried to think about himself, but nothing. Always nothing. Not a goddamn thing up there. He wondered if he could get it up if he had to. He wasn't so sure about that either.

"Let's stop at my place before we head back, Eddie."

"Not tonight, Maura. I don't even know who the hell I am. It bothers me a lot."

"You're Eddie O'Hara from Washington, D.C. That's who you are, Eddie."

"Well, if I am, I don't remember a goddamn thing about Eddie O'Hara. Nothing."

"I've brushed my hand against junior downstairs, and I know he's working, Eddie. And he sure don't care about who he is."

Eddie cleared his throat. "I think you're great, Maura. Any man would be honored, but I'm just not up to it."

He could see the disappointment in her face which was curious. He didn't think he had anything to offer anyone.

She caught his eyes and held them as she poured it on. "Are you sure, Eddie? Who knows when we'll see each other again? I know you think I'm brazen, but I know what I like, and a girl's got to do what a girl's got to do."

Well, she was certainly good for his self-worth, Eddie thought.

Captain Scott lived in a small trailer court not far from the medical center. Eddie couldn't put his finger on it, but he felt that he was trouble for her. The less she had to do with him the better, but he didn't have a reason why he felt that way. And that was exasperating as well.

Later, in the Shady Brook Trailer Court, the 43rd President of the United States made love to Captain Maura Scott who, being a good nurse, carefully avoided any physical contact with his face.

CHAPTER 9

Shelby Mannix was not in a good mood. He liked to do things in an orderly fashion, but here he was on his way to Fort Sam Houston to interview Eddie O'Hara, a minor player in the scheme of things, but a loose end that had to be cleared up as quickly as possible. There were no longer any White House records — the blast had destroyed all the White House files — which didn't bother Shelby. It was a lack of a Social Security number for Eddie O'Hara that was the loose end. No one in the world could work at the White House without a Social Security number.

It was a long shot, but O'Hara could be tied into the terrorists, mused Shelby, as he entered the hospital ward at Fort Sam Houston. Shelby had managed to keep most of the information on the survivors to himself including the discrepancy in Eddie O'Hara's work file. Shelby was very bad at delegating authority, but always justified it to himself as necessary for security. That didn't mean he didn't have a driver or an assistant standing by at the hotel. He just liked to work alone on something as sensitive as an investigation of a White House employee who didn't seem to exist.

As far as Eddie O'Hara's face, it looked to Shelby like it had just been slapped a few dozen times. It was raw looking, and still had the quiver of trauma attached to it. He knew from the neurosurgeon's report that O'Hara had a *closed head injury.* His brain had literally been shaken and bruised. Sixty percent of brain trauma patients lost some memory from this type of injury. Complete loss was unusual, but not unheard of, Shelby discovered.

On first seeing Eddie O'Hara, there was something vaguely familiar about him, Shelby observed, but he couldn't figure out what it was. Shelby prided himself on his instinctive ability, and his radar wasn't disappointing him. There was something about this Eddie O'Hara that was different from the other victims. For the moment he just couldn't put his finger on it. He would figure it out eventually. He always did, he told himself. He had been right to make the trip, he decided.

Shelby introduced himself, sat on the metal visitor's chair, crossed his legs, and then proceeded with the interview. "I understand you can't remember anything about that night, Mr. O'Hara?"

"I can't, sir."

"Not even a smidgen?"

"Not even my name," replied Eddie.

Shelby opened his briefcase and took out a folder. Information was always so official looking that way.

Shelby said, "The White House employment records are lost for now, that much we know, but there's no Social Security number registered to anyone with the name of Eddie O'Hara. Obviously there's a very good explanation for this since you worked at the White House, Mr. O'Hara?"

As Shelby waited for an answer, he studied Eddie's face and then said, "Mr. O'Hara, screw ups happen, I know that, so I'm not that concerned."

Eddie straightened up. "If there is an explanation for it, Mr. Mannix, I don't know it," he replied, pulling no punches. "I understand anyone who could have identified me is dead. Which is probably why you're here."

Shelby didn't like to condescend to people he was interviewing, but thought a slight nod of the head to indicate that Eddie O'Hara was right, was appropriate. It now seemed to Shelby that even Eddie O'Hara's voice was vaguely familiar. It was enough to send shivers though him. Yet the face was brand new. The nose he was told was a masterpiece of modern medicine. 'You can't have more of a new face than Eddie O'Hara's,' the surgeon had told Shelby. 'To be blunt his mother wouldn't know him,' the surgeon had added.

Shelby was all prim and proper sitting upright in the unassuming hospital chair as if he were a school child in his first day of class. He didn't like to admit it to himself, but his *look* was not unlike the author, Tom Wolfe — dandy, but masculine, with a dash of Riverboat gambler.

For the next hour, Shelby asked Eddie O'Hara a number of questions, but was not satisfied with his answers . It almost seemed to Shelby that any answer O'Hara gave was not enough. There was a persona about Eddie O'Hara that was deeply disturbing as well. A grand bearing so to speak. Hardly the demeanor of a maintenance man. Yet the man before him was a stranger. He had never seen him before, of that he was sure.

"So, it's a blank, Mr. O'Hara?"

"I'm afraid it is, sir, much to my disappointment."

"Or is it something else, Mr. O'Hara?"

Eddie tensed. "I don't know what you mean?"

"A false identity. How do I know you didn't come in with the terrorists?"

Shelby observed O'Hara's face. He had discovered over the years that when you surprised a person with a question, the area around the eyes for the first fraction of a second always revealed if this person was lying. The brain didn't have time to catch up at that point. Eddie O'Hara's eyes revealed nothing.

"I don't feel like a terrorist," Eddie answered, his wired jaw making his words sound choppy.

There was an honesty to the answer that impressed Shelby. Eddie O'Hara was most likely not a terrorist, he concluded, but there was something so hauntingly familiar about this man in front of him, yet it was a man he had never seen before. God, it was troubling.

"Some bureaucrat, somewhere has a download of the White House files, Mr. O'Hara. Time will help us get some answers," Shelby said gruffly.

"That wouldn't be soon enough for me," replied Eddie, hating the blankness in his head; the feeling that he would never be whole again.

"It's believed you were on a motorcycle, Mr. O'Hara."

Eddie smiled. "Was I going in or out of the White House?"

Shelby didn't appreciate the response.

"What do you think, Mr. O'Hara?"

Eddie just raised both hands palms out. "I don't know. Honest I don't."

Shelby knew he would have to return to the hospital at a later date and find out more about this enigma that lay before him.

Eddie O'Hara had become the first mystery of Shelby's investigation, and he didn't like it.

CHAPTER 10

It was through investigators like Shelby that he would find his way back to himself, thought Eddie, but he didn't like the man. Underneath the stylish suit and polished manner of Shelby Mannix, Eddie believed, was a government official who would stop at nothing to achieve his goals. He didn't know why he felt this way, but he did.

Eddie O'Hara was also reluctant to admit to himself that his mind was a blank slate. He decided he would have to be on the lookout for any rationale — even subjective — that explained who he was and why he was a victim of an attack on the White House. But he would not believe anything without conclusive proof. Somehow even his name seemed all wrong despite the White House pass found in his pants pocket — *The White House? That was where the President of the United States resided, wasn't it?* And from what he was told about the terrorist explosion, he still couldn't believe he had survived the attack and the President hadn't.

Shelby Mannix tried to unwind at the hotel bar, but it didn't work. The higher he got on gin and tonic the more concerned he got over his interview with Eddie O'Hara. In all his years of prying out people's secrets he had never felt so uncomfortable with a subject.

Shelby went to bed hating the mystery that surrounded Eddie O'Hara. It was unexpected, and taking much too much of his time.

Around 2:00 a.m. Shelby awoke from a light sleep, his body soaking wet. 'Mannix men never sweat' Shelby had been told by older relatives as far back as he could remember. For the most part it was true. Sweating was considered weak and vile in the Mannix family. But Shelby was dripping wet. He had awakened with a horrible, startling, incredible, and absolutely unacceptable thought. What if Eddie O'Hara was the President of the United States somehow injured trying to escape under a false identity? It was not the kind

33

of plan you would expect for protecting the President of the United States, but on the other hand the White House grounds had never been overrun with terrorists before. Could it really be possible that Sam Wainwright escaped with a hastily arranged plan?

The sweat continued to soak Shelby's body. He prided himself on his built-in *shit detector* and kept hoping it would go off and prove him wrong, but it remained silent. In fact, there was not the slightest twinge of doubt that he was wrong in believing Eddie O'Hara was Sam Wainwright.

As modest a politician as he was, Sam Wainwright was a resourceful President, Shelby believed. He wouldn't have been a victim of circumstance.

Now, clearly shaken, Shelby walked to his hotel window and studied the highway in the distance. Each car and truck seemed a world of its own, he observed. There are defining moments in one's life, Shelby believed, but too few people ever recognized those moments. If he was right, one phone call to the White House with his theory about Eddie O'Hara could change everything. He knew there was only one way to find out if his instincts were right — DNA, since Eddie O'Hara had total amnesia from the brain trauma injury — or BTI as it was explained to him by a neurologist.

Even the possibility that he could be right gave Shelby a sense of panic because if he was right, sooner or later, Eddie O'Hara might start to recall his memory, and then it would be all downhill for the former Speaker of the House. A President taking office while his predecessor was still serving his term, no matter what the reason, could only mean legal trouble for Luther Donald and the party that wanted to do so much for America and its roots. It was a cause that Shelby believed in passionately.

Shelby spent the rest of the night on the phone with a close aide.

The next morning, using the authority of the White House, a sample of Eddie O'Hara's blood was given to Shelby Mannix, who sent it by Federal Express to a private firm specializing in DNA for criminal defense lawyers. At the same time Shelby arranged for faxes of Sam Wainwright's DNA profile to be sent from the Bethesda Naval Hospital — where the President had received physicals — to his office in encrypted form. When that was accomplished, his assistant unscrambled the information, and flew immediately to San Antonio with the former President's DNA profile.

In turn, using an alias for Sam Wainwright's name, Shelby faxed the President's DNA profile results to the private firm, and asked the company to match it with Eddie O'Hara's DNA.

Shelby was told he would have to wait 48 hours for the results and was lucky at that. It had once taken weeks to get the same information.

Shelby was not impressed. He concluded that what was at stake was beyond imagination. The possibility that there were two Presidents of the United States, one of whom didn't even know his name. An unconscionable situation at the very least.

Eddie O'Hara was sick of neurologists and neuropsychologists. They couldn't tell him what he looked like before the blast, or what he had been, or when he was going to get his memory back. He wasn't sure what they did to help victims of memory loss, he only knew he was ready to leave the hospital after three-and-a-half weeks.

Maura was startled when Eddie told her he wanted to leave.

"Eddie, you've had serious work done on your face. You've suffered complete loss of memory, and you have burns that are still healing. What's more, there's a real danger of reconstructive hematomas — a pooling of blood beneath the skin. Where the hell would you go?"

"I don't know. Where would I go? Away from here. Florida, I suppose."

"And how do you know there's a Florida?" she snapped, obviously hurt by his remark.

"I don't know. Why can I remember there's a Florida but not anything else? It's a good question."

"And it's why you have to stay, Eddie. Let the authorities find out more about you. Let us help you, God knows you need it."

Eddie smiled. "You can be quite dramatic, you know."

"I know," she said softly. "And what are you going to do for money?"

"They sent me a check which I can't cash because where would I cash it?"

"You have no money?"

Eddie gave Maura a lost-little-boy look.

She smiled. "Do you really want to leave, Eddie?"

Eddie O'Hara didn't know why he wanted to leave. He just knew he had to. Somehow he felt like a sitting duck, and he just couldn't rationalize why.

"Yes, I do, Maura, very much."

He could see the hurt on Maura's face which made him feel even worse.

CHAPTER 11

'There is a match' stated the DNA report. Four words that could bring down the President, and the party that had fought so hard to get on top again, agonized Shelby.

It was times like this that Shelby Mannix believed he was trained for. Instinctively, Shelby recalled the wartime story of his uncle on his father's side as he looked at the DNA report. 'There's a fire on the bridge, sir' Shelby's uncle was told by a panicky Executive Officer as he led a destroyer in the middle of the night into Liverpool Harbor during World War Two; the harbor was crowded with ships loaded with ammunition, and spaced closely together.

The destroyer was now ablaze, and dangerously close to the other ships. Shelby's uncle turned to the panicky officer and said in the calmest of voices, "Then put it out," as he continued to guide the destroyer in the tricky night, his demeanor and confidence giving the men under him the calmness to fight the fire successfully.

There will be no panic, Shelby told himself. None. This was a defining moment, a moment that could change history, and he, a Mannix, would make the best of it he was determined. But under his breath, he heard himself mumble, as if another person were saying it, "My God almighty, the President is alive and doesn't know it."

There was nothing the hospital could do. Eddie O'Hara insisted on checking out, and that was that. Officially he was a material witness but no one in Washington had gotten around to telling him that, because no one was sure what he understood and what he didn't understand.

His departure was a compromise. He would stay at Maura's for a few days before setting out. Maura, in turn, was troubled by Eddie's need to run away from good care and safety. So was Eddie troubled by the fact that he needed to do it; that somehow he felt like a sitting duck. *When did I learn that phrase?* he mused. He knew the phrase *sitting duck*, but knew nothing about himself. It was maddening.

Eddie made an agreement with Maura not to tell anyone where he was. He made sure she understood that it was his life that had to be put together, and he didn't want people like Shelby Mannix telling him who he was or who he wasn't. He was going to put himself together on his own terms, and for the next few weeks all he would do was try and figure things out, and maybe have some sex with Maura.

The thought that memory loss had nothing to do with sex amused Eddie. The thing between his legs knew exactly what to do after his fingers got Maura's juices flowing. There was something to be said for animal instinct, he determined. Survival went beyond procreation, and he believed those very same instincts were protecting him now, telling him to get the hell out of harms way. One neuropsychologist told him the return of his memory could happen at any moment. While a neurosurgeon said, it might never happen, that the amnesia was a combination of physical injury and unimaginable fear.

Eddie rejected that opinion out of hand. Somehow, instinctively, he knew he was not a coward.

CHAPTER 12

Shelby Mannix was deep in thought as his driver drove him through the gates of Fort Sam Houston. Shelby did not disagree with those pundits who believed that a political party that does not gain the majority for a long time has a tendency to have a darker side to it than the majority party. Shelby had been dealing with the fringe of his party for years, in fact nourishing it, because, he believed, it was the fringe that stirred the political pot for new ideas to win power. Simply stated, Shelby knew every extremist in his party. He had used them many times in local, state, and national elections to disrupt the status quo. Every party had its fanatics, but Shelby had access to the top of the feeding chain in zealots; men who did not ask questions when given an order.

Shelby decided to pay one more visit to Eddie O'Hara and then he was done with it. Calls would be made, a plan formulated, with every effort at keeping the reason for the plan limited to himself.

Shelby also tried to not let his doubts about harming the former President creep in, but they did. However, his final decision was not difficult to make. It was based on everything he believed in, verses the life of a man who by all appearances was now a shell.

It would have been a profound weakness on his part not to take the more difficult road, the painful road of knowing he would have to destroy Sam Wainwright while he had the chance. The window of opportunity could be shut at any moment as long as Eddie O'Hara was alive. Possibly, Shelby believed, this decision to harm Sam Wainwright was the most distasteful one ever made by a Mannix, and at the same time the most important.

Bolstered up by his belief in himself and what he stood for, Shelby Mannix approached Eddie O'Hara's hospital bed full of confidence, but like many men used to power, Shelby did not like surprises and took them personally. He was startled and angry to see a very fat lady sucking on a taco in what had been Eddie's bed.

When told that Eddie O'Hara had signed himself out, Shelby threatened to destroy the careers of anyone on the staff that had anything to do with allowing a material witness to leave his hospital bed while suggesting subtly that Eddie O'Hara might have *terrorist ties.*

By the time Shelby demanded Eddie O'Hara's medical records, the head physician was more than eager to oblige. More importantly, as far as Shelby was concerned, was the fact that Eddie O'Hara now appeared to be on the run. He had sealed his fate according to Shelby Mannix's code of conduct. It was time to hunt the former President, and once finding him, to contain him, and once containing him, to keep anyone from ever knowing that for the first time in America's history, there were two active Presidents at the same time.

Eddie O'Hara lay in his trailer bed watching a soap opera still wondering when he would find himself. One nerdy looking neuropsychologist, he remembered, had told him that another traumatic event like the bombing he had been through could trigger his memory, but he hoped not. He had been blown up and couldn't remember it; he didn't want to be involved in another life and death situation that he couldn't remember. The term for his condition, which he kept hearing thrown around, was *Dissociative Amnesia.* One neurologist also told him that if he did regain his *autobiographical memory* there was a good chance he would forget everything that happened in his present state of mind.

"Even a woman I slept with?" Eddie asked.

"Probably," replied the neurologist.

It was a chilling statement as far as Eddie was concerned, but a reminder of how serious his condition was. He supposed the place to start finding out about his life was the place where his accident happened, but he didn't have the strength to do that right now. Nor could he remember what Washington, D.C. even looked like. The tight space of Maura's trailer, however, felt good and he looked forward to seeing Maura every night. But he knew something was still wrong. He didn't feel safe.

The day after Eddie O'Hara's disappearance from the hospital, Shelby Mannix met with a team of four men he had worked with many times. Until that meeting the *brief* for these men had always been the same — destroy the political opponents of the majority party. In other words, get the Democrats anyway you can.

In the back of Shelby's mind, however, he wondered if containing the problem like this was the best way. He had other choices. A quick call to New Orleans would get the job done, but that might be too severe. The New Orleans people were a power in their own right going back to the assassination of John F. Kennedy.

No, he decided, he would try and keep the Eddie O'Hara problem within the confines of the party and work with men he trusted.

One would have thought that the five men in business suits dining near San Antonio's Venice-type canal were successful businessmen.

Over a light meal — none at the table ate red meat — Shelby told his dinner guests that they would have to deal with an unusual turn of events. One of the victims of the White House blast was missing, and was possibly a grave threat to the new administration. Details were *Top Secret*. Officially, the view was that Eddie O'Hara was a material witness being investigated for possible ties to the terrorists. No more had to be said. On the other hand, Shelby believed, the more he made Eddie O'Hara into a suspect, the more information he had to pass on to other agencies, particularly the FBI. So the idea for the moment, in regards to the public persona of his inquiry, was to downplay the *ties-to-terrorists* idea as a wild hunch that had no facts to back it up, while Shelby's team of investigators tried to locate Eddie O'Hara for *his own good*. The taint of Eddie O'Hara having *ties to terrorists* would be brought back to life when Eddie O'Hara was out of the picture, Shelby decided. At the moment he was unclear himself on what out-of-the-picture meant, although he had an idea in the back of his mind that frightened him.

CHAPTER 13

The lock on Maura's trailer home door was no match for Shelby's investigators. They forced the lock on her trailer with little effort.

Eddie was sleeping. He had been doing that a lot lately. Still groggy, he said, "What the hell is going on?"

A large bony man nodded to one of the other intruders who carried a bag. The man holding the bag went to the kitchen sink, removed dishwasher detergent from the bag, and began washing all the dishes and pans.

"Are you people nuts?" shouted Eddie. "Clean the toilet too while you're at it."

"Good idea," said the large bony man.

The four men were dressed in suits and appeared well mannered but frozen faced.

Eddie, now on his feet, said, "I hope you have a good explanation, I mean really a good one, for barging in here like this."

The bony man didn't answer. The two men standing behind him looked serious and had the persona of men who looked like they were going to get their mission accomplished one way or another. They seemed so above-average in demeanor — well educated might be a better word — Eddie didn't know what to make of it.

The large bony man took out a sheet of paper. "Eddie, you're a material witness, and also a witness who is still under the government's care. You've been released into our custody."

"Can you do that?" Eddie asked innocently.

"We have the signature of a federal judge that says we can, Eddie. Now if you'll pack your things and come with us. You wouldn't want any of those bones in your face to be broken again trying to resist a court order, would you? For sure they'd never heal right."

"I have a friend, Maura. She should know where I'm going."

The bony-faced man handed Eddie a sheet of paper and a ballpoint pen. "Print, 'Good-bye Maura,' and sign it," he ordered.

Eddie struggled with the alphabet, but finally was able to print the two words. He could see his captor was in no mood to discuss the matter, so Eddie signed his name. Out of the corner of his eye Eddie could see the man with the bag still washing the dishes in the kitchen. He was wearing Maura's blue latex gloves.

The man at the sink finally said he was finished and removed Maura's gloves. As far as Eddie was concerned, the man looked comical. He still couldn't figure out the reason for the intruder washing the dishes. In fact, none of what was happening to him seemed to make any sense.

The large bony man handed Eddie a handbag and told him to pack his clothes and personal items.

Eddie didn't have much. The man watched Eddie pack, then searched the trailer for anything Eddie would not have likely forgotten. Satisfied, he said, "Okay, we're gone." A Ford Explorer was waiting outside the trailer. Eddie was placed in the middle of the back seat between two of his captors.

Eddie now realized that he was in a lot more trouble than he had originally thought. His survival instincts told him he had to devise a plan, and quickly, but what kind of a plan? Seated between the educated, but hard looking investigators, it seemed his options had run out.

How do you plan when your memory is so selective? It disturbed Eddie further to think that if his memory came back he would not remember Maura. The breakfast they shared together that morning was perhaps the last time he would see her or remember her. It was a disturbing thought and momentarily plunged him into depression. However, only minutes into the ride, Eddie began to lay the seeds of an escape plan knowing his memory was still selective, and not sure what he knew, or didn't know.

"I have to go to the bathroom a lot," he uttered, slightly embarrassed. "It's the medication I'm taking. Just want you to know that."

There was no response.

Two hours into the drive, Eddie asked to go to the bathroom.

"You'll have to hold it," said the bony man from the front seat. "We'll stop when we can."

Survival has no social graces Eddie decided. He knew his only chance of getting away was to get out of the Ford Explorer. So Eddie O'Hara, once Sam Wainwright, President of the United States, turned to his captor on his right and said, "I can't help it. I'll have to take it out and urinate on the floor."

"Can't help what?"

"Excuse me if you get wet."

The man looked down and saw Eddie opening his fly.

"Sir, he's going to pee in the vehicle."

There was a gas station up ahead, the bony man signaled for the driver to pull into it. They were in flat country, rural country, the kind of place where a truck driver didn't have to ask for a key to the men's room.

Eddie was guided to the toilet. Blessedly, he observed, there was only room for one person at a time in the men's room, and just as important a small window just above the height of a small man, and easily accessed by standing on the toilet seat.

In his other memory Eddie had pumped gas in many stations like this one as a teen. Somehow, instinctively, without any memory of that time, he knew exactly what the layout of the gas station was.

"No tricks," said his captor, as Eddie went inside, closed the door, and sat on the toilet seat. His captor looked in briefly, and closed the door. Eddie immediately stood on the toilet seat forcing himself to make grunting sounds. It was a demeaning process as far as he was concerned, but necessary. Carefully, he opened the window slowly, and slipped down the other side of the small, wooden-framed building. Taking a deep breath, he then bolted for a heavily wooded area that skirted the highway. For a man in his fifties he was fast, and it occurred to him that he must have run many times in the past. A few seconds later there were shouts, but he ignored them, and continued to head toward the wooded area, crouching low, zigging and zagging, trying to draw all the energy he could muster.

There was a faster man among his captors, and he brought Eddie down. As Eddie struggled to fight off his kidnappers, the bony man restrained him.

"Very unacceptable behavior," shouted the bony man. "You'll wear diapers for the rest of the trip."

The gas station was also a convenience store. While Eddie, under guard, waited in the clump of woods, his captors were true to their word. They forced him to put on a Pampers. And although they drove all night, and stopped twice to relieve themselves, the President of the United States had to use a disposable diaper. Even in his present memory, Eddie realized that he had suffered unmentionable humiliation. What Eddie didn't know, was his captors didn't know who he was either. He was just a man who matched the description of the man they were supposed to take in: Six feet, slightly underweight, a reddened face that didn't look fully healed. Eddie O'Hara was a major threat to their party, and to the Presidency, and that's all they had to know or wanted to know. At times, however, his captors wondered, how much of a threat could Eddie O'Hara be? After all, they found him sleeping like a baby in a trailer park, and now they had him wearing diapers.

Just after noon, the Ford Explorer pulled into a small sanitarium forty miles northeast of Selma, Alabama, on Route 22. The sanitarium was run over with weeds, and obviously closed.

The Sunshine Sanitarium had seen better days. Its clientele of famous drunks had been equal to any in the country at one time, but now it was held by a medical holding company that was only interested in the bottom line, and was closing facilities like *The Sunshine* as tax write-offs.

A man in his middle sixties, with a slight physique, smoking a filter-tip cigarette, and wearing a white coat that looked like it had just been washed, but not ironed, greeted Eddie's captors.

"You'll stay here for the night," the bony man said quietly to Eddie, "Dr. Jackson will show you to your room. And no funny stuff, Eddie."

The doctor seemed excited, happy to be with a patient again even if the patient was being held against his will.

The room the doctor led Eddie to was at the end of a dirty hallway. The doctor opened the room door with a bit of a flourish. "Our best drunks used to stay in this room, Eddie. It's padded, and utterly dehumanizing. I apologize for that."

Eddie, seeing the bars on the window near the top of the ceiling, and the strangeness on the face of the doctor, knew he had been right to run.

"But, as you can see, there is a toilet. Take your clothes off, Eddie, and put on the gown that's on the bed. I understand they had to put you in diapers?"

"Why are they doing this?" Eddie asked, dropping his pants and removing the foul-smelling diaper. The doctor took the diaper as if it were someone passing him a desert dish.

Dr. Jackson then smirked like an old silent film villain. In a heavy, but cultured Southern accent he said, "Sometimes I think, Eddie, it's because parts of the deep South like ours, still exist. The liberals stepped on us like we were waterbugs, but their heels missed a few of us. We've absorbed all the bitterness that used to be spread throughout the entire South and we're full of patriots that have a Scots-Irish penchant for revenge. Why are they doing this to you, Eddie? Because places like this allow them to get away with it. There isn't a law enforcement person in the country that can get an honest answer out of anyone in this county. Not a one."

"But I still don't understand? I'm supposed to be a White House maintenance man," said Eddie. "I don't get it."

"Why you, Eddie? I don't know. But they could take you right out on the lawn and shoot you, and no one around here would care. People are still being thrown in swamps in this neck of the woods."

Eddie put the gown on then snatched a pair of blue Jockey briefs out of his hand bag. The clean tight-fitting briefs made him feel human again.

Eddie cleared his throat. "You don't seem very worried, telling me all this, Dr. Jackson."

The doctor, still holding the diaper in his hand, smiled. "You wouldn't be here, Eddie, if you weren't a threat to someone, and there are so many reasons to be in that category. Favors are asked for. Favors are done. And favors are returned."

"And what favor are they doing for you?" asked Eddie, dreading the door being shut and locked, knowing they had him for the moment, but nevertheless still trying to make a favorable impression on Dr. Jackson. From some innate part of himself it seemed to be a smart thing to do.

The doctor ignored Eddie's question, smiled, and left the padded room.

Somehow he had to get out of the sanitarium while he could, Eddie thought. The trouble was Eddie O'Hara, 43 rd President of the United States, didn't have much to draw upon. He was a completely new person who understood meanings and phrases, and some cultural mores, but he had nothing to draw upon at this moment. His sudden fear of being in the hospital came from instinct not deduction. He knew that there was an outside to his door, and that things didn't look good, but it perplexed him to think of what to do next. He realized that Maura's place was about as far as he could have gotten from the hospital at the time. He remembered again that if he got his old memory back the present part of his life would probably be forgotten.

On the other hand, he suspected, whatever he had done in his other life must have been bad, or else why was this happening to him? All his musings, however, were academic, he realized. He had the sense of what a prisoner was, and was fully aware that his present situation fit that description.

CHAPTER 14

Shelby Mannix sat at the far end of the conference room table as Luther Donald gave a speech to his new Cabinet about the sweeping new plans he had for America. As Shelby looked around the room, he saw some compromises for the Cabinet that he didn't like, but understood Luther Donald's reason for appointing them.

Shelby wanted so much to tell the President what he had done for him, but that was out of the question. He was a Mannix. He would never implicate the President.

Later that day, when Shelby was alone with the President, Luther Donald became chatty. "How goes it, Shelby? We haven't had a chance to talk much lately. Well, I was finally forced to get a Chief of Staff."

It was Donald's way of letting him down slowly, Shelby knew.

"It goes very fine, Mr. President, very fine indeed."

"You wouldn't bullshit me would you, Shelby?"

"No, Mr. President, I wouldn't."

Luther Donald popped a sour ball into his mouth. "This is a great thing that's happened to the Republican party, Shelby. A great thing. But it has come out of evil, and I don't know if we can contain it."

Shelby tensed. "I don't understand, Mr. President."

"So much power has suddenly come into our hands, we won't want to give it up. We've been on the outside as far as the Presidency is concerned far too long. John Dean called it Blind Ambition, and it is."

As Luther Donald talked, Shelby could already see the President's transformation from party arm-twister to statesman. Was it the power of the Presidency that changed men in office like Donald, he wondered?

"I wouldn't want anything to stain this Presidency, Shelby. We've been given a gift and we should take full advantage of it within the context of the Constitution. The advertising for the Bicentennial a number of years ago said the Constitution was 'The Words We Live By,' and that's so true."

"The interviews are going well, Mr. President. Nothing unusual as yet," replied Shelby.

Donald looked at Shelby and hesitated before asking, "Nothing then?"

"One character who signed himself out of a hospital before he was supposed to, but that's all."

"Then we're home free?" asked Donald, sitting behind his desk, moving the sour ball around in his mouth.

"Yes, Mr. President, we are."

The President leaned forward. "You know, Shelby, I look out my window and I don't see the Potomac, or the Jefferson Memorial. It doesn't seem fair does it? All I get for my Presidency is a temporary office."

"No, Mr. President, it doesn't."

"I'm the first Speaker of the House to become President and I have to run the government from the Vice President's office. That goddamn explosion practically vaporized the White House."

"The White House will look the same when it's rebuilt, Mr. President."

Luther Donald laughed, but it was not a laugh that allowed you to see into it. "That will be two years from now Shelby. And I'll be running for my job. Two years is not a lot of time to change the thinking of ordinary people, but I'm going to do it, Shelby. By damn I'm going to do it."

Shelby stood up. "It's an honor to serve you, Mr. President."

"Keep the barracudas from my door, Shelby. Will you do that?"

"I will, Mr. President."

"You know you used to call me Luther."

"It wouldn't be appropriate, Mr. President."

Donald walked Shelby to the door. "I know you would do anything for me, Shelby, and it worries me sometimes."

Shelby smiled. "No need to worry, Mr. President. We have a tight ship here."

"Good," said Donald giving Shelby a little wave good-bye as if he were a four-year-old waving a miniature flag at a parade.

When Shelby left the office, he was immensely pleased with himself. Somehow, he suspected, the President knew he was plugging up holes.

CHAPTER 15

From his condo at the Watergate, Shelby tried to sense what his next move should be. The muscle he had chosen was from the right wing fringe of the party — they weren't really Republicans, although they liked to think they were. If you had asked any one of them when they went over the line from hard-right politics to enforcing extreme measures against their enemies, they probably wouldn't have been able to answer you. Politics and criminality had become a blur to them. A good guess, however, would be their early participation in undermining Pro Choice. The path from demonstrations to violence can be subtle, or as someone once said, 'Rage can be as subtle as a good-looking suit on a Mafia Don.'

The four men selected by Shelby believed passionately in their views, and believed very much in what the extreme right of their party advocated. At the level of violence they were operating at now, few in the party knew of their existence except powerful insiders like Shelby Mannix. These men did not do this kind of thing for money — never money. They believed to a fault that they were soldiers fighting a terrible enemy — the left wingers who were dragging America down and removing God from everyday life and promoting the killing of human life. The Constitution, they believed, was suffering the death of a thousand cuts. If anyone probed into the backgrounds of these men they would have discovered that all had families, and all were members of good standing in their communities. The bony faced man — who went by the name Elijah, was considered a legend among the fanatical far right but only known through innuendo and hearsay. Elijah's specialty was the elimination of good prospects in the Democratic party from winning any key local or state elections before they got too popular. He had long ago graduated from the picket lines against abortion clinics to political assassination. Usually when political opponents were confronted with whatever trap Elijah had set for them, they dropped out of the race. Occasionally, an auto accident against a member of their family would have to convince them to leave the race or even the death of a close friend. This was war, Elijah reasoned, as holy as the crusades. When patriots like Shelby Mannix needed something to be done, it was done. No questions asked. Because Elijah and his men knew it had nothing to do with money, or self fulfillment, or personal agendas of power, but instead the hope of a better America, or to be more precise, an America that the Founding Fathers would have been proud of.

Elijah and his men were anxious to end their current assignment, but that would be too dangerous, concluded Shelby. As much as he hated to admit it, Eddie O'Hara was still a mystery.

Shelby was concerned about the change of identity. How far did it go? Was it a last minute thing? Was there anyone in the world who knew Eddie O'Hara was the former President of the United States, or arguably, still the President of the United States?

Disposal of the body would be a major problem as well, pondered Shelby. Technically if his holding Eddie O'Hara were revealed, he still had wiggle room and the authority to put a witness under protection for his own good, as long as Eddie remained alive. The District Court order that Shelby's men had quoted to Eddie was a fake, but technically he could have obtained one if he wanted to. Eddie O'Hara alive gave him some options, dead only one — keep it a secret at all costs.

Shelby recalled Dwight Eisenhower's decision-making process for the D-Day invasion. Keep your options open until the last possible moment. Shelby figured that Elijah would not like it, but he would have to deal with that. Containing Eddie O'Hara was enough for right now. O'Hara's memory loss was total. Basically he could not function. There was even a bright side that Shelby suddenly considered. What if Eddie O'Hara's amnesia was permanent? Why not let him walk? But then, somewhere, in some file, someone had known about the President's fake identity or else the White House Pass would have not been issued. No, the unthinkable would have to eventually be done, but he would keep his options open as long as possible. *Did a Mannix ever have to make a more terrible decision?* he thought.

CHAPTER 16

Their pistol holsters strapped to their bodies over their white shirts and ties, made Eddie's four captors look like hoods from a grade-B movie. Only they didn't sit around playing cards, but instead read trendy investment magazines like *Red Herring* which dealt with high technology investing and dot.com chatter.

Two days had gone by since snatching Eddie. Eddie's captors were becoming restless. "Elijah, my family will be worried," one of them said at the kitchen table. He was the intruder who had carefully washed the dishes in the trailer to remove Sam Wainwright's fingerprints and any other DNA that might be around.

Elijah pondered the question for a moment. He was under orders to keep things status quo. He didn't like it, but it was orders.

"This matter is more serious, I understand, than anything we've been assigned, Abel" — each of them had taken biblical first names as a code — "we've been told to hold on."

"The package seems very confused, Elijah,"said a former retired Army officer. He called himself Jacob.

There was a look of disdain on Elijah's face. "I'm told this baggage is extremely important and has to be dealt with carefully. Why do you think a man of your caliber is involved?"

The flattery worked for the moment. Jacob backed off.

The other hard-looking man in the group, Jonah, a former assistant DA from Louisiana, scoffed. "O'Hara is pathetic, Elijah."

Elijah gave Jonah a look of disdain. "Our package is suffering from amnesia. I understand. The party could suffer greatly if he starts to remember things, I'm told."

"He's a White House maintenance man. What could he have seen?"asked Jacob. "Maybe he knows something about the explosion at the White House that he shouldn't. Is that it?"

"Don't tell me we were behind that?"interjected Jonah. "It would be a glorious day indeed."

Elijah stood up abruptly. "Enough, we have our orders. We follow them like always. We sit tight until further notice and that's that."

"I agree,"said the only man at the table that hadn't spoken, a former stock broker. His code name was Nehemiah. His wife had been raped and murdered by a killer who had been paroled for the same offense. He would be the one Elijah would turn to eventually to finish off Eddie O'Hara.

Little attention was paid to Eddie by his captors, but Dr. Presley Jackson — or Press as he liked to be known — seemed to take great pleasure in his conversations with Eddie. Despite his medical credentials, Dr. Press Jackson could easily have passed for a good old boy. Like many people in the state, he had large goldfish eyes and a wide expressive face that smiled easily.

However, Dr. Jackson owed his life to others because of a fierce gambling habit. A former patient with strong ties to the far right bought Dr. Jackson's tab from the mob before they put out a contract on the good doctor. Each favor Press Jackson did reduced his tab, but took pieces out of him as a human being. He had already taken part in the murder of three political candidates around the country, two of them women associated with the Pro Choice movement. Each of the killings was made to look like an accident based on his advice.

He wanted to cleanse himself but didn't know how. His conversations with Eddie O'Hara had now accelerated to honest disclosure.

"They don't worry about me talking to you, Eddie. They own me, that's why," Dr. Jackson said, sitting on a small chair in Eddie's padded room.

Eddie, sitting against the corner of the padded wall, arms folded around his legs, replied, "I didn't have the context to really figure out what was happening. I see it better now, Doctor."

"What do you see, Eddie?"

"I see that I'm in a lot of trouble that apparently has nothing to do with crime. Those creatures outside just don't look like criminals — funny, I know enough to know that, but don't know anything about myself."

Dr. Jackson nodded his head in agreement. "It's why I can talk to you, Eddie. Any second-rate criminal knows that you don't allow anyone in the operation to get emotionally involved with your hostage. Those people outside are delusional. The world works differently for them. They are into causes, not humans."

"You sound like you don't like them, Doctor?"

51

"I despise them, but they own me."

"The gambling you told me about?"

"Yes, Eddie."

"So you are playing with fire talking to me — *playing with fire?* I wonder where I got that from?"said Eddie.

The doctor, sitting on a white, three-legged stool, said "Of course, I'm making it more difficult for myself, Eddie, but I see something in you that fascinates me. I just can't figure out what it is. I'm really at a loss."

Eddie laughed.

Dr. Jackson continued, "Honest, from the moment I saw you, I felt you were someone special. Not so much by your conversation, it's something else I can't explain. I believe the word might be charisma."

"Charisma? I know what that means. I look at myself and feel furthest from that. You understand, don't you, Doctor?"

"I do, Eddie, but time is running out. When they bring you here you don't walk out, but I assume you've figured that out for yourself?"

Eddie shook his head. He was going to die for something he couldn't remember. It just didn't make sense. But nothing had made sense since the morning he woke up in Saint Francis Hospital for Special Surgery.

Dr. Jackson read Eddie's mind, easily. "I can't help you Eddie. When they get the order, one of them will come in here and end it. The best I can do is convince them to let me take your life by injection."

"You're very considerate,"said Eddie facetiously.

The doctor stood up. "I'm sorry," he said, "I really am," and left the room.

No progress there, thought Eddie. *Who am I? Who the hell am I? Why can't I remember?* But only blankness followed.

CHAPTER 17

Shelby felt a little uncomfortable walking into the White House counsel's office. The Chief Counsel was a lean, wiry man who didn't have to wait for a person to finish a sentence to know what they were going to say. His two assistants, both females, were also fast on the draw. Their right wing credentials were impeccable, Shelby knew, but he didn't like any of them. They had never been tested. He liked to group people he worked with in two categories: those he wouldn't want to be in a POW camp with, and those he trusted.

Everyone in the room was courteous, full of smiles, but Shelby suspected more pressure was going to be put on him.

The head of the President's legal team, smiled. "Shelby, I wanted you to be one of the first to know the President's selection for Vice President." When told, Shelby was pleased with the choice. It meant the legacy of the party would continue.

"It goes to the House tomorrow. We don't expect any trouble since it's our House. It won't be like the Wainwright nomination."

"We tied it up pretty good. Damn good thing we did," said Shelby, forgetting his tenseness for the moment. "If there had been a Vice President where would we be today? Very prescient of the Speaker, I would say."

"It's that looking ahead that's always distinguished him, Shelby."

Shelby looked at each of the President's legal team. Their faces were deadly serious.

"Okay, why am I here?" he asked.

"We have a legal hump to get over, Shelby. Technically, Wainwright chose his successor only he was not approved by the House. And, as you know, the Speaker led that fight against Sam Wainwright's nomination . His succession, however, is not sitting well because of that. There are some Democrats just spoiling for a fight because of the Speaker's opposition to

Sam Wainwright's choice for Vice President. Legally, we have them, but they're going to make a big deal about the President's body not being found although they know they don't have a leg to stand on. Can you imagine? There wasn't a human at that dinner party that wasn't practically vaporized."

"There will always be Democrats spoiling for a fight. I don't see any problem here," said Shelby.

The Chief Counsel, a natty dresser who prided himself on never getting ruffled and sitting behind a desk much too large for him, said, "Luther doesn't want this kind of controversy to begin his Presidency. Simply stated, we need conclusive proof that the President died. He wants you to head the search."

"Finding DNA is damn near impossible. You know that," moaned Shelby.

Undeterred, the Chief Counsel said, "They're still finding body parts. Luther wants to make sure we don't overlook any part of the President that might have survived the blast. He wants you on the job. And that's that. Hell, you've been looking at the President's DNA profile."

"I've passed it on to our initial search teams, yes, that's true."

"And they found nothing, I assume," said the Chief Counsel.

"Yes, that would be correct. The shirt should be enough for evidence."

"Somehow Shelby, we need a body part that has the President's DNA."

"I don't know how we can do it."

"It's there Shelby. Has to be, somewhere in that heap of human waste left over from the explosion. I want you to get on some asses, bring in whomever you want, and get some DNA that's from a body part. That will stop our detractors cold."

They're goddamn evil, thought Shelby. Somehow these sons of bitches must know about Wainwright, had to know. Or was it just his conscience? The thought that a Mannix would have a man's foot or hand cut off repelled him. He could not do it, and couldn't order anyone else to do it either, but he reminded himself that he had to stay calm.

"You're looking very pale, Shelby. Were you afraid of blood when you were a kid?" asked the Chief Counsel.

"I've already got an investigation. The President must have told you that."

"He thinks you're going to do much better with the dead than the living. You know how he changes his mind."

God, thought Shelby. *Do these people know? Do they know?* "Well, most of the interviews have been done. I suppose I could turn that part over to one of my assistants."

"Yes, Shelby," said the Chief Counsel, "empower your staff with some responsibility for a change. We all know how stingy you are about assigning it."

Shelby forced himself to appear cooperative, but another fear was looming in his mind as he said, "We can bring in the Air Force team that's still looking for American bodies in Viet Nam. They're well trained in this work."

The Chief Counsel sprang to his feet. "Now that's good, Shelby. Damn good. You always were a pillar of common sense. Find us a piece of Sam Wainwright, Shelby. Any part will do. His pecker even. We don't care."

It's just like the President to have his counsel do his dirty work, thought Shelby. *But did they know?* If they did, his life wouldn't be worth much. He was very versed in the ways of the radical hard right. Were they just waiting for him to get rid of Wainwright? The expression 'caught between a rock and a hard place' came to Shelby's mind. It occurred to him that as long as Wainwright was alive his options were considerable, but dead, Wainwright might turn into a liability.

Would a toe suffice? he asked himself going out the door.

CHAPTER 18

"How long can your men stay on the detail?" asked Shelby over a phone that was cleared for security.

"They're getting antsy," replied Elijah.

"What's the problem?"

"O'Hara doesn't appear to be as important as the men would like, and frankly they want to get back to their families."

"O'Hara is damn important, Elijah. Don't let your men forget that. We have to sit on this a while. Closure will happen."

"The swamps around here know how to keep a secret," Elijah said with confidence.

"Not these days, Elijah. Damn developers are buying up the state. You never know what swamp is going to turn into a bunch of condos."

"Sir, the longer we hold him, the more chance of exposure."

" Give me a few more days. I'll work it out," assured Shelby.

"That's all the time we can give you, sir."

"And your men have done a fine job indeed, Elijah. Now there's just one favor you have to do for me. You'll need Dr. Jackson for this."

Elijah did not like his latest order. No, he didn't like it at all.

CHAPTER 19

They had been holding Eddie O'Hara for nearly three days. In that time, Dr. Jackson had almost forgotten that Eddie was a prisoner.

The doctor always sat on the white stool, and Eddie always squatted in the corner, like an exotic creature.

"I got them to buy you a radio, Eddie."

"That's very good of you Doc. I appreciate that."

"I wanted to take you on the grounds for a walk, but they wouldn't let me."

"You've been very good to me, Doc. Very good indeed."

"I don't like you being here, Eddie, you should know that."

"You're a decent human being, Doc. I can't say that for the others in the kitchen. Packing guns and quoting stock prices. Where do people like that come from?"

"They're from all over the country, Eddie. Maybe television got boring for them. I don't know, but they live two lives. Sort of an upscale version of the Ku Klux Klan. Something to do in their spare time."

Eddie had seen the doctor soften more to his plight each day. "I would like to know why I'm here Doc, that would be a comfort."

"I wish I knew Eddie. You're a mystery to those thugs in the kitchen as well. Somebody doesn't want to give the order on you yet. It's most unusual."

"Maybe I deserve to be done away with. I don't know anything about myself, Doc. Maybe I've done bad things to people?"

"You, Eddie? I don't think so. No, I don't think that at all. You have so much presence, Eddie. I felt I knew you as soon as I saw you. I don't know why."

I wish I knew why, too, thought Eddie.

"The others in the kitchen, they wonder all the time who you are, Eddie."

In his squat, spider position, Eddie shook his head. "Ridiculous, isn't it. The only person who knows who I am is probably the person who ordered this."

"I know it's bad, Eddie. I wish I could do something."

"I'll tell you, Doc, I almost don't care. Honest I don't."

"You can't do that to yourself, Eddie. You have to want to live."

"So those guys in the kitchen can kill me?" Eddie stood up, walked to the small sink, and splashed water on his face. In the mirror he glanced at the doctor's face. If he could hold out a few more days, he might be able to convince the doctor to help him. But that was still a long shot, he suspected. However, his instinct to manipulate was a surprise to him. He wondered where it came from. It didn't seem rusty at all.

That afternoon, Eddie could hear Doc Jackson arguing in the kitchen just down from his jail. The doctor sounded animated, almost hysterical.

Eddie braced himself for the worst.

The doctor entered somber faced, but determined looking.

"What is it Doc, what's wrong?"

"They just asked me to cut off one of your body parts. I don't know why. I don't think they know either, but I'm helping you get out of here, Eddie. They've pushed me too far this time. They want it done right away, but I told them I needed surgical equipment, antiseptic and antibiotics; that I have to go into town to get what I need. I told Elijah I would perform the surgery tomorrow morning. I've convinced him that the morning is the best time to do this."

"Why do they want to do this, Doc?" was all Eddie could say.

"I don't know, Eddie, but it's academic. I'm going to help you."

"You'll get in trouble, Doc."

"I'll feel like a human again, Eddie. That's very important to me at my age. Tonight will be our only chance. Elijah always checks your door around eleven. I'll wait until then, and then unlock it."

Dr. Jackson handed Eddie a key. "This is for the back door. You need a key to open it from the inside. Once outside, turn left and run like hell. There's a freight train going through every hour during the night. Damn whistles never stop blowing when they hit the bend."

"Thanks Doc, I don't know what else to say."

"This is good-bye, Eddie. I enjoyed our conversations."

"Doc, I—"

"Don't say anything more, Eddie. You're giving me a chance to feel human again. Oh, one more thing. I'll leave your clothes outside the door. You'll have to dress and run. Don't waste any time. They're sleeping in the room across from the kitchen, but one of them is in the kitchen all the time, or is supposed to be."

Eddie shook hands with Dr. Jackson. "They pushed me too far this time, Eddie. Too far," Dr. Presley Jackson mumbled.

CHAPTER 20

That night, Eddie could hear himself breathe as he waited for the door to his padded room to be unlocked. The Alabama moon was bright, almost as if it was in on the escape. Eddie was still confused about what the doctor had told him. Why would anyone want a part of his body? What did his other memory know to deserve this horrific treatment?

Eddie pushed his memory as far as it could go, but there were no memory traces, *or seamless integration of neurological functions*, as the doctors might say. He just couldn't remember anything about his other life.

The kitchen was quiet. Maybe they had all gone to bed, Eddie hoped. Suddenly he heard his door unlock.

He waited for a moment, then opened the door. Slowly reaching down into the darkness, he scooped up his clothing and shoes. His body was now dripping with sweat. He dressed quickly and guessed it was about 75 feet to the back door. He held his breath as he stepped into the hallway. He could hear snoring as he crept along the wall still afraid to breathe.

As he inched down the corridor, the kitchen light went on, throwing light violently into the hallway. Eddie froze, turned toward the kitchen, then flung himself to the floor, pressing his face against the dirty cement, flattening himself out as much as he could.

He heard a belch, and a fart, and then the refrigerator door being opened. Next he heard water running, then silence, and finally the harsh light turned to darkness again, but just as Eddie was about to get up, he heard footsteps. Eddie looked up from his prone position. He could not see anything.

Is he there? Or isn't he? Eddie thought. He covered his mouth and waited. His practical side told him to run, but his insides said wait.

Finally, the footsteps continued to the room across from the kitchen. Eddie waited for a moment, then got up and ran. At the end of the hallway, at the door, Eddie slipped in the key, turned, but nothing happened. He took a few deep breaths and tried again. Still nothing. He was trapped. Maybe the Doc gave him the wrong key? Finally on the third try, using all his strength, the lock opened. The heavy metal door moaned, letting out a creaking sound as Eddie jumped to the ground, stumbled, and began running. The Alabama night was steamy, but the sweetness of the air felt good. Eddie fell again as he headed into the woods. For a moment he felt free until he heard his captors shouting after him. In another memory he had done this before, his instincts told him.

He looked up at the sky and tried to get his bearings. He was using everything he had been taught as a Marine, but wasn't aware of it. Finally he heard the sound of a freight train. It guided him to the railroad tracks. The train was still moving around a large bend at about eight miles an hour. Eddie could hear his captors getting closer, exhausted, he waited for the first open box car and then lunged at the opening. Nearly inside, he began slipping until a hand reached out and pulled him up and into the car.

Eddie's captors fired at the box car but could not get the right angle as the car was past them. Inside the car were dark shadows of other riders. One of the shadows slammed the metal door shut, but Eddie could hear the pinging sound of bullets ricocheting off the box car.

The travelers on the train lit a lamp and looked Eddie over.

One of them said, "Got any money?"

"No, I don't," said Eddie uncomfortable again.

"They was chasing you for something?"

"I don't have any money."

"If the screws get you in the yard they'll put you on the chain gang for vagrancy," he continued. "They still have the chain gang in this state." The speaker was young, and mean looking.

"Sure you don't have any money?" the speaker persisted.

"*No*, I don't."

"Well, far as I know the only folks who shoot at other folks in public is the law."

"It wasn't like that at all," replied Eddie, now looking for a way out.

"Then you don't have any money?" said an older man with a whiskey voice.

"Nothing, not even a wallet."

"How about a money belt? You could have one of those?"

Eddie instinctively pulled his shirt out to show he didn't have a money belt. Again, it was an instinct. Money belt was a funny term he thought.

"Damn, you ever see anything like this before, Russell?"

The older man came closer to Eddie. "Cooperate son, and you may leave this box car alive— "

"Leave him alone," said a female voice. "Can't you see he ain't got nothing."

"Sure looks like he has nothing, don't it, Russell?" The younger man grunted.

"I didn't rob any banks, if that's what you think," said Eddie, nodding to the woman in the corner who had stepped out of the shadows. She was young and not unattractive. She came closer to Eddie and took a good look at his face.

"He ain't got nothing. Never had nothing. And won't have nothing," she said. "Ask him to leave."

"Please, I would —"

"They'll be waiting for you when this train pulls into the rail yard anyway. We're doing you a favor, isn't that right, Russell?"

Eddie watched the younger man pull open the metal door of the box car. The train was moving fast, real fast.

"Maybe when the train slows down," said Eddie,

There was a big laugh from the woman. "Shit stranger, we were just having some fun." The two men slapped Eddie on the back and chuckled.

Eddie relaxed. The two men picked him up and heaved him like they were dumping trash into the back of a truck The air lashed Eddie's face. He felt his hands hit a rocky embankment as he slid to the bottom of it, laughter trailing behind him.

Eddie lay in his face-down position for a few minutes. He was scared to move and afraid to find out he couldn't, but except for some minor cuts and bruises, he guessed he was okay.

The area was heavily wooded but Eddie could see street lights in the distance. He picked himself up slowly and began walking. When he got closer to the lights he could see the outline of a leafy village.

He was exhausted, and contemplated resting in the woods, but then thought better of it. They were out there looking for him. He didn't want to make it easy for them.

Near the tree line he noticed a light and a yard with a low picket fence. He stepped over the fence, took a few steps, and huddled against a weather-worn shed. Leaning his back against it, he slid down to the ground putting his knees against his chest and wrapping his arms around his legs. Before thinking about it, his eyes were closed.

CHAPTER 21

When he was five, Shelby remembered a kindergarten school teacher telling him that the South had not won the war. However, that was not the impression he had gotten from his father. He remembered two adults pulling him off the hysterical teacher as he called her a liar. Later, when his mother came to collect him in the principal's office, Shelby expected her to go to the teacher and correct the teacher's misunderstanding. When his mother told him that the teacher had been correct. Shelby would not believe her either. And now, as an aide to the President of the United States, he was again hearing news that he could not believe possible. And again he could only feel rage.

"Did I hear correctly, Elijah? He escaped? From a confined building with four people guarding him?"

"We believe it was the amputation, sir. Dr. Jackson couldn't do it. We believe he allowed Eddie O'Hara to escape."

"You mean you're not sure?"

"It's pointless now, sir. Eddie O'Hara is out there wandering around, but we'll find him."

Dr. Jackson was already swamp meat, but Elijah understood the rules. Shelby would not be told.

Almost raising his voice, Shelby said, "There are important people here, Elijah, that want O'Hara's DNA. Do what you must, but I must have a body part."

"When we find him, sir, that won't be a problem."

"Have you located the authorities?"

"We told them we've been looking for an Eddie O'Hara as a material witness."

"Yes, that would be correct. How far can he get on foot?"

"He hopped on a freight train that's not going very far. We'll nail him."

"Call me when you do," Shelby said nervously then hung up. He knew his identity was safe with Elijah, but wondered if he could have done things differently. Deep down he suspected he hadn't the stomach for the death of the former President, even if the President was a pathetic case with a slim possibility of ever regaining his memory. However, with Eddie O'Hara's escape, Shelby knew, like the Mannix men before him, that he had to reach in for his reserves and finish the task. After all, it wasn't as if he were involved in killing the President, he reasoned. The bomb had already done that in an insidious way.

"Wake up," said a woman's voice. The voice sounded faraway to Eddie.
"Wake up now, do you hear me?" persisted the voice.
Eddie opened his eyes. Before him was an older woman dressed as if she were going to church. He held his hand up to stop the brightness of her flashlight.
"Why are you in my yard?"
"I must have dozed, ma'am. I was on the train."
"Your face is all cut."
"Some people shoved me off."
"You look terrible."
Eddie smiled.
"I suppose you know that anyway?" she said.
She had a nice face, thought Eddie.
"You running from the chain gang?"
"No, not that."
"Then what?" she said shifting the weight on her feet.
"It's complicated," he said, brushing himself off.
"You a hobo?"
"No, I'm not," replied Eddie ready to walk away, but already wondering how close his pursuers were.
"There's something familiar about you, you know that."
"Others have said that to me, too. Supposedly I was hurt in the White House explosion."
She shook her head. He could see she was incredulous, but her face showed great interest nonetheless.
"I suppose you have quite a story to tell if you ended up in my back yard. I'll trade you a piece of pie to hear it," she said.
"I accept," Eddie replied, wanting to get indoors as fast as he could.

* * *

Elijah and his crew were confident that they would find Eddie O'Hara. Homeless people stood out in Alabama. Everyone knew everyone else and their business. Drifters in Alabama were like exotic creatures moving in an environment that did not welcome them.

At the rail yard, Elijah and his men spoke to every drifter they could including Eddie's boxcar bullies. They discovered that he had been thrown off the train. They knew he had no money and no where to go, but worried that he might get locked up for vagrancy before they got to him. When they did find him, Elijah swore to himself, he would take off Eddie O'Hara's body part himself.

The woman in the back yard was a retired executive that had worked for UNESCO, she told Eddie over tea and apple pie. She had seen the world and decided to retire in her deceased husband's hometown of Hardin, Alabama.

Eddie didn't think he had much to lose and told her what had happened to him since the White House bombing, but couldn't tell if she believed him or not.

There wasn't much in the world that surprised her, she told Eddie. But she did make a point of Eddie being the first 'fugitive' she ever had in her back yard.

"And you can't remember a thing?" she said over her third cup of tea.

"I can't."

"Well, if you're telling me the truth, Eddie, you know something someone doesn't want you to talk about. It's plainly obvious. And from what you told me they seem to have some sort of quasi official status. Of course my suspicions about the government go way back to Kennedy."

The name didn't ring a bell with him. On his second cup of coffee Eddie said," I have to find out who I am and what I know before turning myself in. That's what I believe."

"I agree," said Elizabeth Cherry. "You're going to have to go back to the Capital. By now you're probably a suspect in the bombing. You shouldn't have run, Eddie."

"I don't know why I did. Honest, I don't"

She gave him a look as if deciding whether to believe him or not. "Well, we can talk about that later, Eddie, but right now I want you to go upstairs and take a bath. You need one. I don't sleep that well anyway, never have."

Like the rest of Mrs. Cherry's house, the bathroom decor was Victorian. Eddie soaked in the deep tub for nearly an hour. When drying himself off he took a good look at his face. It was an honest face, but still healing. Whoever gave him a new nose had done a great job, he thought. His jaw was still wired and stiff looking.

Eddie used a leg razor and facial soap to shave. When he finished he felt more human than at any other time since his new memory.

Mrs. Cherry then knocked on the bathroom door and slipped fresh underwear, a turtleneck sweater, and button-fly jeans through a crack in the door.

Eddie later learned the clothes belonged to her son who died in Vietnam.

When Eddie came downstairs, Mrs. Cherry had *Time* and *Newsweek* in her hand.

"Read about the bombing. Maybe you'll recall something," she said.

Oddly, Eddie hadn't read anything since waking up in the hospital. He hesitated before looking at the magazines wondering if he could even read, then realized that he had read scads of type watching TV at Maura's.

The covers of both *Time* and *Newsweek* had a picture of President Sam Wainwright with a one word headline, 'Assassinated.' Eddie wondered if he had ever spoken to the dead President. The articles were long, and at times seemed more in mourning for the White House structure itself than the President, who didn't seem that popular. Both major articles inferred that Sam Wainwright had not been the best choice for Vice President, that his lack of ambition was troubling, that he was a 'cold President', and did not inspire leadership.

Mrs. Cherry, crocheting, watched Eddie from across the room.

When he finished reading the articles, Eddie said, "They're out there, Mrs. Cherry, looking for me. You're taking a risk having me here."

Mrs. Cherry smiled. She had such a terrific smile, he thought.

"I'm a very good liar, Eddie, you learn that pretty quickly as a UN bureaucrat. Nothing is as it seems. Lies put people at ease. If they come along, I'll know what to say."

But Eddie O'Hara continued to worry.

It was nearly 2:00 a.m. Eddie didn't want to leave.

Mrs. Cherry studied Eddie carefully before saying, "Take the couch, Eddie."

"Are you sure?"

"Yes, I'm sure." In the next few minutes she supplied Eddie with sheets and a blanket, touching his shoulder before saying goodnight.

Not long after he was snug on her couch. The remaining night was so peaceful, he thought, almost like a dream. There was nothing but stillness, yet he didn't feel safe. Sooner or later they would be around, and then where could he go? There was the safety of Mrs. Cherry to think of as well.

Eddie thought of leaving, but decided against it. Elizabeth Cherry's home, and company, had made him feel human again.

CHAPTER 22

They bugged the home of the nurse in San Antonio and waited for Eddie to call. They issued flyers in the South saying Eddie was a material witness who was suffering from amnesia and wandering about. But Elijah was confident that Eddie was somewhere around Hardin, Alabama. He just had to be patient. It had now become a personal thing. An enemy against everything he stood for had escaped. Why a maintenance man at the White House was so dangerous to the party still baffled him, but if Shelby Mannix said Eddie O'Hara was dangerous to the President, then he was.

Tomorrow, Elijah decided, they would conduct a house-to-house search in Hardin. That was where the drifters said they threw him off the train. Someone, Elijah was confident, had seen Eddie O'Hara. It was the way small towns worked.

At various times throughout the early morning hours, Eddie could hear Mrs. Cherry pacing back and forth. Did she do that every night, he wondered?

After a restless night, Eddie took a shower. It was such a luxury he thought. As he was drying himself off the doorbell chimed. Mrs. Cherry, rushed down the stairs. It must have been no later than eight in the morning, Eddie figured. He stepped into the hallway to hear the conversation at the door.

"We're investigators for the General Accounting Office," he heard a familiar voice say.

Eddie shuddered.

"We're looking for an important material witness to a very serious matter," the voice continued. And then the voice mentioned Eddie's name, and explained how he suffered from amnesia, and perhaps paranoia. He believed people were chasing him to do him harm, when it fact, the authorities wanted to see him get well.

"Can you tell me what he was witness to?" asked Mrs. Cherry. "Nothing ever happens in Hardin, Alabama, you know."

"It's confidential, ma'am," replied the voice.

"Well, you give me your card. If I see him, you'll be the first to know."

"You already have seen him, ma'am, that's what your neighbor said last night."

Eddie darted to a window that faced the other side of the house. A man in a dressy hat and suit was stationed in the back yard. They already knew, he thought.

When he returned to the hallway, he heard Mrs. Cherry say, "That drifter I talked to? He's the one then?"

"Yes ma'am."

"Damn, I wish I had known that. I would have fed him, given him a place to clean up, and sneaked a call to you people. That's what I would have done."

"Then you don't know where he went?"

"I didn't say that," teased Elizabeth.

"Then you know where he went?" asked the voice accelerating in excitement.

"Well, I admit to giving him some money. He said he wanted to take the bus to Montgomery. I didn't believe him, but that didn't matter. He looked like a nice man, really. But that's what he said he was going to do."

Eddie could see the man at the door trying to peek in, craning his neck like a swan, but Mrs. Cherry showed no concern.

When she closed the door Eddie slipped down the stairs holding his clothes. He dressed quickly.

"I think they know something, Eddie," she said in a shaky voice.

He admired her courage — how she had managed to stay so calm when talking to his pursuers.

He said, "They don't know for sure. They'll check the other houses, and then I'll leave."

"Do you know if you can drive, Eddie?"

"I don't."

"But you knew what I meant by the word drive?"

"Yes."

"I'll park my car outside the house and leave the motor running, I'm sure you'll be okay once you're behind the wheel. Take the car and stay away a few days."

"I really don't —"

"I insist, Eddie. It's an old clunker my husband used to love to tinker with. I really won't miss it."

Eddie, moved by her gesture, said, "Why are you doing this for me?"

Mrs. Cherry bit her lip for a moment. "I have a feeling about you, Eddie. Something is terribly wrong with your being here in this situation. I don't know why I feel that way, but I do. And I want to help."

Eddie looked out the window. Across the street was a parked car. Eddie recognized the man behind the wheel. He turned to Elizabeth.

"You're in danger, I've got to go."

"No, Eddie please. They don't know for sure if you're here."

"They're involved with the government somehow. What's to stop them from going to the sheriff? No, I'm going."

Mrs. Cherry grew firm. "You just can't walk out there, Eddie. I'll park the car in front and leave the motor running."

"He's going to see me come out."

"I'll create a diversion."

Eddie didn't know what to think of this woman who was doing so much for him. At that moment he had feelings for her that he hadn't experienced yet with his new memory.,

"Wait here, Eddie." Mrs. Cherry left the room for a few minutes, then returned.

"Here, $350, it's all the cash I have in the house."

"Mrs. Cherry, please —"

"I insist. You'll pay me back I know that."

Eddie slipped the money into her dead son's jeans. "I don't know what to say."

She looked at him, her eyes full of wisdom, and smiled. "Now I've got to get that character out of his car. It's a small town as you know. We can do things in small towns you can't do anywhere else. I'll park just outside. Wait for my signal."

Eddie watched Mrs. Cherry pick up her phone. After a few moments she said, "Jim, there's a stranger having a seizure right in front of the Mellinger house. I can see him right from here. He's shaking back and forth and everything. Better get right over here."

Eddie watched Mrs. Cherry leave the house, walk to her garage, and back out of it in a 1978 Buick Riviera. He could also see Elijah's man straining his neck to see what was happening. Next, a siren went off. The kind that always goes off in small towns at noon — a hangover from the cold war days.

In less than two minutes a fire truck was alongside the vehicle of Elijah's point man.

Elizabeth signaled for Eddie to come out of the house.

Standing at the window, he shook his head.

"Drive the car, Eddie. I know you can do it," she persisted.

Eddie opened the door, crouched down, and sprinted to the Buick Riviera. Without saying good-bye to Mrs. Cherry, Eddie pulled away from the curb surprised at how automatic his actions were.

Elijah's man couldn't follow. Two paramedics were holding him down while another attempted to stick a tongue depressor between his teeth.

Elijah's other man, the one in the backyard, fumed in the distance.

CHAPTER 23

Shelby Mannix sat in his temporary office at the naval observatory, and contemplated his options. It was apparent to him now that he had not served the party or the President well. There would have to be collateral damage. The plastic surgeon that worked on Sam Wainwright would have to go and possibly anyone else that had intimate contact with Wainwright since the attack.

The thought that the 43rd President of the United States looked like a bum from all reports bothered Shelby. Wainwright would be harder to find.

Shelby decided he had been wrong not to finish the job right away. But there was fear in Shelby as well. Eddie O'Hara was on the run, but there was still a chance Sam Wainwright might appear, although the longer Wainwright was without his memory the more likely that Eddie O'Hara's memory would predominate. There were lessons that should not be forgotten, mused Shelby, Watergate being the prime example. That's why he swore he would involve no one but himself. The party and it's new programs for America had to survive. The Republican Presidency was at stake. Sam Wainwright had to be eliminated, he concluded.

Eddie O'Hara drove across an America he had never seen before, although as President, Sam Wainwright was very familiar with the rural South. The gas signs told Eddie that a good portion of the money that Mrs. Cherry had given him would have to be spent on fuel, and that he would probably have to sleep in the car for most of the trip, but he didn't mind. Finding out about himself and why men were chasing him, that was his concern. That's what he had to do.

After driving east most of the afternoon, Eddie gave up on the idea of sleeping in Mrs. Cherry's car and stopped at a small run-down motel just outside of Savannah. The idea of getting a good nights sleep and a warm shower were just too overwhelming.

The proprietor was friendly, maybe even gracious, and obviously used to customers that didn't have much money.

Eddie asked how he could call someone without paying for it and was given quick, courteous directions on how to make a collect call.

Maura answered the phone on the first ring.

"My God, Eddie, you're all right?"

"I'm okay Maura."

"Where are you? What happened? I've been worried sick about you."

Eddie brushed the question aside. "I'm okay, Maura, that's what counts."

"Where are you?"

"In a small hotel just outside of Savannah. It's real run down."

Maura went on about her concerns for him.

Eddie thought how wonderful it was to have someone that worried about him. He explained he was on his way to Washington, D.C., promised to call her again, and hung up.

Once inside his room Eddie was determined to write everything down that had happened to him as Eddie O'Hara, cognizant of the fact that if he did recover his old memory he might not remember anything about his new memory. Men were hunting him. It was important that he know that.

In a schoolchild's notebook purchased at a 7-Eleven, Eddie wrote down everything that had happened to him since the explosion. The trouble was if he didn't have the notebook on him when he recovered his old memory, how could he know he was being hunted? It was exasperating. He decided to take a drastic step.

Shortly after, he asked the proprietor of the hotel where he could get a tattoo, marveling at the fact that he could remember something like that but not remember so many other things such as how to make a collect call.

At the tattoo parlor Eddie decided to tattoo the top of his knee with 'Eddie, you lost your memory, and are being hunted by killers. See the notebook.' The rationale being he would see the message as soon as he sat on the toilet.

"It don't seem right without a serpent wrapped around the letters or something," said the tattoo artist. "Don't seem right at all."

"It will be okay as it is," said Eddie.

"I'm an artist you know," protested the tattoo man. "It'll cost you more this way."

Eddie thought for a moment. "Okay, put a picture of the White House."

"It's still upside down," moaned the artist. "Who will see it?"

"That's the idea. I will," said Eddie, "especially when I take a dump."

And so the 43rd President of the United States got a tattoo that warned his old memory that he was in danger. It was just the kind of practicality and common sense solutions that had helped Sam Wainwright get to the Vice Presidency.

Elijah let out an uncustomary "good" when he heard that Eddie O'Hara had called the nurse in Texas. His men were just an hour away from Savannah. It would take them another few hours, he reasoned, to find Eddie's car. They already knew the license number.

When Shelby was notified he was firm in his demands. "Give me a part of him and make sure no one sees the rest of him ever again."

Later, when Shelby had time to think about what he had ordered, he was shaken by his own hardness. However, he justified his actions to himself with the rationale that Eddie O'Hara would never recover his memory; that perhaps he was doing Sam Wainwright a favor. And anyway, a Mannix never quit a task that threatened the well-being of his beliefs.

After a lukewarm shower, Eddie turned on the black and white TV but still found it hard to relax. The thought that men were chasing him for something he couldn't remember seemed to be a constant punishment and a reminder that his other life had not been normal.

What had he done? Who had he hurt? What had he seen? Over and over he asked himself these questions and over and over he would come up with a blank. Every vehicle that drove into the parking lot made him jump. The headlights cut across the dark shadows of his motel window like searchlights. Exhausted, Eddie couldn't take his own thoughts anymore.

He decided to go for a cup of coffee at a nearby truck stop.

The steamy July air felt good in its warmth and sweetness, but the constant drone of the nearby highway was unnerving.

The truck stop was crowded with truckers and travelers eating meals with lots of gravy piled on their plates. The TV screen broadcast a report about two Saudi glider pilots who were tracked down and who committed suicide rather than be taken in for questioning.

"Terrible thing about the President," said a trucker to Eddie as he sat down on a stool.

"Yes," said Eddie, pretending he remembered who the President was.

"You look beat," said the trucker.

"I am," said Eddie ordering a cup of coffee.

"Computers, faxes, and cell phones were supposed to make our lives easier — look what they've done to us," said the trucker.

"It's not easy," faked Eddie.

The trucker gave Eddie a long look. "You somebody I should know?"

"I don't think so," replied Eddie.

"Well, if you don't mind me saying, you're too beat up to be anyone important, but somehow you're familiar."

"I was hurt in the White House blast."

The trucker almost spit out his food. "You were? I mean you were really there?"

"That's what they tell me. I really don't remember much."

"Then what the hell are you doing in this truck stop, buddy? Make the government pay — pay through the nose. Get yourself a kyke lawyer and sue, baby."

"Kyke?"

" Jew."

"What's a Jew?" asked Eddie, exasperated at how much he remembered some things, but not others, and now realizing he may have made a mistake.

The trucker stood up and gave Eddie a menacing look. "You know what I think?"

"No, I don't," replied Eddie innocently.

"I think you think I'm a Red-Neck fool."

"What's a Red Neck?" asked Eddie observing the truck driver and somehow sensing what a Red Neck was.

"You don't know what a Jew is? You don't know what a Red Neck is? You're trying to make a fool of me."

"Honest, I'm not," said Eddie still waiting for his coffee.

The trucker stepped closer, his eyes bulging, seemingly aware that his peers were looking at him.

Eddie sensed the danger, but didn't know what to do about it.

The trucker pushed Eddie off his stool.

Eddie didn't understand what happened next, but some sort of reflex action kicked in. Before the trucker had a chance to complete his first blow, Eddie had him on the floor, his foot on the trucker's neck. He was as surprised as the trucker, but that didn't stop him from pressing down on the trucker's throat with his foot. It was animal, all animal, and he was confused by his actions.

"Okay, let him up," said another trucker. "And get your ass out of here."

Eddie stepped back. The truckers at the counter and in the booths looked at him menacingly.

Eddie walked out of the truck stop silently, but was more baffled than ever about his other memory and what it knew. On his way back to the motel he had to dodge a number of large rigs rolling in and out of the truck stop, their air brakes sounding like an angry herd of snorting bull elephants. The 18-wheelers seemed to have a life of their own. They were menacing in their size and lack of regard for humans that had to scramble to get out of their way.

The sticky summer air now seemed close and getting closer in its intensity. Eddie began to sweat heavily on his way back to the motel. It was a dark route that skirted the highway leading to the parking lot in back of the motel.

Eddie could have walked straight up the driveway and then to his room in the back, but for some reason he didn't understand, instinct maybe, he skirted the driveway and walked behind a row of bushes at the property line.

There they were, two of them, sitting in silence at the far end of the driveway, their hats silhouetted in the moonlight, waiting for Eddie O'Hara, he guessed. The only explanation he could come up with was Maura. Her phone must have been bugged.

He had to get in his room, but how? All he had in the world was there: His money and the few garments Mrs. Cherry had given him, not to mention the keys to her car and his notebook. There was no turning back. He had to go in.

Eddie backtracked to the front entrance of the driveway and took the obvious path to his room walking as if he didn't have a thing to worry about. When he got inside his room he turned on the light and gathered his things quickly. The good news, he told himself, was that his pursuers didn't know he knew they were outside. He turned on the crummy television set, let the muddy lukewarm water run in the bathroom, and gave every appearance of getting ready for bed. He suspected the vultures outside would make sure he was in a prone position before coming through the door. There was one problem, however. He had nothing to defend himself with.

The 43rd President of the United States scanned the room for anything he could use to defend himself. There was nothing, but he remembered the plunger handle in the toilet. It was ancient, the wood solid. It would have to do.

Putting all he had left in the world in the handbag Mrs. Cherry had given him, Eddie shut out the light, stood near the door, and waited.

Elijah's men waited too. Eddie could hear the couple next door arguing about money and a child crying. Finally he heard a car crawling on its belly, inching toward his room, the muffler letting out little hissing sounds. Then he heard two men whispering. Eddie gripped the plunger handle like a baseball bat. He began to sense that somewhere in the hidden crevices of his gray matter, in his other memory, he had experienced danger like this before.

The car engine outside his room kept running. Eddie guessed they wanted to drag him into the car and get out fast. He only heard one set of footsteps, then the slight jangle of keys. First one key slipping into his lock, then another, then another, then silence, then another, then finally the door creaked open. Eddie tensed.

He couldn't see what the intruder had in his hand, but it didn't look like a gun. As the intruder inched his way toward the bed, Eddie waited for the second man, but he remained outside. Eddie struck.

Elijah's man, blood pouring from his head, screamed, and jumped around as if his head was on fire. The other man rushed into the still darkened room. Eddie aimed for his hat, and cracked his face with the plunger. He could hear the crunch of the intruders nose breaking. There were cries of pain, confusion, and curses in the darkness as Eddie grabbed his handbag, ran from his room, jumped into his Buick Riviera, and raced out of the parking lot, tires squealing.

77

CHAPTER 24

The President was bearing down on Shelby to find a body part. At one point, over coffee Luther Donald said, "Goddamn it Shelby, we need more than a bloody shirt — now how much time do you need?"

Right then, Shelby wanted to come clean, but knew it would be the worst thing he could do. The matter was taking on a life of its own. Elijah's men had failed again. You didn't get any more dedicated than those men. They were the top of the feeding chain for loyalty to the party. After them the downward slope happened — the anti-government people. No, he had to come up with something, he thought, as Donald continued to browbeat him. At one point the President, clearly upset, said, "We're keeping that fucking hole open that used to be the White House, but I have to start building again, Shelby. That hole in the ground is a festering sore. It has to be covered and healed with a new White House and its leader sitting inside. A few wise-ass journalists have compared the hole to my leadership. We've got to get out from under, Shelby. Certainly you appreciate the symbolism that's going on here. If any human remains of the President are on the White House grounds, I want them found — now. Get the National Guard. I don't care."

"You've made that very clear, Mr. President," replied Shelby, knowing what he had to do.

"Is there anything you need, Shelby? Is that the problem?"

"No, Mr. President."

"Then find some DNA, Shelby. And tell the man or woman that finds anything to do with Sam Wainwright's DNA, that the Medal of Freedom awaits them."

"They're patriots already, sir."

Luther Donald gave Shelby a sardonic look. "They're goddamn bureaucrats. You have to kick their ass to get something done. Do I make myself clear, Shelby?"

"Yes, Mr. President," replied Shelby nearly angry enough to tell Donald that Sam Wainwright was on a highway heading east and the only way to stop him was to put out a contract on him.

They were the next generation of Cuban nationalists, ex-CIA, ex-Pentagon, ex-Treasury, and current Mafioso. An organization that stood on the shoulders of earlier men who had either looked the other way, contributed, or carried out the assassination of President John F. Kennedy. If at one time so long ago there were differences in these men, there were none now. There was no beginning or end to them, just a circle of darkness and intrigue that had the assurance that whatever office was involved in investigating a killing executed by one of them, would also have someone in power who would look the other way for any number of reasons. Not the least being ties themselves to this organization's delivery-of-death system. You could no longer say they were Mafia, or ex-CIA, or ex-Pentagon, or second generation freedom fighters, or present government what-have-you. Their obliqueness was their clarity of purpose. It's strength really.

There was a downside, Shelby knew. When the contract was completed, someone would figure out the body-part aspect after President Donald made his DNA announcement. They would know who Eddie O'Hara really was. Then the killing would have to continue until perhaps he was a victim himself. In any case, Elijah and his men would probably be the first to be hit. They would have to be given up for security, but what could he do? New Orleans would have to decide what to do with them. It was out of his hands, he concluded.

After the President's chewing out, Shelby sat in his tiny office and watched the stream of visitors coming in and going out of the Luther Donald's temporary office. Shelby chided himself for his lack of decisiveness and his purist need for the job to have been done by *his people*. There were no *his people* when it came to such matters he now realized. He would have to call New Orleans. Negotiations, of course, would have to be delicate. He would have to be careful. For the moment, the payment he would agree on couldn't be too much for someone the New Orleans people never heard of, yet not enough not to have the job done quickly. The license number of Eddie's car would be enough to identify him, Shelby decided.

The cities flew by — Memphis, Cincinnati, Wheeling. Most were unfamiliar names to Eddie although he had campaigned intensively in all of them as candidate for Vice President. They were in his brain's file of memory that he could not recall.

Finally, after driving eighteen hours and only stopping for gas, he entered the nation's Capital via New York Avenue. *Now what?* he asked himself.

It was a steamy July afternoon, the sun intrusive, glaring, destroying every shadow in sight as if at war with darkness.

The traffic was more than Eddie could handle. He turned onto a side street and searched for a place to park confused about what he was going to do next. He didn't know where to start, where to find out who Eddie O'Hara was or whether that was possible? And would *they* be waiting for him? His pursuers had something to do with the government, he suspected, but he was so damn tired, he had to rest.

Finally Eddie found a parking place. The African-American children playing on the street peered at him and his crummy looking 1978 Buick Riviera, but he didn't care, he was so damn tired.

It wasn't long before a cop on a motor scooter gave the Buick a good looking at, then Eddie, and figured it out. "Not a good idea to fall asleep here," the policeman said in a deep baritone voice. "There's a men's shelter on the next block."

Eddie took his advice and pulled out.

If I lived here, why can't I remember anything about the place? Eddie asked himself. He knew what an African-American was, what a policeman was, but the city was entirely foreign to him, and he just had an inkling of what a men's shelter was.

CHAPTER 25

There was a line of homeless men stretching the length of a spiral staircase waiting to get into the downstairs kitchen. Eddie felt the violent atmosphere of the SouthEast Men's Shelter immediately. The din of beaten men talking loudly was incredible. Next to the line of shattered men was a small office with an open window not unlike a drive-thru.

The clerk in the office asked Eddie what he wanted.

"I need a place to sleep. I'm broke."

"Name?"

Eddie thought about giving his real name, but decided not to. "Sam — Sam Walker."

The clerk in the booth picked up a pen and handed it to Eddie with a form.

Eddie wrestled with the form for a few minutes and then admitted he couldn't answer most of the questions. He didn't know his Social Security number. He didn't have a last address. He didn't know his status with the welfare department. And he couldn't say if he was a veteran or not, or had ever been arrested or for that matter, whether he was married or not.

The clerk shook his head in disgust. "We get funded by the city and the federal government. We have to have this information."

Eddie explained his condition, but left out the White House part.

"Dissociative Amnesia, that's a new one for not wanting to tell the truth," replied the clerk.

"Honest, it's the truth," pleaded Eddie.

Eddie hadn't noticed another man in the small office listening to their conversation. He was a rangy African-American, built like Eddie.

The clerk looked at the African-American who seemed to indicate that Eddie was okay.

The clerk said, "We haven't seen you before, *Sam*, so we'll pass on the information for now. You can have a shower and a bed for three nights."

The man who indicated it was okay for Eddie to stay said, "What was that condition you have called?"

"Dissociative Amnesia."

"You can't remember a thing?"

"No, sir, I can't," replied Eddie thinking the man seemed to really care.

"Been on the road?"

"Yes, sir."

"In some trouble?"

"Yes, sir, but not of my doing."

"Percy will fix you up with a meal ticket. Just remember to stand at the end of the line and be real careful about it."

"Thanks," Eddie replied grateful for the break.

As he climbed the stairs, two homeless men argued about their place in line. Eddie wondered if he was doing the right thing. When he turned to look down the steps, the rangy African-American was looking up at him, still sizing him up. Eddie couldn't figure what was turning in this guy's mind. He had not mentioned the car and wondered if that had been a smart thing to do.

The lunch was wholesome and good. Like many of the homeless men at the tables, Eddie dragged out the time and tried to forget about the drone of anger that surrounded him. He listened to the other men talk and tried to think of what to do next. Nearly two hours had passed when he got up from the lunch table and was about to go upstairs to his assigned cot when a small, wiry, African-American, dressed nattily, approached him and introduced himself as Lincoln Washington. "My mother thought adding another President's name to our surname would propel me to greater heights," he joked. "They stopped giving black folk names like that in the sixties, but that didn't stop my mother."

"It's nice meeting you, Lincoln, but I've got to go," said Eddie.

"Bill Paxton, the man who runs this place thinks you need my help," said Lincoln.

"The man in the office?" Eddie said, surprised.

"He believed you and when he believes you, he doesn't waste any time."

"It is the truth."

"Except maybe your name? I bet Sam Walker is not your real name?"

"Who are you anyway?"

Lincoln Washington handed Eddie his card.

"Private detective? I can't afford a private detective," said Eddie.

"It's gratis until we find out who you are. I owe Bill a lot," said Lincoln.

"Three years ago I was one of those guys sitting in this room. He wants me to help you and that's the way it's going to be."

Eddie didn't know what to think. Someone was actually going to help him. It didn't seem real.

"Now let's take a drive in that piece of shit you have parked outside — damn I hope no one sees me in it," said Lincoln.

Eddie was surprised at how Lincoln had figured out whose car was parked outside the shelter.

"Before you ask, it didn't take much. Out-of-state plates. You just walk in the door. And anyway, I know the owner of most every car that parks on this street. If we get out in time, your car may still be there — bet you didn't tell Bill about the car either?"

"No I didn't," said Eddie impressed that Lincoln Washington was a man who wasted no time. However, Eddie did not open up or tell Lincoln the only name he had known since he woke up in the hospital.

The first stop on Lincoln's agenda for the afternoon was the Vietnam Veterans Memorial.

As they walked across the grass, Lincoln said, "This will jar any mother-fucker up who's been in the service."

"I don't know if I've been in the service or not," Eddie replied meekly, still confused by Lincoln's offer of help.

"You're the right demographics, unless you were one of those educated white assholes who got a deferment."

Eddie noticed for the first time that Lincoln and he were about the same age.

"Were you there, Lincoln?" asked Eddie as they neared the Wall.

"Damn right," he said with a touch of anger.

As they approached the black granite panels that made up the Wall, there was only blankness in Eddie's mind.

Lincoln peppered him with questions, 'Do you know what in-country means?' and, 'What was the term for sex when you were in-country?' but the terms were unfamiliar. Intellectually Eddie knew a war had once been fought in Vietnam, but emotionally he couldn't connect. The war was too much a part of his autobiographical memory, too much of a meaningful part of his reality to make any association with it.

Eddie didn't know it, but there were far fewer visitors to the Wall than there had once been. There had been major conflicts in Africa, the Balkans, and the Middle-East. Vietnam was fast becoming an exclusive memory for a group of Americans who were no longer making things happen, who were no longer the target audience of the media. The baby boomers had to move over for Generation X.

Lincoln touched a few names on the Wall and wiped a few tears from his face, then he turned to look at the blank look on Eddie O'Hara's face. "Are you going to come clean with me, or not?" Lincoln asked.

Eddie, touched by Lincoln's feelings for his comrades, replied, "I'm running for my life, Lincoln, and I don't know why."

Then feeling a connection to Lincoln that he didn't quite understand, Eddie decided to tell Lincoln everything he knew.

The President seemed relaxed," thought Shelby as he stood before him.

"We've got our man confirmed for Vice President — we're a tidy package now, Shelby."

"I'm so pleased to hear that Mr. President," said Shelby trying to resist any feelings of relaxation.

"We're doing great things for the country, Shelby. I'm going to have a tax package that's going to knock the socks off America. And I'm initiating legislation that will allow every American to have their own private pension plan that moves with them when they change jobs."

"That's wonderful, Mr. President."

Luther Donald reached for a sourball. "Of course, I need the country behind me, Shelby — hell, I'm the first Speaker of the House to ever succeed to the Presidency. There are problems as you know."

Shelby tried not to miss any cues. "I don't think it's that bad, Mr. President."

"Well, for starters, Shelby, it was never supposed to happen. If the Congress had selected Sam Wainwright's choice for VP after he filled the President's shoes, I wouldn't be here. But goddamn it, Sam Wainwright picked that abortion-loving fairy from California as Vice President and I wouldn't have it — anyway there's some grumbling."

"I don't understand, Mr. President," said Shelby knowing quite well where the discussion was going.

"The succession law is clear. If there is no President and no Vice President then the Speaker gets the brass ring, however, the 25th Amendment is tricky: the President had a heart attack, Wainwright got the job, but it's up to Congress to approve his appointment for Vice President. Well, we didn't approve it, thanks to our party's firmness on the matter. As I've stated, theoretically, it would have been Wainwright's choice for Vice President that became President, but that didn't happen. I'm here goddamn it and I'm staying."

Luther Donald stood up and peered down at his aide. "If only we could bury this Wainwright thing."

Shelby became anxious. "I'm doing everything I can, Mr. President."

"I know you are Shelby, but until we find some DNA it's hard for me to get this country going. There's even been a proposal that we hide ourselves in the 25th Amendment which is called the Presidential Disability and Succession law. That's what allowed Wainwright to nominate that Pro-Choice fairy from California in the first place —I really can't stand to mention his name."

"I understand, Mr. President."

"Well, we've asked the few surviving members of Wainwright's former Cabinet to forward us a letter with each of their signatures stating that Sam Wainwright is not around to lead the country — of course that's plainly obvious, but they won't do it. Can you imagine? The Chief Justice has sworn me in, and they still won't do it."

"How would that document have helped, Mr. President?"

"It's a technicality, that's all. It gives us added weight should by some sort of miracle Wainwright shows up some day."

Upon finishing the sentence, the President locked his gaze on Shelby. Shelby grew uncomfortable.

"That could never happen, Mr. President."

Luther Donald stood up. "I know that, Shelby, and so does Wainwright's former administration, but my critics want a body part, Congress wants a body part, and I want a body part."

"We're sifting every ounce of earth around the White House, Mr. President. Everyone involved is aware of the importance of the search."

Donald walked to his window. "You know my feelings, Shelby, about occupying a temporary office space. I'm between a rock and a hard place. The polls show the public wants the new White House built immediately, but would feel better about finding conclusive forensic evidence of Sam Wainwright's death. Under a worse case scenario, if Wainwright were alive — and we know that's not possible — he could hand the pro tempore of the Senate and the new Speaker of the House a letter saying he's ready to serve again. We would argue against that — hell, I've already been sworn in — and Congress would have twenty-two days to call a session and determine by a two-thirds vote who the President is, him or me? A letter by some ranking members of Wainwright's administration saying he wasn't around to serve would lock things up for us. Of course the process would be destructive to the country and a goddamn mess. This 25th Amendment has muddled up the whole succession law, Shelby. It was meant for Vice Presidents to be appointed immediately, but was Congress ever prescient about anything?"

Shelby was confused. The President's worst case scenario, seemed inordinate to the facts at hand. God, did Donald know? he thought. Was that possible? Or was it one of Donald's well known panic attacks? He had once seen Donald flip out over a badly printed publicity photo of himself about to be sent to an admirer.

Donald sat on his desk, the same one used by Ronald Reagan, and looked down at Shelby. "Of course we know Sam Wainwright is gone, don't we Shelby?"

"Yes, we do, Mr. President."

"One of my legal people said what if he were walking around in a daze, didn't know who he was — ridiculous, isn't it?"

Shelby tried not to sweat, but couldn't help himself. He was drenched in nervousness.

"That can't be possible, Mr. President. No one could survive that blast — and hasn't," he forced himself to say.

Donald smiled. "Of course, everyone knows that, Shelby, but they want something, anything. Give me a fingernail, but give me something."

"I feel that we're getting closer, Mr. President, just can't explain it really."

"Fine," said the President walking back to his window. "I know you'll come through for me," he said looking out at his substitute White House view.

As Shelby was about to leave, Donald added, "What we've discussed is just between the two of us. No one else will ever know? Is that right, Shelby?"

"Of course, Mr. President," replied Shelby, feeling more pressured now than at any time in his life.

CHAPTER 26

After his visit with the President, Shelby Mannix was shaken. How far would the killing spread? Would he have to call New Orleans and amend the contract to include Elijah and his men as well? And what about the woman who helped Eddie O'Hara? No, the contract on Eddie O'Hara was enough for now. That was all the dirty work he was going to do for the party. Tying up loose ends stopped at the people he knew. But if the New Orleans people figured out who their victim was, there would be trouble. The sooner Eddie O'Hara was found the better for all concerned, Shelby mused, but he believed there wasn't much to worry about. The New Orleans people were efficient, and swift. They had O'Hara's license plate, his car model, and the general location he was in. More importantly they were powerful, a silent, festering, sore that had infected the powerful agencies of government since the Bay of Pigs; a sore with the ability to erupt at any moment.

They were sitting in Starbucks. Lincoln Washington looked at Eddie O'Hara . "That's the biggest bullshit story I ever heard, Eddie."

Eddie looked at him, smiled, and said, "It's the only story I can tell you, Lincoln."

"Running for you life is one thing, but you don't look like no goddamn maintenance man. Bill, in the men's shelter, spotted you right off. You're fucked up but it has nothing to do with drink and drugs."

"Thanks for the compliment, Lincoln."

"You notice how much I've been on my cell phone this afternoon?" questioned Lincoln with a warm smile.

"I have."

"Well, you don't exist Mr. Eddie O'Hara. You're not a veteran. You don't even have a Social Security number. I can tell you right now that Eddie O'Hara is a bullshit name — you dig me, a bullshit name."

"I can't explain it," replied Eddie.

"Where is that White House pass anyway? I want to see it."

"It was never returned to me."

"Saint Francis?"

"Yes, that's where they first brought me."

"Didn't even know I could get a new face there. Let's go."

Lincoln didn't say much on the ride to the hospital. Eddie wondered if he could help at all. If anyone could help.

At the hospital's front office, the Head of Admissions, a woman in her late forties with an out-of-shape body, looked at Lincoln and Eddie with an air of indifference as if she had seen it all, heard it all, and nothing could rattle her.

When Eddie asked for his personal effects, the answer was abrupt.

"Everything that could have been handed back, was, Mr. O'Hara," she replied tersely.

Eddie explained that he was transported to a military hospital without having any of his papers returned.

"I can't help you, perhaps they're part of the GAO investigation? —or the White House investigation? —or the subcommittee on terrorism? —or the FBI investigation? God knows, this hospital has been turned upside down because of our gracious acceptance of White House bombing victims."

"You'll have a copy on file. I know how these places work," said Lincoln, seemingly undeterred by bureaucracy.

"Please, it would be so helpful," added Eddie.

The hospital bureaucrat studied Eddie and Lincoln for nearly a minute before agreeing to help.

It took an hour, but a copy of Eddie O'Hara's White House pass was produced. There was one catch. The administrator would not hand it over. She held it in her hand like a winning lottery ticket.

"The photo doesn't look like Eddie," she exclaimed. He had sideburns, different color hair.

"Does the record show what Mr. O'Hara was in here for?" asked Lincoln with a bemused look on his face.

"Yes, it does."

"His nose was practically blown off I understand."

"Yes, that's what the record says."

"Then how the fuck is he going to look like his picture?"

It was a knockout punch by Lincoln, but the bureaucrat still refused to hand over the pass.

Outside, in the car, Lincoln said, "That motherfuckin' photo didn't look like you, she's right."

"I don't understand," said Eddie, suddenly depressed and confused. The confusion was partly because of his Dissociative Amnesia.

"But it could have been you," said Lincoln, somehow pleased with himself.

"I don't know what you mean?" said Eddie, gripping the wheel, not sure what he would do next.

Lincoln slapped himself on the knee. "Damn, that's it. That photo wasn't supposed to look like you. You got too much hair in it, not to mention sideburns. It's you disguised to not look like you. Now that's a motherfucker riddle if I ever saw one."

"Then my name has to be bullshit like you said?"

"Without a doubt."

"Then who am I?"

"Probably a fuckin' yuppie terrorist, or something like that. Why else would people be chasing you?"

"I don't know."

"I know you whites think blacks have this conspiratorial theory about government, but I think you saw something you shouldn't have seen — damn, we better get rid of the plates on this car. How do you think they found you at that motel?"

"They had the phone to a lady friend bugged, I believe."

"That's what I'm telling you — there's a lot of money being spent on finding you."

Eddie was impressed with Lincoln.

"There's one thing I didn't tell you about, Lincoln. I sometimes can't remember things even with my present memory."

"Give it to me," said Lincoln, his face emanating a look of distrust that usually accompanies such a remark.

Eddie told him that they wanted to cut a part of his body off.

"To prove they did the job," Lincoln said glibly. "DNA does the rest."

"I got the feeling it was for something else," Eddie contradicted.

Lincoln adjusted his expensive-looking hat. Until now, Eddie hadn't realized how natty Lincoln really looked.

Looking over his shoulder, Lincoln said, "It wouldn't make any sense if it was for anything else, now let's get the hell out of here Eddie whatever-the-fuck-your-name-is."

At the men's shelter, Lincoln convinced Eddie that it would not be a good idea to leave his car in the street overnight, that he would take care of it, and pick Eddie up in the morning.

The request seemed reasonable so Eddie agreed. In a way he was happy to have someone like Lincoln thinking ahead for him. These days it seemed like such a hard thing to do.

The rows of cots at the men's shelter contained about seventy sleeping men who were snoring, screaming in their sleep, farting, and some even having sex. The air was heavy with sweat and confining. Eddie was uncomfortable with its suffocating closeness. The entire room reeked with the smell of defeat. It was hard for Eddie to believe that this was the only alternative to the street. But he knew if he left he would not be able to get back, and right now he needed someplace to stay.

Somehow, Eddie managed to doze, only to be awakened at dawn by the security guard.

"Bill wants to see you," the guard said sternly.

"Me?"

"Yes, you."

Eddie wondered why the manager of the shelter wanted to see him so early in the morning. When Eddie stepped into the hallway at the top of the stairs, he saw the man who had helped him standing at the foot of the stairs, looking agitated.

Eddie took a deep breath and climbed slowly down the stairs.

"The guard said you wanted to see me," said Eddie at the foot of the stairs.

"Get your things and get the hell out."

Eddie was confused, hurt even. "Why? I don't understand."

"Someone planted a bomb in your car last night. Parts of Lincoln are all over the street. It's almost as if the bastards who did it wanted it that way."

"Is he —"

The manager of the shelter looked away, his face twisted in torment. "Goddamn, I got him killed because of you."

"Oh no," moaned Eddie. "Look, it was his idea to —"

"It doesn't matter," said the manager. "He got killed because of you and I want you out."

"How did you know?" Eddie asked, his voice full of desperation.

"Lincoln had my name in his wallet in case of an emergency. He told me about the car last night, about your name. He was worried about you."

"Do the police know it's my car?"

"No, but if you don't get out of here, I'm angry enough to tell them."

What a horrible feeling to be responsible for someone's death, agonized Eddie He couldn't imagine his old memory ever having experienced such a feeling. He looked at the man who had helped him. "I wish I could explain."

"Nothing gets better, nothing," moaned the manager of the shelter.

Almost overcome with emotional pain, Eddie returned to the gym-sized room to get his handbag which contained the clothes of Elizabeth Cherry's son. Death was everywhere Eddie now thought, and so much a part of his life.

The handbag, however, was not under his cot where he had left it. Someone had taken it, including the 7-Eleven schoolbook with all his notes.

All Eddie had now was what he was wearing: a long-sleeve shirt, jeans, belt, and a pair of army regulation socks and shoes. He had only known Lincoln a day, but felt like he had lost a member of his family.

Eddie left the men's shelter in a daze.

CHAPTER 27

Constantly looking over his shoulder, the 43rd President of the United States walked the streets of Washington, D.C. for hours trying to sort things out. Why were people chasing him, trying to kill him? What had he done?

Eddie repeated these words over and over, until it felt like a sickness. But the answer was always the same — no answer. Eddie was feeling desperate again. He suspected it wouldn't take his pursuers long to locate the shelter that had been so much a part of Lincoln's life. Eddie hadn't intended it, but somehow he found himself approaching the White House grounds. He could feel his heart beat pick up speed as he approached the barricaded site. It was obvious that something awful had happened to the White House. Eddie gazed at the empty hole in the ground where the White House had once stood. He had no memory of what it had once looked like, only a sense that it was there. It was a cross current of confusion that made him feel awful inside; the trickery of his condition that made some things so easy to recall, and others only followed by blankness.

Dozens of men and women in uniform were sifting the earth with small pans. They looked like a bunch of miners searching for gold.

The police guarding the gate were edgy. "You'll have to move away, sir," said a young D.C. cop.

"I once worked there," said Eddie.

The policeman studied Eddie for a few seconds. "Sure buddy, now you'll have to move on."

"If I wanted to talk to someone from the White House, who would that be?" asked Eddie, moving away from the gate to show his cooperation.

"You wouldn't be able to get the Chief of Staff," said the policeman, still studying Eddie, seemingly not sure whether Eddie was worth a complete sentence, "but the President does depend on Shelby Mannix a lot. He's supervising the clean-up mess He probably could be reached through the White House telephone exchange."

Shelby Mannix? The name sounded familiar. Wasn't he the person who interviewed him at the hospital? Eddie hadn't liked Mannix from the first moment he met him, but maybe Mannix could help him meet some former aides of the President? People who might know who Eddie O'Hara really is.

As Eddie walked away, the policeman as an afterthought said, "You probably could e-mail him also. He has an address on the White House web site."

Eddie needed a moment until the *memory trace* of web-site and e-mail came to him, until he fully understood the comment.

Although Eddie didn't know it, it was the same pattern repeating itself: The more distance the person, place or thing from his *autobiographical life* the easier it was for Eddie to recall. Which is why anything to do with White House was a total memory loss, while web site and e-mail, were terms that he understood.

Eddie continued walking until he spotted a coffee shop with a computer chat room. He also realized that his appearance was not that impressive basically because he hadn't shaved that morning. He made a mental note to try and do his best not to give the impression that he was a drifter.

In front of the coffee shop Eddie reached into his pocket and pulled out what was left of Elizabeth Cherry's generous loan — just under $100.

This was as good as time as any to send an e-mail to Shelby Mannix, he decided.

CHAPTER 28

Eddie rented a computer near the back of the shop, just out of sight of the street. Once he started, the basics of using a PC came easily enough. But as cozy as the chat room was, Eddie just didn't feel safe.

How long would it take for his pursuers to know that they blew up the wrong man? he wondered. Or was it a mistake? Lincoln was a private detective, he must have had enemies, Eddie rationalized, but a deep feeling in his gut told him that a mistake had indeed been made, and Eddie O'Hara for some godforsaken reason was the original target of the bombers.

The attendant at the shop was courteous and showed Eddie how to set up a temporary e-mail address. Eddie decided to struggle with the rest himself.

It took some doing, but Eddie finally found the name of Shelby Mannix and his e-mail address under White House Bombing Investigation. The web site invited witnesses who had not been interviewed by the White House to send in their statements.

Before sending Shelby Mannix an e-mail, Eddie nervously leaned sideways and looked out the front window of the coffee shop. How far away were his pursuers? he thought anxiously. Then pulling himself together, Eddie composed an e-mail to Shelby Mannix.

Dear Mr. Mannix,

I was one of the victims of the White House bombing. Do you remember? We spoke in San Antonio at the hospital . I wonder if you could help me locate any person from the former White House staff that could tell me about myself. However, there is a problem. It seems as if there are people trying to harm me. Do you know of any reason why this is happening? Have I done something awful and don't know it? Can you help me get to the bottom of things? I would be so grateful.

Eddie O'Hara

P.S. I'm sending this from a coffee shop chat room so you'll have to respond quickly.

Why would Shelby Mannix know anything about the men chasing me? Eddie thought, but it was worth a try. As he waited at the computer Eddie considered turning himself in but thought better of it. Somehow, for reasons he couldn't explain, the men chasing him seemed connected to official authority — what if he was turned over to them? No, he had to find out if he really was Eddie O'Hara and why people were trying to kill him?

There were two other customers on computers, a Chinese girl in her twenties, and an Indian man about the same age. They were so lucky, Eddie thought. They knew who they were.

Eddie leaned over to look out of the window again. He spotted two men sitting in a Volvo. Call it instinct, but Eddie turned around to see if the coffee shop had a back exit. It did, right next to the men's room. Eddie decided not to wait for an e-mail response from Shelby Mannix. Instead, he got up and walked into the men's room to regain his composure. There was a good chance they couldn't see him go for the exit, he rationalized. He exited the men's room, ducked down, and slowly opened the back door until it was just a crack. He could see a man in his thirties standing in the alley with his hand in one pocket.

Eddie closed the door ever so slowly and noticed a box of dirty linen. Scrambling through the dirty linen, he put on a greasy white coat, and pants, grabbed a tray of Danish off a rack stacked with pastry, took a deep breath, and walked through the store and out into the street as if he were making a delivery. He held the tray of Danish close to his face and forced himself to walk at a slower pace than normal.

For a few moments everything was okay, and then he heard a man's voice yell, "Thief."

Eddie O'Hara dropped the tray of Danish and ran. Glancing over his shoulder he saw the Volvo that had been parked outside of the coffee shop chat room driving toward him. He heard one of the men in the car shout, "Motherfucker, keep still." Eddie hit the ground just as the sickening sound of four shots shattered the plate glass window of a shoe repair store.

95

Stumbling to his feet, Eddie darted across the street to where the traffic was headed the opposite way. The gunmen, defying the traffic, made a U-turn. Eddie bobbed and weaved like a good middleweight as he ran through the African-American neighborhood. The children smiled in bemusement, probably because they had never seen a white man chased before in their neighborhood.

Some spectators, standing on stoops, could not hold back their smiles and whoops.

It was amusement for them, and terror for Eddie.

Eddie turned around to see the Volvo screeching and swerving, coming at him like a wounded animal anxious to pounce on him and finish the kill.

"In here bro," said a young African-American holding the door in front of a scummy-looking row house.

Eddie ducked in, the door closed.

"Whatcha got for me?" said the young man. The hallway smelled foul.

"I don't understand."

"Money."

Eddie pulled eighty-six dollars out of his pants.

The young man snatched the money from Eddie's hand like a lizard snagging a fly with his tongue. "Okay, let's go," he added with great authority.

They walked through a series of rooms that had human-sized holes in the walls which connected to other row houses. Used needles were everywhere.

Finally, they climbed the stairs of an apartment building. The smell of urine was gagging.

When they reached the top landing, Eddie's guide said, "Stay here until it gets dark. They ain't gonna find you, man."

As the young African-American headed back down the stairs, Eddie said, "Thanks." But there was no answer.

The 43rd President of the United States slumped in a corner and waited until dark.

Shelby Mannix's assistant, Ruth Hoffman, handed him a hard copy of Eddie O'Hara's message.

"The person I interviewed in San Antonio?" said Shelby, trying to play dumb.

"Yes sir, I believe that's who it is. The witness who left the hospital. You were very upset I remember. He thinks people are trying to harm him."

"I saw that, Ruth — I wonder how he knew my e-mail address."

"We're on the White House web site, sir. You specifically asked for that — witnesses we may not have talked to. You thought it was a good idea."

Shelby leaned forward. He had been studying the 25th Amendment, the Presidential Disability and Succession Act.

"Strange he would contact me, don't you think?"

"Yes sir, I wonder why he left the hospital in the first place?"

"Where is this e-mail from Ruth?"

"I have someone on it. Right now all I can tell you it's somewhere in the South East district. It's such a coincidence."

"What is, Ruth?"

"The FBI has been asking for information on our witnesses. They want all the information we have, and then this Eddie O'Hara shows up."

"To hell with the FBI," grumbled Shelby. His out-of-character voice startled Ruth. "When we're finished, they'll get a report."

"Yes sir, but isn't it strange that someone is trying to harm him?"

"It could all be in his imagination, Ruth. The doctors told me his type of injury could bring it on."

"Well, I answered that we got his message and told him to wait for your reply."

"Ahead of me again, Ruth?"

Ruth kept a straight face.

"This O'Hara might be a suspect in the bombing. We've never been sure," said Shelby. "I'll have to give some thought to what we do next."

Ruth, more than familiar with the investigation, left Shelby's small office, the e-mail still on her mind.

Shelby was furious. A connection had now been established between him and a man who was about to be murdered. If he ignored Eddie O'Hara, it would look suspicious. If he had contact with O'Hara, he would be included in the investigation of O'Hara's disappearance should that ever come up. *What to do now?* Shelby agonized.

He also realized that he was suffering from some memory loss of his own. Somehow he didn't like to think of Eddie O'Hara as the 43rd President of the United States. He was not the target. A broken-down man with a new name and a new face who could not remember anything about himself was the target.

Shelby continued to look at the 25th Amendment.

Theoretically the Speaker's succession only mattered if Wainwright was dead, it appeared. The 25th Amendment was only relevant to Luther Donald if Wainwright had transmitted a written document to the House stating that he was unfit to perform the duties of his office, or at the least his Cabinet had done so. Shelby concluded that Luther Donald, despite being sworn in by the Chief Justice, was on shaky ground. Something else was even more horrifying: Even as Eddie O'Hara there was a possibility that Sam Wainwright might be able to retain the office of the Presidency.

Ruth entered the room again. "No one is answering the e-mail, sir."

Shelby relaxed for a moment. "Like I said, Ruth, it may be all in his mind."

"He's still a question mark, isn't he, sir? I mean the Social Security thing? The Secret Service says since he had a pass there's no way he's not legit, only the records have been destroyed."

Ruth was always throwing curve balls. He wondered why he hadn't fired her years ago.

"There must be some logical explanation, Ruth. Only I don't know what it is."

Ruth gave Shelby what he considered one of her *superior looks* before saying, "You'll get to the bottom of things. I know that, sir."

Sometimes she reminded him of a female Columbo — never satisfied with an answer.

"Look, Ruth, why don't you leave early. Take the rest of the day off. I know how hard you've been working."

"Are you sure?"

"Yes, I'm sure."

"What if this Eddie character contacts us?"

"I wouldn't worry about it, Ruth."

Shelby watched the pain-in-the-ass leave, not sure whether she bought the brush off. He now realized that he had to find out where O'Hara was staying, and give the people from New Orleans every assistance that he could. Too much was at stake not to.

CHAPTER 29

It was night before Eddie thought it was safe enough to leave his rooftop hideaway. He took one look from the rooftop. The Capitol building glittered in the steamy night.

Downstairs, on the street, the sidewalks Eddie walked on felt like a sore that oozed fear, yet they were less than a mile from where the White House had once stood.

Eddie was broke now, and realized that his situation seemed hopeless. If he gave himself up, the authorities might turn him over to the same people that were trying to kill him. But if he didn't turn to the authorities for help, he probably could be on the streets the rest of his life.

Eddie asked a policeman where the Vietnam Veteran's Memorial was located. Thanks to Lincoln Washington, it was the only place in Washington that he was familiar with.

The walk to the Vietnam Memorial didn't seem that long to Eddie. He liked the night, it kept other people from seeing him.

When he reached the Memorial, there were no visitors, but in the near distance he could see a group of men standing around a small fire near the statues of three infantrymen. He had heard somebody refer to them as the *Grunt Statues* on his last visit with Lincoln Washington.

Eddie approached the men then stopped. They turned instinctively and looked at him. One of them said, "Come in from out of the boonies, brother."

The veterans were heating some cans of food over a fire. They looked very hard. Each was wearing a beret and a fatigue shirt covered with decorations.

"You're welcome to share our rations," said a friendly voice.

"Thanks, I appreciate that," said Eddie, surprised at the generous greeting.

As Eddie ate a tin-can frankfurter, he couldn't help but notice that the veterans had a vocabulary all their own. They used terms like *beehive rounds*, *chicken plates*, *snoop 'n poop* and *white mice*, which meant nothing to Eddie.

He told them he didn't think he was a veteran, but couldn't remember too much about himself. They seemed to relate to his remark and were friendly. It was hard for Eddie to tell whether they were homeless or not. They seemed to enjoy each other's company immensely. They spoke of their friends on the Wall with great affection.

In his new memory Eddie hadn't met such men before. There was something that he liked very much about them. Yet he couldn't relax. For some reason he sensed that his adversaries were not far away.

One of the vets shouted out, "Looks like trouble."

Eddie turned toward the Wall. He could see the dark silhouette of two broad-shouldered men wearing raincoats coming towards him. They appeared menacing in their slow, deliberate, gunfighter walk.

"D.C. detectives," someone in the group said.

"No, they've come to kill me. And I don't know why," said Eddie.

The vets, under the light of the crinkling fire, studied Eddie's face. In turn he looked at them. Their faces showed no fear, only confidence. Although he had only said a few words, Eddie could feel their trust in him.

One of the vets pulled up his pant's leg and untied a pistol strapped to it.

"They're not making their body count tonight, my friend."

Two other vets also held pistols which seemed to materialize out of nowhere.

The two dark figures continued to walk toward the men, the Vietnam War Memorial looming in the distance behind them.

"Kick out the fire," said the vet who had pulled out the first pistol.

The two dark figures, about twenty-feet away, stopped.

"What's the password?" the vet shouted to the dark figures.

"Password?"

"So you don't get your balls shot off if you take another step."

"We're looking for Eddie O'Hara. He's wanted for questioning. Is he here with you?" The accent had a slight southern drawl.

"Never talked to an Eddie O'Hara."

"We think he's in the neighborhood."

"Not this neighborhood. Only heroes are in this neighborhood."

"We'd like to take a look at you guys, anyway."

"You can arrange for an appointment at another time."

"You guys are in over your head. We talk to who we want to talk to, do you understand?"

As if the remark was a cue, the veterans cocked their revolvers at the same time. The sound in the night was unmistakable. The fire was dead. Now there was only darkness.

"You guys sound like Charlie to me," said another vet.

"Charlie who?"

There was laughter.

Eddie heard one of his pursuers say, "Son of a bitch."

"I don't think he's here either," said the vet who was first to take out a pistol.

"You guys are fucking with the wrong people," seethed one of the men in the raincoats.

The vets began spreading out, one of them touched Eddie on the shoulder and signaled for Eddie to follow him.

There were lots of trees and zigzagging, but Eddie soon found himself staring at traffic.

"Why did you trust me?" said Eddie to the vet who had led him to safety.

"You got the vibe, brother. You either got it or you don't — most don't."

"What vibe?" asked Eddie, having trouble understanding the word.

The vet just smiled and slipped away in the charcoal darkness.

Eddie crossed the wide street anxiously and was confused about which way to go. Finally, a tourist with a cell phone helped him get the address and directions to the SouthEast Men's Shelter.

Before leaving the area, Eddie hesitated for a moment, and wondered if he would hear gunfire, but there was none.

CHAPTER 30

It began to drizzle. The streets were glossy, full of bleeding colors from headlights and store lighting. Eddie still had to stop a number of pedestrians to ask further directions to the SouthEast Men's Shelter, but eventually found it. Bill Paxton was just finishing up after what looked like a long day.

Paxton gave Eddie a hard stare.

"I'm sorry about Lincoln, I am."

"I don't want you around here O'Hara," said Paxton locking up his desk.

"I've nowhere to go. People are trying to kill me and I don't know why."

Paxton came into the hallway. "You got Lincoln killed."

"I know," said Eddie, looking down, rubbing his brow, clearly shaken. "Something's crazy. I don't know who I am, or what I am, and most of the time, where I am."

Paxton looked straight at Eddie. "If I thought you did, I would have told the police about you, Eddie. But I know you're having problems you can't handle."

"If I could use your computer, I might have a start," pleaded the 43rd President of the United States.

Paxton, holding a bunch of papers, his once white shirt soiled from the day, gave a big sigh. "You're trouble Eddie, I can't have you here."

"Just let me use your computer for an hour. That's all I ask."

"You remember how to operate one?"

"Yes, this condition I have is strange. The doctors told me my *autobiographical memory* is what's gone. Some things come to me, others don't."

Paxton's lips came together in doubt. "What in the world do you need a computer for?"

"There's someone on the White House staff that can help me get some information. I can reach him through e-mail."

"The White House?" replied Paxton, looking at Eddie incredulously.

"Yes, I was supposed to have worked there at one time."

Paxton, seemingly fighting the urge to say no, said, "Okay, but you're out of here as soon as you finish."

"I'll need to be here in the morning for a reply," said Eddie, meekly.

Paxton handed Eddie a meal ticket. "Then have breakfast but be out of here after that. Is that a promise?"

Eddie shook his head. He realized at that moment that nothing seemed real to him including the conversation he was having with Paxton. It was the unrealness that was getting to him. The feeling that he would wake up at any moment and Eddie O'Hara would disappear.

After Eddie sent the e-mail to Shelby Mannix, he walked to the door with Paxton. He didn't know where he was going to sleep, but didn't care. Somehow making contact with the White House gave him intense gratification.

"I'll put you in a hotel tonight, Eddie," said Paxton. "There's one in the neighborhood that owes me a few favors."

Eddie thought about Paxton's offer for a moment, then declined. He had been enough trouble for Paxton, he decided.

It was only 7:45 in the morning, but Shelby could immediately see by the look on Ruth's face that something important had happened. She handed him a copy of Eddie's latest e-mail.

"He's persistent, isn't he, Ruth?"

"I think we can't afford *not* to talk to him, sir?"

What to do? thought Shelby. "What's his official status, Ruth?"

"Fuzzy. A download of the White House files haven't been found anywhere. I guess we now know the Secret Service does a good job that way. Simply stated, sir, he doesn't fit in anywhere."

Why should he? Shelby thought. *He's the goddamn—or was—the President of the United States. Of course he doesn't fit in.*

"You look angry, sir."

"I'm not, Ruth, just tired of the whole thing."

"We should talk to him, sir."

Shelby got up and walked to his window. The President was right, not even a view of the Jefferson Memorial — and now he was a prisoner of a man who should be dead. Any more contact with Eddie O'Hara would implicate him further, as well. What to do?

"As I remember, Ruth, there is no file on him. All the people who could have briefed me died that night."

"His fingerprints are not on file anywhere as well, sir."

Shelby turned from the window and looked at Ruth menacingly. "How do you know *that*, Ruth," he said, trying to keep his composure.

"We recently found out that some bureaucrat at the White House ordered the hospitals to fingerprint every victim that wasn't vaporized by the blast that night. We received Eddie O'Hara's prints last week, but by then you were trying to find a piece of Sam Wainwright in the ground. Since I had been helping on the original investigation, I sent Mr. O'Hara's fingerprints to the FBI. I didn't want your report to be incomplete for any reason. Well, he's not on file. Never served in the Armed Forces, or has been convicted of anything. Funny though."

"What's that, Ruth?"

"He would have had to be fingerprinted to have a White House pass. The only person in the White House who doesn't have his fingerprints on record — including the Armed Services — is the President."

"We checked the pass. It's authentic," interjected Shelby. "He might have been new, not processed yet. And I'm sure his prints are somewhere."

"No sir, they check fingerprints first before anyone goes on staff."

Shelby sighed. "I've long suspected that the FBI is overrated on being able to find the identity of any fingerprint forwarded to them, even with that new wonder computer they have, Ruth."

Ruth seemed to be reading his mind.

"I didn't mention to the FBI that he had a White House pass, sir, so there was no follow-up. I was waiting to talk to you about it. I know how you feel about other agencies meddling in on your responsibilities. I said Eddie O'Hara was just a hospital victim. And that was the truth."

Shelby looked at Ruth. She suddenly had that look of leverage so common with power brokers in Washington.

"Well Ruth, you've made a good case for why we should find out more about Eddie O'Hara. On the other hand, it could be embarrassing for the President if O'Hara turns out to be associated with terrorists."

"I just have a hunch about him, sir. Something's not kosher."

Shelby sat back and sighed. Ruth was a Jew, born and raised in Ireland. It was impossible, he learned, to try and change her mind, but that wouldn't stop him from trying.

"I couldn't find anything about this O'Hara character, that was the problem," Shelby replied.

"Maybe his being chased is not mental, sir."

Shelby was ready to explode, but managed to contain himself. "Send him an e-mail. Tell him we'll do everything we can, whatever that is?"

"Don't you think you should interview him again, sir?"

"Yes, of course, Ruth. Let's take this one step at a time."

Ruth was like a hunting dog who got a scent from afar and couldn't rest until she went after it. He also suspected that the *alive Eddie O'Hara* was just slightly more dangerous than the *dead Eddie O'Hara*. The matter was no longer a can of worms, but a stadium full of boa constrictors, he concluded nervously.

Eddie walked all night, sometimes resting on a park bench, but he didn't mind. He felt he was connecting to something about himself for the first time.

In the morning Eddie returned to the men's shelter. He could hear the men rising, their coughs rattling like kettles. He turned on the ancient Apple computer like Paxton had showed him. He could feel himself holding his breath as he selected mail and waited for the connection to the server to receive the mail. He knew immediately that he had gotten a response by the e-mail address that appeared on the screen. It had been sent just minutes before he had gotten to the shelter. The message said, 'Will do everything I can. Reply for an appointment. Shelby Mannix.'

Eddie thought, *my God this feels good*, but just then Bill Paxton burst into the small office, half out of breath, and full of fear. He held the door open. "They're outside, Eddie, just driving around the block— two thugs."

"I got a response, Bill — look."

"Eddie, please go."

"Damn it, Bill, I *need* to reply."

"And you need to get out of here. Take the stairs at the back of the upstairs sleep area. Go down to the basement. It will take you to the street in back of us. Remnants of this building once housed runaway slaves. There's a lower passageway just before you hit the exit door. There's a big toilet-paper carton on top of it."

"I appreciate that, Bill, but I've got to reply first."

"Damn, I can't believe you. Okay — reply, but then get the hell out of here."

Eddie typed his message, 'Have to hurry. Will call. Thanks for your reply. Can you e-mail me your direct phone line?'

Eddie got up. "I'll be in touch for their response, Mr. Paxton."

"You're going to get us all killed, Eddie. I just don't understand." Paxton's face was noticeably tense.

Eddie wondered if fear was accumulative. He didn't feel any more afraid than he had while running from his kidnappers. All he could remember now was running, and fear, almost to the point of being numb. There seemed to be a desperation to his attackers now. And somehow that felt like weakness to him.

There was a gun shot. Bill Paxton made a funny sound and collapsed in front of Eddie, blood oozing out of the back of his head. Eddie didn't know why he knew, something he had seen before but he knew, Bill Paxton was dead.

Eddie rushed into the hallway and darted up the stairs. The darkness of the stairs was a momentary advantage as he heard a rough voice say, "Get that son of a bitch. Remember we need the body."

'Need the body.' What did that mean? thought Eddie, as bullets splintered the wooden steps he was climbing up two-at-a-time.

When Eddie entered the large sleeping area, a few men were sitting on their beds smoking. The room was still dark. For a moment after seeing Bill Paxton fall, Eddie wanted to stay but knew that would cost him his life. He didn't feel good about himself as he zig-zagged around the foul-smelling cots of the homeless like a quarterback with great blocking. There was great confusion in the room as Eddie continued running down the back steps.

He went straight to the cellar as Bill Paxton had told him, but he couldn't find the light. His eyes needed time to adjust, but he couldn't waste a moment, he knew that. He plunged forward bumping into various objects, brooms, pails, and what not, but no big box of toilet paper rolls. None that he could see anyway. He groped his way through the long cellar, finally spotting the exit door, and to his right, a large box of toilet paper rolls.

Eddie was out of breath and weak but managed to push the box aside. Underneath was a square hole barely large enough for a slightly-built man. It was a place darker than the basement he was in. Eddie's lanky frame had trouble climbing into the hole, but he finally wiggled through thanks to all the weight he had lost. He felt his way to the bottom of the steps and began his trek through the tunnel. The stone underneath was damp. Suddenly Eddie heard cursing. Something like "You fat bastard, let *me* try."

Eddie could hear shots fired though the hole as he crouched as best he could. When the volley of gunfire stopped, Eddie moved forward in the slimy sweating-rock tunnel that was nearly the height of a man.

CHAPTER 31

Shelby was told over a secure line that Elijah Smith and his three men had been *removed*.

"By what authority?" Shelby protested in a restrained voice, but he knew it was no use. The process he had started now had a life of its own. He was no longer the only one who knew about Eddie O'Hara.

They had probably used him just as they had used Oswald; just as they had used others. Most likely they would try to make it look like a mob hit when they caught up with O'Hara, and then, who knew?

A hard copy of Eddie O'Hara's latest e-mail was in Shelby's hand. The message was innocent enough. O'Hara was a man searching for his identity. But the cost was too high, Shelby believed intensely.

Shelby was contemplating his next move when the President called. Shelby could tell by the President's voice that it was not going to be a good conversation.

The other President of the United States groped his way through the runaway-slave tunnel for about sixty yards until being stopped finally by a metal door. Eddie tried to pull the door open, but it was locked. In desperation Eddie slapped his hand on the door a dozen or so times. The men chasing him could not squeeze through the opening, he guessed. That opening could only accommodate starved slaves, or thin people like himself, but he knew he couldn't go back.

Eddie closed his hand and hit the door viciously, but with little hope. Who would be there to answer?

Eddie leaned his head forward, pushed it against the door, and wondered when he would die.

He was startled to feel the door moving.

"Hold on," he heard a muffled voice say.

The door opened. The light that struck Eddie's eyes hurt. Standing before him, was a willowy African-American who stared at him in disbelief. "You're the first white man Bill has ever sent through the tunnel," he said in a deep, gutsy voice that could have belonged to a blues singer.

"Can I come in?" Eddie asked.

"You must be in trouble like all the rest were," the old man said. "Yes, you can come in. Who's chasing you? Usually it's some fat white cop coming down hard on one of the brothers."

"There are men looking for me. They'll find this place."

The old man gave Eddie a hard look. "You know where you are mister? This is the Shiloh Baptist Church. No one is coming through our doors unless we want them to. And anyway I can send you through another tunnel."

"You can?"

"If Bill sent you, I can."

"Bill sent me alright," said Eddie nervous about standing still.

"How's Bill?"

Eddie had dreaded the question coming up.

"He was shot by the same people chasing me."

The old man grimaced for a minute. "Then it's real serious isn't it?"

"They're trying to kill me and anyone who's in their way," replied Eddie, realizing now that he was in a basement.

"What did you do?" asked the old man looking over his nose.

"I don't know. I can't remember a thing about my past life — I have amnesia."

"Is Bill going to be alright?"

"I don't know."

Eddie could see the old man deciding. Finally the old man said, "Bill must have thought you were okay or else he would have never told you about this tunnel."

"That's good to know," Eddie said, getting anxious.

"These tunnels have helped people in trouble even before the Civil War," the old man said. "They only know how to help people, want to help people, must help people — you a junkie?"

"No, I'm not," replied Eddie, startled by the question.

"I didn't think you were. Sometimes the junkies get down here —"

"I don't mean to be rude, but can you show me the other tunnel," said Eddie, knowing seconds were precious.

The old man smiled. He seemed so wise. "We have another tunnel behind the stairs. It will take you to a manhole cover two blocks from here. You'll need this." The old man handed Eddie a cheap flashlight.

Upstairs Eddie could hear someone banging on the door. The old man smirked. "After I show you the other tunnel, I think I'll go out the way you came in, safer that way."

The old man opened a brick door behind the staircase that seemed to be a part of the wall.

"Bill must have trusted you," the old man said to Eddie as he entered the tunnel.

Chapter 32

It was agreed by most Democrats that Sam Wainwright had been ineffectual, maybe even insipid. He had more responsibility than he could handle and didn't like the idea, was their conclusion.

On the other hand, Sam Wainwright was President when the bomb went off and just as important, he was a Democrat. It was generally agreed, and gaining some momentum among Democrats, that the transition of power from one elected official to another had been blurred, particularly with the House Speaker becoming President.

The 25th Amendment should have prevented that, but didn't. The President's body was not supposed to disappear, and it had.

There was no provision for this kind of situation in the Amendment. They could have all the committees they wanted, but a committee could only declare the President dead. Reasonable enough if his plane was lost over the ocean, but a stretch when hundreds of bodies are involved in the crime scene. If there had been a Vice President in place, perhaps the tragedy would have been acceptable, but that had not happened.

Among Democrats not thrilled with the constitutional process that allowed Luther Donald to become 44th President of the United States was Congressman Billy Louis Jr. from the 15th Congressional District which included Harlem. In recent weeks he had become a bane to the right wingers in the Republican party.

Back in the 1970's there had been a famous commercial that pictured a peppy old woman, part gnome and part toughie, who cried, "Where's the Beef?" every time she looked at the competitor's burger. Billy had adopted her approach, although it was more than thirty years later, with "Where's the body?"

No one in Congress took Billy seriously in the beginning, but uncertainty can be catching. His attacks in Congress made Luther Donald downright miserable.

The President was chewing a sour ball when Shelby Mannix entered his office. Elbows resting on his desk, head not moving, pudgy face flushed, the President was in his fighting position.

Shelby entered the office gingerly as if that would keep the President's temper in check.

"Goddamn it, Shelby, we're not making progress on this DNA thing, are we?"

"We're sifting through every inch of ground, Mr. President."

The President took a deep sigh. "The son-of-a-bitch is not alive. You know that. I know that. The Democrats know that, but they still want to make it miserable for me. That's the trouble with these bastards inside the beltway. Everyone's got a political agenda."

"I agree with that, Mr. President."

"They won't let me start building the White House until every millimeter of ground is searched. They're trying to embarrass me. Keep me in this shit Vice President's office, away from the people — there's got to be a goddamn sample of his blood somewhere, Shelby."

The statement caught Shelby by surprise.

"The Naval Hospital in Maryland where all Presidents get their yearly physical would probably have a sample of Wainwright's blood," replied Shelby. "They could give us a DNA printout but that would be it. Anyway I understand our political opponents wouldn't be satisfied with another blood sample — remember the shirt. They know there's a few blood samples floating around from previous tests given to Wainwright."

President Luther Donald moved a photograph of his wife slightly. It appeared to Shelby the President was trying *not* to say what was on his mind.

"You would have thought of that anyway — I know that Shelby. You're always thinking on my behalf; you have been for eighteen years."

"Twenty, Mr. President."

"There are probably things you haven't told me as well — and I appreciate that, Shelby."

Shelby felt a slight shudder. It wasn't possible. The President couldn't know?

"We're on the high ground now Shelby, and we have to keep it that way. You know, three past Presidents I've known — excluding Wainwright that closet liberal — told me they always felt a cold chill when they pushed too hard in any direction that might upset the *people* who really run this country — you know what I mean, Shelby? Seems like those people want me in this job, and I'll take that Shelby, because that means progress for us. No assassination attempts, peaceful co-existence, I don't give a goddamn what the mob does, they'll always be around. The violence that's affecting our youth — that's what I want to do something about."

Shelby was familiar with the *Cold-Chill Syndrome* that almost every President experienced since Kennedy's assassination. It was imagined in different forms, in different combinations of criminal elements conniving with various conservative causes ranging from Cuba to anti-life, but the *Cold-Chill Syndrome* did have a life all it's own, and it was now a part of Shelby's life. Was Luther Donald in his own insidious way letting him know he knew about Wainwright?

Were these people who gave Presidents cold chills so clever they could even arrange terrorist attacks? Shelby doubted he would ever know, but the pressure to find the other President and eliminate him was now so great, he had trouble keeping a steady breath. A Mannix was not expected to get too excited about anything and that only added to the pressure Shelby felt.

"If we could get some DNA — a fingernail even — then that would satisfy the goddamn constitutionalists. Do you understand, Shelby?"

"I do, Mr. President."

"I want it by tomorrow and I don't care how you do it. Is that clear, Shelby?"

"I'll do my best, Mr. President."

The President stood up abruptly. In all the years Shelby had worked for him, Luther Donald had never raised his voice to Shelby. The President drew up his body and said in a tone of voice that was unfamiliar to Shelby, "I don't want your best. I want Sam Wainwright's DNA. Do you understand, Shelby?"

"Yes, Mr. President."

"Then for God's sake, get it done."

There were no further words. Shelby left with the President moving the picture of his wife to another location on his desk. Shelby wondered if the President would ever get over the affair she had with a young artist when she headed the National Arts Council.

Eddie emerged from a manhole in front of a dirty lot sandwiched between two abandoned buildings. There were children cooling themselves under the spray of a fire hydrant. They waved and giggled under their mini-waterfall. Eddie wondered why Congress and the President hadn't done more for these children as he set out to find the office of Shelby Mannix.

When Shelby emerged from the President's office, Ruth looked despondent. "Eddie O'Hara's not following up, sir."

"No reply?"

"None."

"It's Friday. Ruth, take the rest of the afternoon off."

"But —"

"I insist."

He watched her unattractive, ample body mope back to her office. He now realized how dangerous it was for her to get any more involved with Eddie O'Hara.

Back in his tiny office Shelby tried to approach his problem logically, but he had done just that so many other times. Even trying to see if the hospital had saved a piece of Eddie O'Hara's nose after surgery. O'Hara had to be brought down, and quickly. There was no other solution, he determined.

The phone rang. Shelby hesitated for a moment before picking it up. It was the Marine guard at the front gate. He said a man named Eddie O'Hara wanted to talk to him, said he was a White House bombing victim. Shelby's mind raced for a solution knowing he had only seconds to come up with an emergency plan.

"Put Mr. O'Hara on."

"This is Eddie O'Hara, Mr. Shelby — we talked before."

"Yes, Mr. O'Hara, I know."

"I wanted to find out more about my position at the White House, perhaps talk to former employees. I need to know more about myself."

"We can discuss it. Can you do that, Mr. O'Hara"

"Yes sir, I can."

"Our temporary security position prevents you from coming through the gates, Mr. O'Hara, but we can meet. Now I don't want you to repeat what I say for security reasons, but meet me at the Capitol YMCA in one hour. I can debrief you there."

"Debrief?"

"Tell you all that I know about you."

"I understand, sir."

"It's only a few minutes walk from our location."

Shelby then instructed Eddie on how to get from the Naval grounds to the YMCA.

When the Marine guard got back on the phone, Shelby said, "Don't ever have anyone off the street phone me, do you understand?"

"Yes, sir."

"Now ask this character to leave, but politely, and let's not have a repeat performance. This is no longer the residence of the Vice President."

"Yes, sir."

As Eddie was escorted from the front gate, he was confused by the severe attitude of the guard. He thought it was clear that he had made contact with Shelby Mannix.

"Next time I'll have the Secret Service take care of your ass," said the Marine as he pointed for Eddie to start walking.

CHAPTER 33

Shelby rushed home to his apartment at the Watergate, dismissed his driver for the weekend, changed into jeans and a short-sleeved Hawaiian shirt, and put on a baseball cap to cover his impressive gray mane. He had an urge to call New Orleans and tell them where Eddie O'Hara was meeting him, but the location would not be conducive to getting the DNA sample. No, a more secluded place was needed for Eddie O'Hara.

Shelby took a taxi to a location three blocks from the Capitol YMCA.

"This is desperate, I know, but what can I do?" Shelby mumbled to himself.

Eddie had no trouble finding the Capitol YMCA, but now he wondered if Shelby Mannix would show up because of the way the Marine guard had treated him.

The "Y" was like all "Y's" that came to his new memory: young travelers, cheap food, and decent prices. It was odd, Eddie thought, but for the first time he thought about money and the fact that he didn't have any. He noticed a full glass of water at an empty table, sat down in front of it, and took a few sips. He wondered why Shelby would pick the "Y" to have a meeting, but blamed it on his own confusion. *Where was the right place to have a meeting with a man who couldn't remember who he was?* It wasn't long, however, before he began to feel uncomfortable. People were looking at him. Even he could see that he didn't fit in. He was unshaven and dirty from his tunnel escape.

"You'll have to leave," said a managerial type.

Eddie was about to reply when Shelby Mannix jumped in, "I'm buying him dinner. I hope you don't mind."

"No sir, we don't. Sorry to bother you."

Shelby Mannix did not look anything like the first time they met, observed Eddie.

115

"It's not a very auspicious place to meet, Mr. O'Hara, but I suspected you didn't have taxi fare and it is comfortable here. Let's get something to eat."

Eddie followed Shelby to the cafeteria line. This was not the facile gentlemen he first met in Texas, Eddie thought, as he went through the chain of servers tossing food on his tray like priests giving a benediction. He couldn't help but wonder if his pursuers were waiting for him outside.

When they were seated, Eddie said, "Thanks for the food, but it's not what I'm here for, sir."

Shelby seemed nervous. "You're here to find out who you are, and so am I, Mr. O'Hara. That's the paradox."

"I thought you could help me," said Eddie, more hungry than he realized.

Shelby leaned forward. "We can figure this out together. I'm sure of that Mr. O'Hara. After all, I have the resources of the White House."

Eddie looked up from the tray of food. "White House, I know is for Presidents, and I have a sense of its importance, but my connection puzzles me — I don't feel like a maintenance man."

Eddie watched Shelby's face turn red.

"Something wrong?"

"To be frank, Mr. O'Hara, I'm not sure who you are. You were found near a dead secret-service agent. There's every indication you were employed by the White House, but you're an enigma. No Social Security number. No finger prints. And what would you be doing at a reception for the Israeli Ambassador? Perhaps you don't want to remember your part in a terrorist attack on the White House?"

Eddie dropped his fork. "I'm not that kind of a person. I know that."

"Then have the courage to face your past, Mr. O'Hara. Let's work together. There is a Congressional appropriation for victims. You don't have to worry about money."

"That's why I'm here, sir — to face the past. But things just don't make sense. People are trying to kill me. Why, for being a bombing victim?"

Shelby pursed his lips, and gave Eddie a look of doubt that he had honed over the years. It could totally deflate a person. "There are psychological considerations that we have to get past as well, Mr. O'Hara."

"Meaning, I'm nuts?"

"No, Mr. O'Hara, perhaps confused from the blast. One memory fighting another and maybe even both trying to forget what happened. Why, in your state you could imagine all sorts of things."

Eddie smiled. "Like people coming after me? That's your point?"

"It might not stop there, Mr. O'Hara."

"What could be more paranoid than that?" replied Eddie, surprised at the word paranoid. How did he know that word?

Shelby, in his facile manner, toyed with a piece of meatloaf and said, "You might have delusions of grandeur Mr. O'Hara. Think you're somebody important. The doctors told me that could happen."

Eddie looked up and froze in position. "I don't remember any doctor saying that to me. I don't remember who I was, but that doesn't mean I think I'm somebody I'm not."

"Very good, Mr. O'Hara."

"For *who?*" replied Eddie, finishing his plate of food.

Ignoring his remark, Shelby said, "I'm going to give you some cash, Mr. O'Hara. There's a cheaper hotel a few blocks from here named after General Grant. You won't need a credit card. Register yourself at the Grant Hotel for the evening and then expect a call from me in the morning. I would prefer if we kept this to ourselves for the moment. Other agencies could get involved and that might slow progress down considerably."

"Then you really are going to help me?" asked Eddie, relieved.

"Yes, of course Mr. O'Hara. Who knows what other information your former memory has about the bombing? I'm duty bound, actually. And like I said you're entitled to emergency funds."

"Cash?"

Shelby smiled. "Normally a voucher would be issued first, but you've been through enough. Giving you cash is just a few more minutes paper work for me. I'm pleased to do it."

"How much?"

"The first payment is $500, Mr. O'Hara. Get yourself some clean clothes. This "Y" has a decent sportswear shop, in fact."

Eddie smiled, but inside something was ticking away. Something didn't seem right.

"This is the weekend, Mr. O'Hara, but when Monday approaches I'll have my staff work full-time on your matter. You might be a key witness and not even know it, so I do have more to gain than just the pleasure of helping you."

"You scratch my back and I'll scratch yours is what runs this town, I assume," said Eddie.

Shelby smiled again. It was a superficial smile. He was trying to hide something, concluded Eddie, now nervous again.

E.N.J. CARTER

Shelby chose to say good-bye in the lobby. As he watched Shelby walk away, Eddie noticed a young woman without makeup near the sports shop looking at him with great interest. *A woman? Have my pursuers turned to her?* he thought, now desperate to run, but knowing that it would draw attention to himself.

CHAPTER 34

Damn, there isn't much time, thought Shelby. He stopped his taxi half way to his Watergate apartment, and used a public phone to call New Orleans. When the call was completed, he wondered if anyone would care about Eddie O'Hara disappearing, and concluded they wouldn't.

The former President was in worse shape than he could have imagined. He looked like a bum and even smelled like a bum. Shelby rationalized that the New Orleans people had a more difficult task than just elimination. They had to take a piece of Eddie's body without being obvious — well, that was their problem. He had delivered Eddie O'Hara to them and would expect the mission to be completed this time.

Watching the young woman out of the corner of his eye watching him, Eddie purchased underwear, running pants, running shoes, and a Notre Dame jersey. He entered the "Y" restroom to change when the same young woman walked in right behind him.

"I'm sorry, Mr. O'Hara. We have to talk."

"Who the hell are you?" Eddie asked. A surprised Indian smiled as he came out of a stall.

"My name is Ruth Hoffman. I work for Shelby Mannix. Although it's embarrassing to admit, I followed him here."

"And?"

"And, I've taken it upon myself to get involved in your matter."

"And what would that be?" asked Eddie, entering a stall to change.

Ruth raised her voice. "I believe you. I believe people are trying to kill you. I saw your e-mail."

The stall door opened. "You do? Why?"

"My boss never seemed to work hard enough to find you after you disappeared, yet you were the one enigma in the bombing. It just didn't make

119

sense. It's what he does best. He just let you slip through the cracks, yet you are the one question mark in the whole bombing: No files, no Social Security number, no prints. What's more, the White House pass they found on you was official, not forged. Nothing's kosher when it comes to you, Mr. O'Hara. When you were sending e-mails to us, *Mr. Cool Southerner* broke out in a sweat. He never sweats. Butter wouldn't melt in his mouth as the expression goes."

Eddie closed the stall door and took off his soiled clothes. He was naked now, but it felt good changing into fresh underwear.

"Why would you risk your job for me?" Eddie asked.

"Frankly, I don't like Mannix, or the rest of those conservative bastards he wheels and deals with every day. I stuck it out because I didn't want to see another Watergate. I believe this new bunch of bastards in the White House are more than capable of it. How they managed to get the former Speaker of the House into the Presidency is beyond me, but they did."

Eddie's voice was full of surprise as he slipped on his new trousers. "That's who is President — the former Speaker of the House?"

"Yes, Luther Donald — who I'm sure will sell out Israel when he has the opportunity."

Eddie stepped out of the stall. "Then you're not just worried about me, Ms. Hoffman. You, like most in Washington, have an agenda."

"I see you haven't lost all of your memory," she replied facetiously.

"I don't feel like a maintenance man, but that's what everyone tells me I am."

"That's what your White House Pass says, it was the only thing recovered from you. Your clothes were shredded wheat."

Eddie, without blinking, looked at Ruth. "Why are you here?"

Ruth looked momentarily startled by the question, then seemingly gathered herself. "I'm afraid for your safety, Mr. O'Hara."

"Call me Eddie for now," the 43rd President said, taking a step toward the door.

Ruth said, "Shelby put you in a cheap hotel, didn't he? Some place where losers go. Cash only, of course?"

Eddie turned. Ruth Hoffman's eyes were blazing with concern.

"You really do care, don't you?"

"Very much, Eddie."

"After you," Eddie said.

They exited the men's room together. A few tourists seem startled.

"Then what do you suggest?" asked Eddie.

"Stay at my place until we can sort this out. It's the last place anyone would look for you."

Eddie grimaced. "Shelby Mannix is my connection to my past. For God's sake he works for the President. Why would he harm me? For what motive?" said Eddie, looking around.

Ruth's face scrunched up, her brow furrows of deep crevices. "I don't know. I don't think anyone knows but Shelby Mannix."

"Conjecture? Is that what they call it?" said Eddie, trying hard to believe her, but concerned that this was his last chance to get help from Mannix.

"My boss has done his best to keep anyone else from having any information on you, Eddie. What happened after he visited you in San Antonio? You disappeared."

"I was taken prisoner by a bunch of creeps who used biblical names. I escaped. That's when they really became serious about killing me."

Ruth grabbed Eddie by the arm. "Who else would have known your location? Obviously, you're a very important man to Shelby Mannix. If only we could find out why."

She was convincing, Eddie thought.

It was decided in New Orleans that this was no job for *goombahs*.

A new team was sent from New Orleans. It was now apparent that the target was too intelligent for a normal hit.

The power of branding reached into the mob's decision on who next to send. One of the new assassins assigned was the grandson of the hit man — it was generally accepted — who delivered the bullet into Kennedy's head in Dallas. His father, as well, had earned a reputation as a hit man who could be used for important assignments. He had killed two foreign Heads of States — one in Columbia, and one in Indonesia.

To prove that killing John F. Kennedy was nothing personal, Kennedy's assassin named his son after the martyred President. In turn his son, who really preferred to whack wise guys instead of Heads of State, gave the name Kennedy to his son as well.

Kennedy Cristiana, Jr. — known as Kennedy — was instructed by New Orleans to not only take out Eddie O'Hara, but to take a piece of Eddie O'Hara's body for himself after the hit. The mob by now had their suspicions that Eddie O'Hara was big game.

Kennedy's backup was chosen because of his quick intelligence.

Both sipped 7-Eleven coffee while waiting in a late model Toyota Land Cruiser for Eddie O'Hara to register at the flea-bag Grant Hotel.

"Can you imagine? They sent Aldo and Charlie," said Kennedy.

"Probably because of the hacking-off part," said Mason Alexander, ex Army Ranger.

"They actually shot at O'Hara in the street. Assholes! Then what were they going to do?"

"He's not showing," said Mason.

"How do you know?"

"He has no place to go, and was given an opportunity to register at a hotel, and doesn't show up, that's how I know."

"The information is absolute, I understand."

"The only absolute I know is vodka."

Kennedy touched his waist just to feel his Glock 9 mm automatic with 6.5 inch suppressor. Revolvers didn't come with silencers. That only happened in the movies.

Mason knew what Kennedy was thinking.

Sometimes there were set-ups. New Orleans was not past doing that, they knew. Set-ups were necessary. Set-ups killed trails and smothered evidence. Set-ups provided logic. Set-ups kept the public from ever finding out the truth.

"They would have used Charlie and the other meatball if this gig wasn't what it was supposed to be," said Kennedy.

"Then where the hell is he?" countered Mason, checking again to see if his weapon was where he wanted it to be. Always checking.

CHAPTER 35

Shelby Mannix watched the white phone on his desk ring fiercely without picking it up. It was hard to imagine his not picking it up. After all, it was the President calling. But he had no news to tell Luther Donald and would have no news until tomorrow. It was a waiting game. Eddie O'Hara would have to be snatched, murdered, and dumped where no one else would ever find him. Easier said than done.

There were other problems as well. The White House team of sifters and sorters still searching for the President's DNA were grumbling now. It was hard keeping a determined look when he spoke to them. Damn hard. Their antenna wasn't up for the work and they knew it, but he had to keep them digging until the job was done.

The phone kept ringing as if the President knew Shelby was at his desk. Shelby finally picked it up.

"How we doing, Shelby?"

"I think we're onto something, Mr. President."

"It's about time, Shelby. Billy Louis is causing a lot of problems. Hell, I used to wipe his nose."

"We're closing in on a DNA sample, Mr. President, I can assure you of that."

"Well close in as soon as you can, Shelby."

Shelby took a deep breath at the click of the President hanging up. Working with Presidents was all about breathing, he had concluded. In a sense you allowed them to control your air intake: when to take deep breaths, when to be calm, when to even stop breathing at the appropriate time. They pretty much knew how to switch you on and off, but Shelby knew if they didn't get Eddie O'Hara this time out, he could kiss his career good-bye, and from what he could read between the lines of the 25th Amendment, Luther Donald's Presidency might be in jeopardy as well.

* * *

Eddie O'Hara watched Ruth Hoffman squirt chocolate syrup in a coke glass, add milk, and fill it with seltzer.

She handed it to Eddie. "It's an egg-cream."

"I didn't see you put an egg in it."

"Just drink it. You'll feel better."

Eddie sat down on a sofa full of cat hairs.

"We're going to find out all about you, Eddie. I promise." Ruth said, sitting in an oversized leather chair across from him.

Eddie took a sip of the egg-cream. "Good. But why are you risking your life — I still don't get it."

" Let's just say I have my motives as you so aptly pointed out to me earlier."

Eddie finished the egg-cream. It was different like Ruth was.

He put the glass down. "To use your term, Ruth, then you think something's not kosher about my White House experience?"

Ruth leaned forward. "Something's not kosher is a mild way to put it, Eddie! Something's not kosher with Luther Donald running this country."

She paused for a moment. "You see, Eddie, everything fit — the terrorist attack, the fatalities, everything fit but you, Eddie. You don't fit and coincidentally people are trying to kill you. Some coincidence. So who are you?"

Eddie laughed sarcastically. "I don't know. By the way the egg cream was great."

"You know, there is something familiar about you, Eddie, I just can't put my finger on it."

Eddie leaned forward. "People keep saying that, but I find it frustrating. I obviously wasn't anyone important, or else they would have recognized me even with plastic surgery."

"Maybe *you are* the maintenance man. A lot of people walked through the White House — I was over there several times, myself. Wainwright was decent enough, but in a fog. Never wanted to be President. Ran for VP because the party insisted."

"Maybe it's good he's not President."

Ruth gave Eddie a discerning look. "Luther Donald is owned by the extreme right. Sooner or later he's going to do exactly what they want. It frightens me, really."

The phone rang. It was sitting on a table just out of Ruth's reach.

"Don't answer it," said Eddie.

"I have to," she said, composing herself before picking up the receiver. Then looking at Eddie she mouthed the words *Shelby Mannix.* "No sir," she said, "I wouldn't have a clue where Eddie O'Hara is. Yes, I went right home. No, he would have no way of knowing where I live. Yes sir, I'll be on the lookout."

Ruth put down the phone. "That was Shelby. He's furious. He called the hotel and discovered you hadn't checked in."

"Why is he so angry?"

She plopped down on her oversized chair. "More and more I'm becoming convinced, Eddie, that my boss was stupid enough to get involved with your situation in a negative way. And he seems convinced that there's something wrong with your head."

"Now you're hurting my feelings, Ruth. I didn't get that impression," he said, thinking Ruth was not the kind of person who missed too much.

"Get some sleep, Eddie, you look tired."

"I am, real tired. So tired of not knowing about myself."

Eddie closed his eyes and curled his body on Ruth Hoffman's hairy couch. He was so tired of running, so damn tired, but just as he was about to doze off he saw Ruth's cat jump into her lap. That's what he wanted, he thought, a normal life, with the opportunity to pet animals and just live life like a human being instead of a hunted animal.

He fell into a deep sleep.

Someone was shaking him.

"Get up, Eddie — please."

"I just fell asleep."

"You've been out for hours. We have to go."

"Go?" Eddie said, the sleep fog beginning to clear.

Ruth was standing next to her window holding the curtain. "Take a look."

Eddie crossed her small room, half putting on one shoe, holding the other under his arm. It was already dark.

"See that Toyota Land Cruiser? It's circled the block three times. then two men got out and entered my building."

"You've been standing guard?" Eddie asked incredulously.

"I knew Shelby didn't trust me, but he sounded too worried for my blood — shit, he must be in this up to his ankles. We have to get the hell out of here,

Eddie."

Think, think, think, Eddie said to himself.

"We're safer behind a locked door for the moment. Do you have anything to defend yourself, Ruth?"

"A small revolver — but no, please Eddie."

"Get it, hurry." Eddie tied his shoe laces. He could hear Ruth open a drawer in the bedroom. He waited for the door bell to ring.

"I have it. Now let's go," said Ruth.

"No, we're safer here right now. Hand me the revolver."

The revolver seemed so natural to Eddie, but it was made for a woman's smaller hand. Eddie guessed it didn't pack much wallop. He checked the clip, now realizing that in his past memory he must have known about guns.

"There are no bullets, Ruth."

"Oh God, where did I put them?"

She went back into the bedroom. Eddie wondered how much of a chance they really had. He suspected, however, that Ruth was right; the two men in the Toyota would be coming after him. After all, people had been coming after him ever since his new memory. If they were, they would come through the door, he was sure of that.

"Here's the bullets," she said, her voice full of fear.

"Turn out the lights, Ruth. We'll wait. We may have the element of surprise on our side." Eddie held out his hand to her. He could feel it trembling. Could he fire the weapon in his hand? he thought.

"I don't know what's going on," Ruth whispered in the darkness of her apartment. "I wanted to be involved, and now I am — smuck that I am."

Time, as it usually does in such a situation, passed slowly until Eddie finally heard them at the door whispering and fiddling with the lock.

Eddie nudged Ruth into her bathroom and then crouched behind the sofa facing the door.

He could hear them mumbling back and forth, probably suspecting that he was taking a nap or having sex. Then he heard something being inserted into the key slot.

"Oh Eddie, I'm afraid," Ruth said from the bathroom.

So am I, thought Eddie.

Ruth's front door creaked as it opened slowly. In the halo light from the hallway Eddie could see two men in their early thirties, both thick necked and stocky. They had revolvers in their hands. He knew he had to speak before they turned on a light.

Ruth started to sob.

"May I ask what you two are doing?" Eddie said, crouching in the darkness.

"Who's that?"

"Who the hell are you?"

"This is my apartment," Kennedy answered.

"And what apartment number would that be," Eddie asked, watching them turn their heads slowly.

"5B"

"This is 4B"

"Oh," Kennedy said, "then I guess I made a mistake."

Eddie moved from his crouch position just as Kennedy opened fire. The shots sounded more like popcorn in a microwave.

Eddie returned the fire. There was a sudden silence. He heard one of his pursuers say, "Jesus! I'm hit, son-of-a-bitch."

The other intruder dragged his partner into the hallway. Eddie rushed at the door and closed it.

Dropping back, he waited until he heard the elevator door open.

"C'mon Ruth, up the fire escape. This building is old enough for one, isn't it?"

There was no answer from Ruth. Not again? he thought.

She was standing by the window looking out, seemingly detached.

"They're coming out of the building, Eddie — look one of them is dragging his partner into the sports vehicle."

"Good, then we can get out of here. Are you alright?"

"I'm not coming, Eddie. I'm too afraid."

"You've got to Ruth."

"Oh damn, he's coming back into the building."

"Stick with me, Ruth. For the moment, anyway."

Eddie changed his mind about the fire escape and guided Ruth into the hallway.

"Stay on the above landing, Ruth."

"Eddie, I'm afraid."

"Just do it, Ruth. I'm going one down."

"Now hurry."

He watched her go up the stairwell, then climbed down to the landing below. Eddie guessed his pursuer would take the long way up.

Stairwells, so many dark stairwells a part of my life now, Eddie thought, as he waited in the clammy darkness. He could hear his pursuer climbing, snake-like in his silence. This dangerous situation seemed oddly familiar to

Eddie, not knowing that as Sam Wainwright that he had fought building to building in Saigon during the Tet Offensive.

Can I time things just right? he asked himself. He wasn't so sure he could.

He waited patiently as the killer slinked up the stairwell. For a brief moment, Eddie saw a large pinkie ring as the killer hugged the banister. The killer was moving very slowly.

Eddie stepped back into the darkness.

The killer rounded the steps and headed for the next landing.

Eddie placed Ruth's revolver into the small of Kennedy Cristiana's back. "I want to pull this trigger I really want to," Eddie said.

"Don't be foolish, Mr. O'Hara."

"Hand me your piece over your shoulder before I get too nervous and pull the trigger."

Eddie could smell Kennedy's cologne. It was very tasteful, not for some reason like he was used to smelling.

Kennedy handed Eddie his revolver. It was still warm.

"We're going up to the roof and talk a little — Ruth, are you there?"

"I'm okay, Eddie."

"We're coming up."

"I don't want to see him, Eddie."

"Go up the next landing, take the elevator, and get out of here — okay?"

"Okay, Eddie — I'm sorry."

"Don't worry, Ruth."

"I'm alone again," he thought.

CHAPTER 36

You could see the Capitol building from the roof. There was some light from a roof bulb. Eddie got a chance to look into his pursuer's eyes.

There was almost a sneer on Kennedy's face.

"Why?"

Kennedy smiled. "It was nothing personal up until now."

"Up until now?"

"My partner is dead — died in the SUV."

"And before your partner died and it became personal?"

"A special contract."

"What was so special about it," asked Eddie waiting for his prisoner to act.

"I'm duty bound not to say anything, so pull the fucking trigger."

"You're a young man, yet."

"I don't mind."

"Maybe I'll just march you to the police station."

Kennedy laughed. "When my organization gets an assignment, things work differently. And I think somehow you know that."

Through the barrel of the gun, Eddie could feel his assailant coiling like a predator about to attack. Eddie suspected he was probably going to have to pull the trigger, but was searching for a way out. Tell me, why am I so important?" Eddie asked.

"I don't know."

"What were your instructions?"

Kennedy shook his head. "Pull it, I don't give a shit."

"I think you do. Look at you. So well dressed. You could pass for a junior partner in an up-and-coming law firm."

Kennedy smirked. "You people think you're the only ones with values. Where I come from we die for what we believe in."

There was a moment when neither man moved, then Kennedy lunged.

Eddie couldn't pull the trigger. In that moment of weakness the younger man was all over him, smothering him, methodically probing for the weapon that he had knocked out of Eddie's hand, as both wrestled on the rooftop for it. Eddie was weakening. He had run out of tricks. He heard a gun cock. A dark shadow crouched next to his pursuer.

"Hold on lady," said Kennedy, seemingly more concerned about the gun at his head than the one Eddie held.

"We can lock the roof from the inside," said Ruth. "Now we have to go, Eddie."

They were in Ruth's green Saturn, riding down Pennsylvania Avenue.

"I'm so sacred, Eddie, I'm sorry. I thought I had the stomach for this stuff, but I don't."

"You saved my life, Ruth. I'm grateful."

Ruth dismissed Eddie's compliment. "I'm driving to my sister's place in Florida. I have some time coming. If Shelby is involved, he'll know about me and what happened here. If he doesn't, he'll be glad to get rid of me for a few weeks. I just can't face him right now — I'm sorry Eddie. I do believe something is terribly wrong. Maybe I can do some research on the Internet?"

"You've done enough for me, Ruth."

"I'm frightened for you, Eddie. These people always seem to get their way in situations like yours. I guess I've always realized that intellectually, but now I feel it emotionally. You must have seen something that some powerful people in Washington didn't want you to see."

"What could that be, Ruth? Did you hear that killer? He acted as if he was untouchable."

Ruth frowned. "I'll drop you off, Eddie. I'm not going back to my place, no matter what. Not for a while anyway."

"Any homeless shelter would be fine, Ruth."

She didn't reply, but seemed to know where she was going. Finally, she pulled alongside a building called Baptist Mission Shelter.

Ruth didn't say anything when Eddie got out of the Saturn. He could feel her disappointment at quitting, but she was wrong, he thought. He wasn't disappointed in her. He was grateful to her. He watched her pull away without a word.

It was another steamy Washington night. Eddie suspected there would be a vacancy at the shelter. Although he had the money for a better place thanks to Shelby Mannix, he felt more secure among the homeless like himself.

Registering at the mission was no problem, he just had to promise he would attend the church service after breakfast. He had heard the men grumble about always having to trade off their time. Nothing was *free*, not really, not even for men and women with nothing, Eddie was discovering. He registered as Jim Hoffman.

The Baptist Mission didn't seem as loose to Eddie as the other shelter, and it had a lot more Caucasians.

Like the SouthEast Men's Shelter, there was a large room full of Army cots on the top floor. There were a few overhead fans in the dimly lit room, punctuated by the usual coughs, mumbling, and farts that Eddie had come to expect in such a place.

Eddie was sitting on the cot assigned to him when an African-American man in his late sixties said,

"Can I sit down?"

"What for?" Eddie said defensively.

"It's not for your body. I promise you that."

Eddie raised his hands in resignation. The man sat down. "I hope you appreciate what I'm doing for you," the man said.

"What could that be?" replied Eddie, now uneasy.

"There's police looking all over for you. The Lincoln Washington car explosion, the Bill Paxton murder."

Eddie tried to hide his surprise. "How do you know that's me."

The man looked down between his legs and shook his head.

"Look, I was at the other shelter when that shooting went down. I saw you running through the dormitory. I know they're looking for you. Sam Walker, that's the name you gave."

"Then you must know I had nothing to do with Bill Paxton's shooting?"

The man laughed. "Sheeeet. That don't matter down here. They got to pin it on somebody. I saw you running that's all I know."

"There were men chasing me," Eddie said defensively.

"I know that, too. But they'll try to get you on something."

Eddie tried not to look at the man. "Then why are you helping me out?" he said, trying to appear calm.

"Folks down here don't necessarily have to have a reason to help someone. If you have a few bucks I would appreciate it, if you don't, don't worry about it. I'm not going to turn you in. You're running from something, but that don't mean you're guilty of anything."

Eddie looked at the man. "What's your name?"

"Jesse Jones."

"What do you think I should do, Jesse?"

"If I saw you, someone else did. Leave Mr. Sam Walker, although I suspect that's not your name."

Eddie laughed, but in a way that said he didn't mean it. "I don't even know who I am Jesse, or why I'm on the run. Can't remember a thing. This is all new memory."

Jesse pursed his lips. "Memory problems is not uncommon down here. People down here have lots of reasons to forget things. Drugs don't help, of course."

"I'm tired Jesse, real tired."

"I could stay up and keep *chickie* for you, watch out if there's something wrong, but it'll cost you."

"That would be fine, Jesse."

"Twenty dollars."

"Okay."

"In advance, but don't take it out here. Slip it to me later when they turns the lights out."

"That would be great, Jesse."

Eddie could feel the exhaustion overtake him. He slipped his money into his underwear and, still wearing his running pants and Notre Dame jersey, curled up on the cot and went to sleep.

In the morning Eddie's money was gone except for change and so was Jesse Jones. Eddie O'Hara was broke again.

From his condo at the Watergate, Shelby made a call to New Orleans and discovered that there had been no confirmation on the target, and even worse news, his secretary had helped Eddie O'Hara escape.

Was it over for him? Shelby thought. But that was not the Mannix way of thinking. Cool down. Think. There's no way Ruth could be sure he was involved. All she could be sure of was that he had given Eddie O'Hara a few bucks to get a hotel. How she managed to find Eddie O'Hara was anyone's guess. He would keep his cool like he always did.

Later that morning, Ruth Hoffman had still not shown up for work. Instead, she left a voice mail that said she had to take a sudden leave of absence because of illness in her family, a general enough situation to be uncheckable, thought Shelby. He should have fired that little Jewish-Irish bitch years ago. She was always looking over his shoulder, digging, always digging. He could never figure out why.

She wasn't unlike a lot of people in Washington. Paranoia existed everywhere. Loyalty was the rarest virtue inside the beltway, but she had gone too far. What would happen next was out of his hands. That's what happened when you dealt with New Orleans. He would keep her voice mail and move on. That's what a Mannix did. Move on.

In the harsh, ozone-damaged sunlight of D. C., Eddie considered his options. There really only seemed to be one, get in touch with Shelby Mannix again. If he was the enemy, he had the answers. If he wasn't the enemy, Shelby Mannix could help him.

The White House switch board was pleasant enough and connected Eddie to Shelby Mannix's secretary who said she could only take a message. Eddie gave her the number of his public phone, and waited, pretending to fish for change to keep others from using it.

The phone rang promptly enough.

"I called the hotel. You didn't check in Eddie."

"I stayed somewhere else."

"Are you okay?"

"Fine, sir."

"Are you sure?"

"Yes, sir."

"Have you spoken to anyone connected to my office?"

"Someone called Ruth Hoffman contacted me at the "Y."She said she could help me. I went to her place, but we must have been followed. I really can't go into details right now."

"Is Ruth okay?"

"Yes, sure. She said she needed a few days off. A very nice person. She deserves a raise," said Eddie, making Ruth sound like an innocent bystander. He wondered why he was so good at lying.

"I still haven't made headway, Eddie, but I'm working on it. Can you be reached at all?"

"I want to see you right away, Mr. Mannix."

"I'm afraid that would be impossible, Eddie. I'm a Special Assistant to the President. One step below Cabinet level. I just can't walk out."

"If I were you, I would, sir."

"What do you mean, Eddie?"

"I've discovered that the other agencies conducting their own investigations don't even know I'm on your witness list. That's for starters, Mr. Mannix."

"It's not what you think, Eddie, but we can talk about it."

"I'll meet you at the Vietnam Veteran's Memorial. There are always people there, Mr. Mannix."

"That's too public for me, Eddie. How about a compromise? A coffee shop just off Maryland Avenue and Third Street S.W. called Shapiro's."

"Sounds okay."

"Good."

"I'll see you there in — oh — an hour?"

"Yes sir, that would be fine."

Eddie hung the receiver up slowly. Was it possible? Could this man really be the source of his problem? And if he was, why?

A few tourists passing by gave Eddie dirty looks. It was obvious that they would have bet their homes that he wasn't the 43rd President of the United States.

Shelby let out a big sigh. Eddie had come to him — God, why was he thinking of him as Eddie? This was the 43rd President of the United States. Sam Wainwright might or might not get his memory back, but the plan had worked so far: Eddie O'Hara had been left off most witness lists. He was, by all accounts, a non-entity. *And Eddie was the right name.* After all, Sam Wainwright didn't exist anymore, Shelby concluded.

This time, however, he would have to be careful. He would have to go with Eddie, bring him to the New Orleans people. It was dangerous, but the Presidency was at stake. Under these circumstances it had to be done. *No Mannix would ever turn away from that responsibility,* he told himself, as he watched the President's busy staff with their worker-bee mentality carry out the normal business of the Presidency. In some regards, Shelby Mannix felt superior to the others around him. He was, after all, helping to safe-guard the Presidency.

CHAPTER 37

There didn't seem to be any other choice but to meet Shelby Mannix, thought Eddie, as he looked out the window of the coffee shop.

It was Saturday afternoon in the Capital. There were lots of tourists and Eddie was envious of them. They knew who they were and he didn't. *It must be wonderful to know what your face is supposed to look like*, he thought. He got a sudden urge to look at his face. He got up from his seat and went to the restroom.

There were still a few stitches in various parts of his face that hadn't dissolved and were getting ready to fall out. There seemed to be small scars everywhere that were still healing. By most standards he didn't look bad, but he didn't even know how old he was. They had given him a *tuck* one of the surgeons had told him as sort of a compensation for the awful wounds that he had suffered. Well, this was his first real look at himself, and he wasn't pleased or displeased. The surgery appeared excellent, but his face had never felt right. He could sense that things had been moved around. It was a decent-looking face and what more could he expect, he decided.

Eddie sat down again at the booth, nursing his coffee, wondering what Shelby Mannix was all about. Ever since he woke up in the flop house, the face of Shelby Mannix seemed to burn into his brain. He couldn't get rid of it. He wanted to trust Ruth's instinct, but found her rationale hard to believe. Shelby Mannix was a Special Assistant to the President of the United States. Maybe a bureaucrat, at worst a snob, but certainly not the man who was responsible for hunting him down. It just couldn't be, Eddie decided.

Eddie watched Shelby enter the luncheonette. It was an entrance. There was nothing casual about Shelby Mannix even though he was wearing jeans and a polo shirt. *A man who sounds and moves like Shelby shouldn't be wearing jeans,* Eddie thought.

Shelby sat down at Eddie's table, and smiled.

Eddie took a close look at the face of Shelby Mannix. There was something so familiar about him, but then a blank.

Shelby said, "You never stayed at the hotel, Eddie. How am I supposed to help you if I can't contact you? Running off with someone who claims to be my assistant, Eddie — odd behavior don't you think?"

"Ruth was trying to help me. I didn't know what to think."

"What happened?"

"Two thugs tried to kill us."

Shelby flashed his best bemused look at Eddie.

"It was terrible, I may have seriously hurt one of them."

"And this person Ruth saw this?"

"Yes, sir."

"Then someone must have followed, her?"

"Maybe."

"These charges are serious, Eddie. Can you prove them?"

"Ruth could vouch for it, but right now, Mr. Mannix, I've got to find out why I'm being chased. Who am I? What do I know? Ruth says that perhaps I witnessed something about the bombing I shouldn't have seen."

"Suppose I told you no one by the name of Ruth works for me, Eddie? Suppose I told you that as real as things seem, they're not. To a degree your entire brain is virtual reality. It can't tell the difference between real and imaginary. Look at you. You're beaten into the ground. You need rest and extensive counseling, all of which the government is willing to provide."

"Ruth Hoffman?"

"Never heard of her, Eddie."

"But —"

"And if she's real, Eddie, she could be working for the people you claim are chasing you. On the other hand, you have no proof of anything. Nothing may be what it seems in your condition."

Eddie didn't know what to do. Shelby Mannix was mixing him up.

"I understand the next stage of your condition could be delusions of grandeur, Eddie. You could even think you were someone important in government. That way you could rationalize your injuries."

Eddie took a big sip of coffee, cleared his throat, and said, "I'm not comfortable with the description of maintenance man, if that's what you mean."

Shelby reached across the table and touched Eddie's arm. "Look, you need help, Eddie. The government has allocated monies for bombing victims.

There's a hospital in Virginia specializing in trauma cases like your own. I could take you out to the hospital, throw my weight around, get you help, then look into every possible aspect of your identity — get to the bottom of things."

Eddie looked at Shelby's eyes.

"There's no Ruth Hoffman working for you?"

"Never heard of her, Eddie."

Eddie bowed his head. He was going mad and there was little he could do about it, he thought.

CHAPTER 38

Shelby Mannix was calm as he drove past the gates that once housed the White House. He could *feel* the confusion emanating from Eddie-slash-Sam as he liked to think of him now. Nobody could fuck with your mind like Shelby Mannix, it was often said. It was a skill he had learned early on. Disorient your opponent's reality and you have a mind that can be molded to accept any argument. Admittedly he had panicked, Shelby acknowledged to himself. But Eddie-slash-Sam was at the bottom of the feeding chain. Nobody would miss him, or ever notice him. When Eddie-slash-Sam disappeared that would be it. Ruth Hoffman, however, would have to be watched ever so carefully.

The New Orleans people had already told Shelby what to do. He called a number from the driver's seat, listened to the message, and then pretended his cell phone wasn't working properly. The risk he was taking was enormous, but what Mannix hadn't taken great risks? He had depended too much on strangers to do his work. Well, that was *fini*. The 43rd President of the United States was going to be personally handed over to the New Orleans people and he would wait in the next room for the DNA sample. Crude but necessary at this point. Of course, it helped considerably that Eddie-slash-Sam was in the homeless category. Even if he was seen talking to Eddie, so what? He had an investigation to conduct and was not responsible for the whereabouts of a former White House employee who had suffered severe injuries and was now drifting in and out of different memories.

Shelby suddenly caught himself. He didn't like to pump himself up with too much rhetoric. It clouded judgment.

Shelby didn't talk much for the first hour of the drive, but then opened up. "Eddie, your condition is called Dissociative Amnesia. It's even possible that different memories may merge into one."

They were riding on a rural Virginia road which passed many family farms.

"Beautiful country isn't it, Eddie?"

"A lot of green, yes." *And a lot of family farms for sale*, Eddie thought. It just didn't seem right.

"When we get to the hospital I'll have to take a statement, Eddie. A number of blast victims are recovering there. You'll like it."

"Seems as if a Special Assistant to the President of the United States wouldn't go through all this trouble for a maintenance man."

"You're a key witness, Eddie. I talked to some doctors about your case. A few suspected that you may identify strongly with the former President. Your presidential role-playing may be indicative of some sort of guilt. A feeling you could have helped the President and didn't."

"Sounds like a lot of intellectual crap to me," said Eddie, feeling hollow. Shelby smiled.

"For example, the motorcycle you were on, or could have been on, might have been intended for the President."

"I can't remember if I was on a motorbike or not," replied Eddie, looking out at the countryside, still wondering how he had managed to lose his mind.

"There's a small farm just up the road. An old friend of mine is trying to make it as a farmer. I think we could use a pit stop."

"Sure."

"Good. I have to make some calls anyway. My damn cell phone is out."

It was a pretty farm. Just like you would want for yourself, Eddie thought, looking at the rows of corn. The farm house was big, rambling, and full of good smells.

There were facts about small farms running through Eddie's head, but he had no explanation why he knew the price of growing certain crops was more than the price in the local supermarket. If a farm wasn't big enough to sell its crop at a set price before it was harvested, it couldn't survive. The corporate farmers blamed it on the global economy and reaped huge profits.

Certainly the President and Congress should be doing something about it, Eddie thought.

There was no one in the kitchen which didn't seem to bother Shelby.

"I have to make those calls, Eddie. Make yourself comfortable, okay buddy? My friend and his wife are probably out in the field — he'll spot us alright. His wife makes a terrific cup of coffee."

Eddie studied Shelby just before he went into the next room. It was that moment of doubt on Shelby's face on which direction to walk that caught Eddie's attention. Somewhere inside of Eddie there was a feeling that you don't ignore this kind of instinct.

Shelby was in the next room. Eddie could hear him talking.

Eddie walked over to the window and pulled up the old yellow oilcloth shade. That's when he saw two men coming out of the barn, walking quickly, heading toward the farm house. They were young men, thick-necked, dark in complexion. They wore city clothes. They certainly didn't look like farmers.

When they got closer, Eddie saw the face of the man who had tried to kill him in Ruth's apartment.

Shelby was talking into a dead phone when he heard the New Orleans people enter the kitchen. He had prepared himself to be there. He had put everything on the line. It was what was expected of a Mannix. He was almost proud of himself. He had taken the bull by the horns so to speak. There was no Sam Wainwright any more he reassured himself. Just a lump of humanity called Eddie-slash-Sam. He closed his eyes and hoped it would end soon. He had been instructed to wait in the next room while the deed was done. Good conspirator that he was, he had almost enjoyed the subterfuge including his make-believe conversation with the majority leader of the Senate. In his imaginary conversation, Shelby gave the Senator hell for not supporting the President.

Shelby had made it clear to the New Orleans people that he wasn't leaving without one of Eddie's hands. It would be difficult enough taking it back to the White House grounds — there could be no dry-ice to destroy tissue — as well as a dozen other pathology considerations before it was buried on the White House Grounds. Then nature doing its business before it could be *discovered* was required. However, knowing he was going to eventually dig it up would be a great help when the President exploded about the poor progress on the matter.

Shelby braced himself for gun shots that were never fired.

Eddie ran as hard as a man in his fifties can run between rows of corn. People were trying to kill him, and that was the only conclusion he could come to. If he was crazy, so be it, but that's what it looked like. Why on earth Shelby Mannix was involved was beyond him. It was all he could do to keep in focus. Somehow it didn't feel like the first time he was running for his life in the fields. Somehow he had done it before.

Exhausted from running, Eddie stumbled out of the corn fields and felt the softening of the ground. Instinctively, he knew he would run into some marsh. Seconds later he could see a patch of languid water. Eddie waded in the marsh until he hit a stream, then he kept moving. The city boys behind him, younger, stronger, but without Eddie's heart, finally gave up and determined that cutting Eddie O'Hara off at the road was the way to get the job done.

When Eddie finally dropped to the ground, he was exhausted beyond being able to move. He was unsure of where he was or who he was and had no memory of just being chased through a corn field.

Shelby watched the backs of the two hired killers running in their city clothes, bobbing up and down in the dust, and knew that Eddie-slash-Sam had figured it out.

Shelby decided that staying around might be dangerous, but not knowing the whereabouts of Sam Wainwright, might even be more dangerous. However, the idea of waiting for the two assassins, bothered Shelby's sensibilities regarding the conspiracy factor. He was only willing to risk being in the same room if a body part was handed to him, and under no other circumstances. A darker corner of Shelby's mind even suspected that the killers might be angry and take it out on him. He paused to wonder how the farm house became empty to begin with but changed his mind.

Shelby left the farm hopeful that Eddie-slash-Sam would be caught in the next few hours, but did not count on it.

CHAPTER 39

Sam Wainwright was stained with mud, wet, and exhausted when a Thomas County patrol car pulled up to him as he tried to cross a dirt road while crouching in a stealth position.

"Can you place your hands on the vehicle?" said one of the officers in stilted, correct English.

"I'm no threat to anyone, officer. How could I be?"

The officer frisked Sam.

"You have no wallet?"

"I'm confused about being here myself."

"Why were you crouching?"

"Just my way of getting to the other side of the road. I don't even know why I was doing that."

"Damn suspicious. Billy, check the perimeter."

The other officer poked around for a minute or so on both sides of the road. "Nothing Jake."

"Well, he's a vagrant. He's got no money."

"You haven't even asked me my name?"

"Okay, who are you?"

"I'm Sam Wainwright, the President of the United States."

Spreadeagle, with his hands on the police car, Sam couldn't see what was going on behind him, but he could hear the two county policemen chuckling.

Ruth Hoffman called Shelby at his Watergate apartment.

"What are you up to, Shelby?'

"Ruth, I thought I would be hearing from you. Pretty brazen to be calling your boss by his first name, or is that the politically correct thing to do?"

"Someone tried to kill Eddie O'Hara in my apartment. There was only one person who knew where Eddie was an hour before that happened."

"Crazy coincidence, Ruth. I'm working for the President of the United States. How dare you make accusations? And maybe Eddie's pursuers — if they really exist — followed you?"

"Boy, Shelby, you're good at making black and white into gray — real good."

"And you're unemployed as of this minute."

Ruth began crying.

"Now what's the problem?"

"I don't know. I'm confused. You know how much I love my job."

"Then we should talk about it, Ruth. Because I don't love the *way* you're doing your job."

Ruth became defensive. "It just seems that you've kept this O'Hara guy under wraps. I mean none of the other agencies know anything about him. I've always found that odd — Sh — sir."

"Purely political. If Mr. O'Hara had anything to do with the bombings, I wanted the White House office to get first crack at him."

"I almost believe that."

"You damn well better believe it, because it's the truth. I can't believe you followed me."

"I didn't say I did, sir."

"Then how did you manage to bring Eddie to your apartment?"

"Okay, you figured it out, but I can't go back to the apartment. Whoever is after Eddie knows my address."

"You actually saw the killers?"

"Yes."

"They came after you?"

"Yes."

"No wonder O'Hara never checked in. Although I still find the whole thing hard to swallow."

"I'll be in touch sir —"

"Wait a minute — where can I reach you?"

"You can't."

There was a dial tone. Shelby placed the receiver back slowly. His problem had grown. It was a cancer now. Sam Wainwright on the loose. Ruth Hoffman trying to find a way to undermine him.

The things one does for one's country, Shelby mused.

"When did you begin to believe you were the President of the United

143

States?" asked the psychiatrist at the Thomas County Correctional Facility.

"When the Chief Justice swore me in."

The County Psychiatrist glanced at the two officers who had brought Sam Wainwright in. "I don't find this very funny, gentlemen."

"Sorry sir," they said barely able to hold their snickers.

"You look exhausted," said the doctor.

"I am."

"What you're telling me could have dire consequences, you know that?"

"Meaning…"

"Meaning we may have to have send you to another facility for observation."

"You think I'm crazy."

"That word has not been used by anyone in my profession for fifty years."

"Disturbed."

"That might be more logical, but I would not use it."

"Loony," shouted Sam, angry at his life. "Insane. Fucked up, perhaps."

The psychiatrist was a tall man, and not very well coordinated. He moved clumsily. "You have committed no crime, Mr. *Wainwright*. It would be a shame if I had to put you before a judge and have her decide whether you should be put away for observation. I sense no dementia yet you persist in your story."

Sam and the psychiatrist were sitting in an interrogation room. The two officers who brought Sam in were standing behind a glass partition, giggling every time Sam mentioned that he was the President of the United States.

If asked why the prisoner's answers were so funny, they would answer that the prisoner seemed so normal otherwise. Perhaps their giggling was a nervous reaction not meant to be mean. On the other hand…

"There was a blast. I was escaping from the White House on a motorcycle, then on foot, that's all I remember now."

"The blast that killed the President?"

"I'm the President."

"I see that your face has had recent surgery. Other than that you don't look like the President."

"It probably explains why I don't look like the President."

"You suffered a head injury, didn't you?"

"Yes."

"You should be in a hospital not here, Mr. *Wainwright*," said the psychiatrist touching Sam's shoulder. You know what I'm going to do for you, Mr. *Wainwright?*"

"No, I don't"

"There's a government web site for White House Bombing Victims. I'm going to e-mail them about you and ask them if a bomb victim has left the hospital sooner than he should have."

"Maybe I could think of some names, telephone numbers? Maybe we can start there," said Sam.

"If you're a bomb victim, I have to notify the White House. Any mention of the bombing under any conditions and the web site must be consulted. That's what you indicated you were, a White House bombing victim, is that correct?"

"Yes."

The psychiatrist left the room to talk to the two arresting officers. "My feeling is let him go. He's going to cause us reams of paper work."

"What if he hurts somebody? They'll sue our ass, sir. *Whackos* off the street, that's the new policy. I'm not about to lose my pension for that asshole. Sorry, but that's how it is, Doctor."

"Then find someplace to stick him, but not with any prisoner. The judge is going to ream our ass on this. I'll tell you, if he wasn't dressed like he is, and looked like he does, I might believe him."

"C'mon, sir. He's a drifter. He probably wants to be sent to a county facility."

"I'm going to check on him anyway. There's something coming through that just doesn't happen in these cases."

The two arresting officers waited for the psychiatrist to be out of sight before looking at each other and saying, "Another genius?" They both laughed at the same time.

They put the 43rd President of the United States into a cell with a transvestite wanted for stabbing a truck driver in New York City.

He introduced himself as Arthur and said, "I should be with the women. They know the humiliation I'm suffering. I warn you don't make fun of me."

"I won't," said Sam, who unlike Arthur, was still in his civilian clothes.

"I'm supposed to wear women's clothes in the afternoon. It's the law in New York if you're going to get the operation. Welfare already agreed to have my Adam's apple removed. Then they go south on my body. Fucking redneck delivery man made cracks about my legs. For weeks he tormented me. Well, he won't be doing that any more. I gave it to him right in his fucking gut and twisted the knife a little once I had it inside."

"I'm sorry for your pain," said Sam.

The prisoners in the other cells were making sucking sounds and arguing about whose *gal-boy* Arthur was going to be. Arthur still had some makeup on and moved like a woman.

He said, "I'm not taking that crap from anyone. All my friends are dead, or have HIV, and my family won't have anything to do with me. I just exploded."

"You'll be okay, Arthur."

"Thanks, but I don't need your sympathy. What would you know about being a person trapped in a body you didn't want?"

"How about a body that doesn't have a memory?" said Sam sitting on the bunk, waiting for Arthur to object, but he didn't.

"I guess that's just as bad," said Arthur who suddenly grew silent.

Sam rested his face in his hands and chided himself for thinking he was President of the United States. Why did he believe that? Yet names were beginning to pop in his head, names that could confirm whether he had lost his mind, even names of childhood friends who were orphans themselves.

He began to picture the Oval Office, his staff, his enemies, Heads of State — goddamn it, he was the President of the United States. Or was it possible for a mind to make this stuff up? After all, he was sharing a cell with a transvestite from New York. If he was the President, how could he have been overlooked in the blast?

It was the memory closest to the blast that Sam Wainwright had the most trouble with, but now there were images of him being on a motorcycle, then running, then something awful happening.

Arthur was sitting on the upper bunk. Sam began talking.

"Suppose I told you I *am* the President of the United States. What would you think, Arthur? Suppose I told you I was escaping from the White House when the blast went off. Then everything went blank. I must have had surgery on my face and that's why no one recognizes me."

"Upstate mental facility would take you in a sec."

"My story is too unbelievable then?"

Arthur jumped off the bunk, stood back from Sam as if he were a canvas, and said, "Your face has had a lot of surgery. Stand up for a minute. He looked at Sam and touched his face as if it were a bronze bust. "You know, I thought President Wainwright was an asshole. The man was a zombie. Didn't care about anything. You wouldn't want to be him."

His voice desperate, Sam said, "Look at me, Arthur. Tell me I'm crazy."

"Why didn't you have a wallet when they found you?"

"A wallet was given to me just before the blast. There were credit cards in it. Someone said, 'You're Eddie O'Hara maintenance man,' I remember that."

"Then why do you think you're Sam Wainwright?"

"Because I don't feel like Eddie O'Hara, maintenance man."

Arthur, seemingly intrigued, said, "The attack happened during a big dinner for the Prime Minister of Israel, I remember. Why would a maintenance man be there?"

"Exactly," replied Sam.

"Unless they were trying to conceal your identity."

Sam thought about Arthur's words for a moment. "Conceal my identity? Of course? That's it. Now I remember the conversation I had with Secret Service — God, yes." Impulsively, Sam kissed Arthur on the head. The cell block went wild.

Two guards raced to the cell. "You two guys doing it?"

"Nooooooo," said Arthur.

"I kissed him on the forehead," said Sam. "Arthur has helped me considerably. It was just a sign of gratitude."

"I catch you doing it, there's going to be hell to pay."

"We understand, officer."

"You two fairies better understand."

When the guards left there were a series of ugly remarks by the inmates.

"I'm with the President of the United States. He's going to remember this when he gets out," Arthur shouted back, half in tears.

There was more laughter, but Sam Wainwright had become a new man not only in his feelings of sympathy for Arthur, but his sense of sureness for the first time that he was indeed the President of the United States.

CHAPTER 40

The query about a 'John Doe' prisoner claiming to be a victim of the White House bombing was faxed to Shelby at the Watergate. Shelby had paid little attention to the White House Web Site regarding bombing victims. It had really been Ruth's baby, but Mannix men had always been lucky in love and war, Shelby reasoned.

The Thomas County Correctional Facility was less than an hour's drive from Washington. There could be no official contact, but sooner or later Sam Wainwright would be released.

Shelby called his weekend staff and instructed them to send a reply to the good doctor that all victims of the attack were accounted for. That the *John Doe* claiming to be a victim was a trickster and should be dealt with accordingly. Next, on a secure phone he called New Orleans. They told Shelby *their people* were well aware of Eddie O'Hara being picked up and sent to the Thomas County lock-up. He would be reached shortly and Shelby could expect a Fed Ex package no later than 8:00 p.m. tomorrow.

"Remember, I want a hand," said Shelby, completely oblivious to his desperation minutes before the call. "The body must be alive when you take the sample. Forensics will know the difference if the tissue is dead when the sample is taken. Do you understand?"

"These things never work out like you want them to," said the voice on the other end of the line.

On Monday morning the farmer and his wife were found tied up in their barn. *John Doe*, caught running in the general area, was held for a line-up. Now under suspicion of armed assault, Sam was fingerprinted, photographed, strip-searched, and given an orange jump suit to wear.

Like all bureaucrats who get the same pay whether they do a good job or a bad job, the lieutenant in charge of the assault at the farm stood stone faced and seemingly unaffected by the psychiatrist calling for Sam's release.

"This man has done nothing," said the psychiatrist.

"They've all done nothing until they get identified," said the lieutenant.

"It was two men, well-dressed. This is pathetic."

"He's a *nutso*, thinking he's President. He stays until the victims see him in a lineup and say he's not the guy."

"They would have to say he's not the two guys," the psychiatrist said facetiously.

"He stays."

"He's in a cell with a violent offender."

"I'll try and have him moved, but you know how full we are, Doc. If I have to, I'll get him in front of a judge. He was seen in the general area of a serious crime. The assailants were going to kill that couple. They're lucky to be alive — something happened and they didn't come back to the barn."

"What has this to do with a homeless man who thinks he's President of the United States?"

"We'll have to see, Doc."

"Honestly, I don't know what this is all about. You're doing everything you can to keep him locked up."

"He's a victim of his mental state. You know that, Doc."

"Too disturbed to be released, but not disturbed enough to be sent to a hospital."

The lieutenant flinched. "Let's see what happens in the lineup."

"He gets a lawyer if you go beyond the lineup."

"For sure."

In his suggestive state, the psychiatrist was afraid of what Sam Wainwright might be convinced he did. On the other hand, as a prison psychiatrist, he could only do so much, he rationalized.

Sam Wainwright was troubled. During the congo-line walk to the chow line he felt uneasy. Maybe it was the way the men looked at him. He couldn't pin it down. There was something going on. He could feel it. There seemed to be a group of men holding him in. A grid so to speak. The din of noise was frightening. The guards were few and far between.

Sam was beginning to recall what he knew about modern prison life in America. The prison leaders did pretty much what they wanted as long as they didn't create problems for the guards. During the night Sam heard a prisoner screaming not to be raped. No one came to his rescue. Sam swore if he ever got back to the Presidency that would never happen again in an American prison.

As Sam stepped down into a long hallway leading to the prison cafeteria, he was jumped. He was an old Marine. He had a few judo tricks which surprised his attackers, but eventually they got him down. Sam, however, had taken more time than expected to be subdued.

Three prisoners stood guard. Each shouting, "C'mon, C'mon." Two prisoners held Sam's arms, another held his hand over Sam's eyes and mouth. Sam rolled and kicked until finally one of Sam's attackers managed to slice a piece of Sam's pinkie off. Sam had no way of knowing the prisoner was a former veterinarian.

"This will have to do," shouted the ex-vet. All of the attackers then scurried away like jackals, leaving Sam lying in a pool of his own blood.

Sam was grateful he was still alive.

Later, in his prison hospital bed, under medication, Sam tried to rationalize what had happened to him but couldn't. The room was stuffy. He put his right leg over the sheet, and for the first time since being Sam Wainwright again, noticed the tattoo on his leg. He was still groggy from medication and called the orderly over to read it to him.

"It says, 'Eddie, you lost your memory and are being hunted by killers. See the notebook.'"

"I don't have a notebook."

"That's what it says," said the orderly, a man who had obviously seen everything. "You're really screwed up, aren't you?"

"I guess I am," said Sam, trying to make sense of the madness around him that had taken one of his fingers.

Sam didn't see the tall man approaching his bed.

"You'll be able to sue," said the psychiatrist.

"I'll remember you," said Sam. "I know you've been trying to help me."

"You're lucky to be alive."

"I know. It seems they had an agenda, get a piece of me first. Have you seen this kind of thing before?"

"No."

"Still think I'm crazy?"

"I never thought you were crazy."

"Do you know what it takes to be me, knowing who I am, and knowing I might not live long enough to prove it."

"It would take a strong man."

"Why would anyone want a piece of me? It makes no sense."

"I don't know. It might have just happened, but I think they might have killed you if they had more time. I understand you gave them quite a fight."

"I was an ex-Marine."

"It was extremely organized," said the psychiatrist looking down at Sam's tattoo. "Who's Eddie?"

"Unless I'm making it up, a code name to hide my real identity. I'm assuming I must have been told that if I recovered my old memory, I might not remember anything about my newer memory — that people were trying to kill me."

"Why?"

"That's it, I don't know. Obviously I was running from something when the county police picked me up. It seems the experience jolted me back to my old memory. I know it's hard for you to imagine, but I am President of the United States."

"I almost believe you," said the psychiatrist.

"Almost?"

"You have to sympathize with me, Mr. Wainwright — if that is your name. In the history of our country no active President has ever been in your situation — people believing he's dead, but he's alive. The odds are against it."

"But?"

"But the circumstances surrounding you are the strangest I've ever run across. Only organized crime could have arranged your attack in here in such a short time. I admit, Mr. Wainwright, you have my mind buzzing."

"Then help me, Doctor. I think they'll come after me again."

"What do you want me to do, Mr. Wainwright?"

"Let me run."

"I can't do it. I would lose my license."

"It's my face, isn't it? It doesn't look like the Sam Wainwright you've seen?"

The psychiatrist studied Sam. "No, that's not it. Your face has had extensive surgery. It's just that the odds are so against your being right. I do believe, however, that you believe what you say."

"There are tests...DNA...just let me get to the people that can have this done. That's all I ask."

"I can't. My career would be over if you turned out to be a crackpot."

"Find a way, Doctor. I beg you."

"The name is Richard Levine."

"Help me, Richard."

"I'll try, Mr. Wainwright."

Sam watched the doctor leave. The orderly was far enough away not to have heard anything, yet he made a face as the doctor walked through the exit door.

CHAPTER 41

Congressman Billy Louis expected no less than to get his ass kissed by the President of the United States.

"No calls, no interruptions," said the President as Billy entered his office.

Luther Donald signaled for Congressman Louis to sit down. "You were a hell of a college ballplayer," said Donald.

"Thanks Mr. President, but it will only be progress for African-Americans when my people hear remarks like 'You were a hell of a mathematician' or 'you were a hell of a banker.' It's disappointing that we're still in the *You-were-a-hell-of-a-tap-dancer* era."

"I understand, Billy, but look at the progress your people have made."

"I'll tell that to the Alabama sharecroppers or the families on Lenox Avenue."

"You know why you're here, Billy."

"I think I do, Mr. President."

Luther Donald popped a sourball in his mouth.

"I understand the politics of opposing parties, Billy, but I'm dumfounded at this 'Where's the body?' business. This country has to move on, Billy. Admittedly, my politics have been conservative, but now I'm the President of all the people of America. Yet, you raise doubts about my legality. How can I lead? And with troops fighting terrorism?"

Billy Louis could feel his muscles tighten, his body grow tense. It always did for the President of the United States especially when he was going to disagree with him. "There should have been a Vice President, but you opposed Sam Wainwright's nomination, Mr. President. Also, as the 25th Amendment stipulates, there was no letter forwarded from the President's office stating that he was unfit to serve as President until a later date."

Donald snapped, "Wainwright was vaporized in the blast."

"Which is why there should have been a Vice President to take his place," countered Billy.

"What do you want, Congressman?"

"I want some pork barrel in Harlem for a change. I want some federal spending in Harlem that will make your conservative colleagues green with envy. I want my people who've been put out of work by illegal immigrants to start working again. I don't care if you have to put a post office on each block, or build a tank factory for the Pentagon. And I don't want anything that has to go through the Mayor's office. Work it out. Come up with something that will make me feel good when I talk to my constituency."

"Any suggestions?"

"I would like to see what your folks come up with first, Mr. President."

"I bet you're the kind of poker player that checks over betters?"

"You could say I let my opponents make the first move, sir."

Luther Donald could only imagine his Cabinet agonizing over a major pork barrel deal for Harlem. Their careers were built on keeping military bases opened and defense plants booming. Whoever heard of keeping Harlem open?

"And I want to know about it before I read about it in the papers," said Billy Louis shaking the President's hand.

Luther Donald watched Billy Louis leave and sighed. If only Shelby could come up with some DNA, he'd tell Louis what he thought of pork barrel legislation for Harlem.

CHAPTER 42

Shelby was not prepared to find out that Sam Wainwright was still alive, but the news that a sample for DNA had been taken calmed him down for the moment.

The Federal Express package with Sam Wainwright's pinkie in it was delivered the next day to a mailbox service on Third Street. Shelby collected it, returned to his apartment, and put it in a flower pot with soil collected from the White House lawn. It was an act that would make any normal person gag, but it gave Shelby great relief.

He had researched all the forensic information he needed and knew exactly when to put it in the ground to be *discovered* by the Air Force team.

He did, however, have some momentary worry about the forensic pathologist in charge of examining bomb flesh. She was a political appointee of the President, a Harvard graduate. You never knew what those Harvard people would do. They could be quite unpredictable.

As of this date, he knew she had tested every speck of flesh that had been found at the White House site. Newer, smaller samples were being dug up every day by the Air Force recovery team. It was an exhausting process for all concerned.

The families of the victims were particularly a problem, wanting parts to bury of their loved ones. Shelby had put his foot down The Presidential DNA was *the priority*. How far would a pinkie fly in the air? he wondered. And exactly how deep should he plant it?

After a few weeks it would be pretty hard to tell the difference between a few weeks and a few months his overworked pathologist had told him. Still, he would take no chances. He would have her test for DNA, and only DNA.

Luther Donald popped a sourball into his mouth. He was doing that more and more these days.

"You look like the cat that swallowed the you-know-what, Shelby. It's good news then?"

"It will be, Mr. President. Traces of blood in samples indicate a mass is somewhere in the vicinity of the grounds."

Luther Donald leaned forward. Shelby knew that hundreds of times a day Donald would look out of the corner of his eye and be disgusted that his office wasn't oval, but right now he was looking at Shelby. "You're not shitting me?"

"I can assure you, Mr. President the longer we wait, the closer we get."

"How long?"

"How long can you wait, Mr. President?"

It was plain now to Shelby that Luther Donald was desperate. He as much told him that the sample needed a little decomposing time and Donald was pondering it.

"You don't think he's entirely vaporized then?"

"We got blood and it flowed from somewhere, Mr. President."

"What does that Harvard pathologist think?"

"Whatever you want her to, Mr. President — I hope."

Donald rolled back in his chair. "This could be the beginning of a great Presidency, Shelby. Proof at last. I'll give them 'where's the body' right up their *gazoos*."

"You just have to be patient, Mr. President. We don't want to miss anything and we're searching the area very carefully."

Luther Donald leaned forward. "Sam Wainwright was an orphan, Shelby, in more ways than one. All his people went up in that blast and he was a loner to boot. You know Shelby, there are American citizens that didn't even know he was President. That asshole he ran with dominated everybody. There are Americans who still think he's in office, can you imagine?"

"It will be over soon, Mr. President."

"I appreciate that Shelby."

"It hasn't been easy, Mr. President."

"I expect it hasn't, Shelby."

"I'm glad for the strong possibility of good news, Mr. President.I want the party to succeed very badly."

"The Mannix family lives and breathes loyalty, doesn't it, Shelby?"

"It does, Mr. President."

The persona of Luther Donald seemed to change on the next question. "Shelby, I want you to do one other thing for me."

"What's that, Mr. President?"

"You tell those people doing research for you that if they mess with me I'm going to ask the Attorney General to have their balls for breakfast."

Shelby was stunned. He had never expected the President to acknowledge anything that suggested outside criminal help. It just wasn't done inside the beltway. After Watergate, saying something without saying it had become an art form. But he had heard it, and he was ready to pass it on. Of course in a sense there was some denial by the President, still.

Luther Donald at this moment in his Presidency could never allow himself to believe that Sam Wainwright was still alive. No sitting President would ever be able to do that, not even Nixon, Shelby believed.

Ten thousand dollars for putting this piece of macaroni out of business, thought the hospital orderly in charge of watching Sam Wainwright. All he had to do was wait for the right moment and walk away. How fuckin' lucky could he be? Watch the turkey, get him on your side, relax him, and then bingo.

Sam could feel the eyes of the orderly watching him, sly like a smiling Viet Cong waiter on Tu Do street waiting for the right moment to plant a bomb.

Sam struggled to make a mental note of people who knew him personally and could vouch for him. From what he had been told already, most everyone he had any personal dealings with had gone up in the explosion. The trouble was he had never been his own man. He had run on the coat tails of the former President. Even his aides had been borrowed from his predecessors staff. He was a shadow, a man nobody knew. Not even his Congressional peers really knew him.

He was sorry for the opportunities missed and the waste of his short Presidency. Only his fingerprints and DNA proof would save him now, he speculated.

"Hello."

Sam smiled. In front of him was a young, out-of-shape woman with a large pair of breasts, dressed in a blouse and jumper.

"Hello yourself."

"You don't know me?" she asked.

"No, I don't believe I do."

"Are you sure?"

"Yes, I'm sure."

Knowing about Eddie O'Hara's memory problem, Ruth Hoffman sat down on a small metal chair and told the former Eddie O'Hara how she knew about him from an inquiry sent by the County Psychiatrist to the White House Bombing Site. She had developed the site and knew all the passwords to obtain information. She also told him about their previous experience together running from killers, but left out the fact that he had probably killed one of his pursuers in self-defense.

Sam, admiration in his eyes, said, "I'm grateful, Ruth. I owe you my life."

Ruth looked down modestly.

Sam said, "Can you tell me more about the man you work for — Shelby Mannix — and your suspicions."

Ruth told Sam she thought Shelby was deliberately trying to keep Eddie O'Hara from investigators. And maybe worse.

"Then I've had dealings with him?"

"Yes, Eddie or whatever your name is."

"What do you think my name is, Ruth?"

Sam could see it was a question that Ruth didn't want to answer.

"My imagination is running wild, sir. When I was told you had been assaulted and a piece of your finger cut off, I could only think one thing. But that is so unlikely, yet I still thought of it. And worse, the course of recent events seemed to suggest it as well."

"There's no pressure here, Ruth. Tell me what you think."

"Everything points to you being the President of the United States."

Sam let loose a big sigh. "And that's who I think I am as well, Ruth. What do you say to that?"

Ruth eagerly drew close to Sam Wainwright's bed. The orderly grew suspicious.

"Look at this." He bared his leg and showed her the tattoo. "Don't know why I even thought to include the White House."

"Oh, Mr. President, how honored I am to be here."

"Thank you, Ruth, but you're the only person who believes I'm the President except for a transvestite called Arthur."

"No, I know you're the President, Mr. President. It explains Shelby Mannix's actions. He must have known who you were and that you had somehow survived the blast and ended up with a new face and name."

"It's why people are trying to kill me, Ruth. Isn't it?"

"I believe so, Mr. President." Ruth got closer, as she did one of her breasts touched Sam's shoulder. He found himself enjoying it.

The pleasure was only momentary. Sam looked over at the orderly, who called himself Fish. He could see Fish's eyes running over the new plan to get Sam Wainwright.

"Who will believe us, Ruth?"

"DNA. That's what they wanted the pinkie for. They couldn't kill you, but they got what they wanted — DNA. In a few weeks they'll dig up your finger and say there is now definite proof that you were killed in the blast."

"Yes, of course," said Sam, thinking it all made sense now. "If my memory serves me correctly, Shelby Mannix worked for Luther Donald. Don't tell me the Speaker is President?"

"He is, Mr. President."

"My God, he couldn't know about the doings of Shelby — could he?"

"It's possible, Mr. President. He's a desperate man. Americans are very uncomfortable with the way he became President. The 25th Amendment was suppose to assure us that we would always have a Vice President to fill the President's shoes."

"Luther stopped my nomination for Vice President, but I'm sure he doesn't want to know what Shelby is up to. Shelby Mannix is another story. Even from a distance on the House floor I never liked him."

"Your other memory can't remember what you know about Shelby Mannix, Mr. President."

"I'm afraid so. God knows what Eddie O'Hara has been through. It was just a fictitious name to give me another identity in case terrorists overran the White House. I can't imagine how Shelby found out."

"Probably with your DNA," said Ruth, "when he visited you at Fort Sam Houston in San Antonio."

"They're going after me again, Ruth. I can see it in his eyes." Sam tilted his head toward Fish.

Ruth turned and looked at Fish.

"What can we do, Mr. President? There's a lawyer I know —"

"The psychiatrist is on my side, Ruth, I feel it. Work on him. We have no time for lawyers. They were supposed to put me in a lineup and they haven't done it. Work on that. And I'll try not to close my eyes for the immediate future. Please, Ruth, hurry."

Fish did not like the way things were going. *What are they plotting?* he thought.

Ruth Hoffman had learned that playing by the rules could be deadly inside the beltway. A long time ago she had earned a degree in law, even passed the

New York Bar exam, but that was a long time ago. When the stakes are high, you have to do what you have to do, she rationalized.

In his small office at the Thomas County Correctional Facility, Dr. Richard Levine had a startled look on his face when Ruth Hoffman came charging into his office like a Jack Russell chasing a rat.

Levine was seated in a Herman Miller chair designed for bad backs. A framed photograph of Karl Jung was placed respectfully between his diplomas earned from a City College and State University.

Ruth introduced herself, and thought, *He's a psychiatrist who probably had big dreams once. Didn't they all?*

"I'm startled to see how fast Mr. Wainwright obtained counsel," Levine said. "But shouldn't you be talking to the County Prosecutor's office?" Levine put his fingertips together the way professionals sometimes do.

Ruth had decided that the *fuming method* was the only way to go. The careers-can-be-ruined approach. A persona of vengefulness with a touch of righteous indignation.

In her peppery style, Ruth said, "You've got my client in a Catch-22. He's not charged with anything, yet he has to go in front of a judge to decide his mental health, yet he can't do that because he's in the hospital. But that's not enough. He's actually being held for a line-up that hasn't taken place. This keeps up, I'm not after retribution, Doctor, I'm after careers."

The doctor looked on, mutely.

"You don't approve, do you?" said Ruth. "You know something is wrong. They're using this mental thing while they scramble to put together enough to get him charged, that's it isn't it?"

Dr. Levine seemed resigned: "He gave them the ammunition. Two farmers almost murdered, homeless, questioned in the vicinity of the crime, then identifying himself as the President of the United States. The police smelled blood, they still do."

"He's in immediate danger. Do you understand that, Doctor?"

"The sudden attack on him surprised me — yes. I don't understand it counselor. There seems to be every effort to keep him here. I'm troubled over it as well. No explanation for it."

Ruth Hoffman leaned forward. She had scared many a witness before Congress, sitting at the side of her influential Senator, looking like she knew what the truth was and what it wasn't, and ready to whisper it into the Senator's ear should the witness falter.

"What I'm about to tell you, Doctor, is going to shock you — *he is the President*. Or was the President." Ruth's voice was clear, determined, unwavering.

An incredulous surge of confusion fanned over Dr. Levine's face.

Ruth grew confident at the doctor's unsureness. She knew he would never expect a statement like that from someone as sensible looking as her. It didn't hurt that both shared the Jewish faith as well.

Levine's face contorted a little, his mouth moved, lips opened and closed.

"You find a way to get him out of here and I'll see that you get the Congressional Medal of Freedom. You can say good-bye to the prison system, Doctor."

Dr. Levine was on his feet, staring at Jung, staring at his graduate degrees. "Please Ms. Hoffman, I'm not prepared for anything like this."

"You have the authority. I know *this*. He hasn't been charged with a crime."

"How can I believe a homeless man is the President of the United States, Counselor?"

Ruth gave him a determined look. "In addition to what I already know, it could be why they took a piece of him. They want it to be found at the White House bomb site. No other explanation fits."

"Nothing like this would ever happen to me," agonized the doctor. "If it were *true*, it would be an enormous event. Momentous. Nothing like that would happen to Buzzy Levine's son."

"Stop being Buzzy Levine's son," Ruth analyzed.

"No, this can't be possible."

Ruth took out her White House pass and handed it to the doctor.

"I'm not his lawyer, but nobody knows more about the doings of the present White House than me, Dr. Levine. This *prison* is holding the President of the United States, of that I'm certain."

Levine fell back into his chair and crumpled a piece of paper.

"Ethics, morality, or being a bureaucrat? Which do you prefer, Doctor?"

Ruth was confident that her White House pass had been the final convincer, the permission to believe.

Levine said, "A psychiatrist who believes a homeless suspect is the President of the United States — see it from my perspective, Counselor, or whatever your title is."

Ruth countered, "There's only one way to see it — a terrible injustice is being done. The man lost his memory and was hunted like an animal. Bad enough for the average citizen, unthinkable for the President of the United States. Come up with something, Doctor, I know you can. I'm sure you've learned a few tricks."

"I have to call my analyst. I need to put this in perspective," Levine said. His face was clouded with doubt.

Ruth leaned forward. "You'll be responsible for the President of the United States being murdered because you never expected something like this to happen."

Levine signed deeply. Got up. Looked at Jung again. "I don't know what to do."

Sam Wainwright could see Fish watching him, wondering when the time was right. Probably during a change of shifts.

Fish walked over to the bed. The room was isolated. "How you feeling, Pres? *Pres*, that's what they used to call Lestor Young. My grandfather was a jazz musician, good name for someone who thinks they're President as well."

"I'm feeling very well, Fish. Fish — how did you get that name anyway?"

Fish's thin body relaxed. "Always fishing around. Can't keep my nose out of anything. Compulsive."

"How much are they paying for me, Fish?"

Fish's face exploded in indignation. "Paying for you?"

"You know, Fish, I am the President of the United States. Protect me and I'll give you something you want the most — a pardon. Your sins forgiven, because I know what the pressures are, and how you would have to have a giant leap of faith to believe me."

"You don't look like President Wainwright or sound like him. I heard him on the radio a few times."

"My jaw is wired, Fish. It makes me sound different. My face has been reconstructed — look at the scars."

"If you're the President, everyone would know it, even after a fucking explosion."

"I had a code name, Fish. We thought the terrorists were headed toward the White House. No one recognized me after the blast."

"I'd like to believe you, Pres, but I can't. It defies logic."

"Why do you think they're trying to kill me, Fish? A homeless man wandering around the countryside, yet they take one of my fingers. There are people in our government who don't want me found. Can't you see that, Fish?"

Fish waved his hand in disgust, turned around, headed toward his stool in the corner, and sat down. "If I believed you, that would make me crazy too," Fish shouted across the room in a *so-there* attitude.

Everyone in the prison but the guards and the warden knew the *crazy guy* would be taken down at 4:00 a.m. The New Orleans people wanted it, and whatever the New Orleans people wanted, they got.

And it wasn't just the money, it was the *respect.* You did not go against these guys They were everywhere. The crazy guy would go down at four, that's the way it was.

CHAPTER 43

Ruth Hoffman continued to wait while Buzzy Levine's son decided what to do. His thoughts are passing in front of his eyes like news flashes on a building in Times Square, she imagined.

"Please, Dr. Levine, I know it's a bold step, but one that must be made. Time is our enemy. You've got to get him out of this prison."

Levine clasped his hands and put his lips to them. He was in turmoil. She could see that. A psychiatrist was not trained for irrational events like this. He could have ruled out a patient claiming to be Napoleon, or Caesar, in a flash. But a President whose body had not been found?

Finally, he said, "At the least I'll be suspended."

"You'll be written about for you courage and foresight," countered Ruth.

"My colleagues will never let me live it down."

"They'll be praising you for your guts."

"If they're going to do something, it will be on a change of shifts. Frankly, I would have to bluff our way out of the ward."

"I know you can do it, Doctor."

Warden Jim Rowe was a professional. Like any good Christian he didn't like overcrowded prisons or men being gang raped, or a few prisoners pretty much controlling things, but what could you do?

It wasn't his job to decide who was guilty and who wasn't, but hell, get a man who claims to be the President of the United States roaming around the area of two murders and you got yourself one hell of a suspect. Talk to him enough and sooner or later you got 'the devil made me do it' in one form or another. Still it had been 24 hours and John Doe, alias Sam Wainwright, hadn't been charged yet or gone before a judge — and had already been attacked within the system. Yes, it was a sticky one.

The Warden looked up at Richard Levine. "Hell, they haven't been able to put him in a lineup, you know that. Or bring him in front of a judge — you know that too, Richard."

"If I have him transferred to a mental facility on a temporary basis, all our asses are covered," said Levine. "I can have him sent there for 48 hours. The DA's office can get their shit together by then, can't they?"

Rowe smiled. "Shit together? This place is getting to you, isn't it, Richard? And how can you have him transferred? Richard, I know of no emergency transfer or regulation that allows you do that before he sees a judge."

"It's the harm to yourself clause."

"We got a man watching him."

"A prisoner. If something happens to this guy again, you're open to a lawsuit that could be bigger than the state budget."

"You sure you have the authority?"

"Yes, Jim. We've got to get him out of here. He's been attacked in a county facility without being charged for anything."

"I thought the same thing, Richard. The County Prosecutor will be on my ass, so will the locals who brought him in, but I know you know what's best. Frankly, I don't know how you ended up here in the first place, a man with your credentials and ability. Okay, get him out of here, Richard. God, wouldn't it be something if he really was President. I don't think I'd be able to get a job washing windows if that turned out to be true."

"You've got nothing to worry about, Warden," said Levine. But he felt like he was lying when he said it, and that was good he told himself.

Fish could hear the clanging of gates being opened and closed. The laundry detail was coming. All he had to do was unbolt the door to the main hospital ward and look the other way. He didn't want to know who was going to do it, but he guessed it was somebody already in a hospital bed. This fucking guy thinks he's President. He's gonna parole me — what bullshit. The sooner they shut him up the better. Fucker was making me nervous.

Fish was already thinking of the *crazy guy* in the past tense.

Fish unlocked the door and leaned his back against the wall. Why not watch?

"Hell, Fish what you doing opening the door like that?" said the Captain of the Guards. Fish surveyed the situation. Standing next to the captain, holding a cheap-looking suitcase, was Dr. Levine.

Holy shit, they're moving the crazy guy. No, please, don't do that, thought Fish. *Please don't do that.*

"Are you sure you want to take him by yourself, Doc?" said the Captain

165

of the Guards. He was standing on the driver's side of the county car, his head leaning inside the window. He looked at Sam Wainwright. "He's a *nutso*. I just know it."

Levine's face grew serious. "He's agreed to be put under observation, Orville. He can ride up front with me like a human being. I know the County Prosecutor has other plans for him, but that will have to wait."

"Warden says its okay, it's okay," said Orville. "God knows why anyone inside would want to harm him — don't understand it, really. Hey, we put a guard on him. I understand we're prejudicing his rights. Can you explain that to me?"

"He hasn't been charged, Orville."

"Oh, I know that, but he was in the vicinity of a near murder, he has no alibi, and he claims to be President of the United States."

"That doesn't make him any less innocent, Orville."

Orville just shook his head. "He'll be back. The County Prosecutor is not going to let him get away."

As they pulled out, it was raining hard, the windshield wipers had all they could do to keep up with the downpour. Sam Wainwright waited a few minutes before talking. "You have a lot of guts, Doctor."

"I'm honored, Mr. President."

"Then you believe me?"

"Ruth Hoffman presents a pretty good case."

"We just have to get in front of the right people, Dr. Levine. Let them take all the DNA and ask all the questions they want."

"People are trying to kill you, Mr. President. If this were a political thriller, I wouldn't believe you had much of a chance of reaching the right people."

The doctor glanced over at the President. "We're not going to the state mental facility, sir. Ruth is going to meet us at the next McDonald's. And that's all I can do. As far as the boys at the county lockup are concerned, I was wrong about you, you jumped out at a stop light, and took off. Of course, that won't help matters if you're caught."

Sam shook his head. "I'm amazed at how much you're risking, Doctor. I don't know what Ruth told you, but I'm going to make it my business to see that you're rewarded for your courageous act — I'm curious, was I a good President?"

"Lousy. No leadership. You didn't seem interested in the job. Somehow you seemed frozen. I suspect the pressure was too much. I would guess the Vietnam war had a lot to do with it."

Sam took a deep breath. "You're a very wise man. I don't know what the legalities are, but if I'm given a second chance I can assure you, and the country that I won't be asleep at the wheel again. I'm awake now."

Sam wanted to talk about Shelby Mannix, but he held back. It might be good for releasing his anger, but it wasn't good for the country. No, it was better to keep the whole matter under wraps until a clear decision could be made on who was really President. Yet already having two intelligent Americans believe in him was a great comfort. *If only I can stay alive long enough to prove my case*, Sam thought.

CHAPTER 44

"I promised him the Congressional Medal of Freedom, Mr. President," said Ruth pulling out of the McDonald's driveway.

Sam smiled. "Well, *something* did the trick, but he's going to be in a lot of trouble until then."

"Luther Donald must know," said Ruth, making a sharp turn.

"I can't believe that, Ruth."

"Well, I'll put it in Washington terms: he doesn't want to know. Shelby will be playing the discovery of your finger, or tissue, for all he can get. Oddly enough, your little pinkie will be the concrete that Luther Donald builds his Presidency on. Scary, and disgusting, I might add."

Sam frowned. "Is Shelby capable of putting out a contract on me? Or is it more than that?"

Ruth smirked. "Luther Donald is capable, Mr. President, but the way I see it, Shelby figures it's his job to keep the new Presidency protected at all costs. I'm sure no one expected you to turn up alive, but once you did, Shelby Mannix knew what he had to do."

"It's hard for me to imagine that such men still exist. Who are these men trying to kill me?"

"It's known by some here in the beltway as the *Cold-Chill Syndrome*. Every President feels it when he begins to do more for his country than the lobbyists, capitalists, and well-connected want him to do. You start to feel the chill in the White House. You start to feel like someone is aiming at you every time you go out in a crowd. Then you discover that the less you do, the less there is to worry about. The lesson is *you know* there are people out there who can be hired at any moment to stop you, and you kind of compromise your ideals once you know that. No one, in fact, knows those people better than Shelby Mannix, Mr. President. He helped Luther get the job of Speaker by whacking his opponents, if not physically, certainly by getting the dirt on them. The Right Wing has always had a pipeline to them."

"They seem to act as if they're not worried about the consequences," said Sam, impressed by Ruth's acumen.

"That's real power, Mr. President."

"There are respected statesmen that I can turn to, Ruth. We'll go through them."

Ruth made another sharp turn. Sam could see that driving was not one of her better skills. "The way I see it, Mr. President, there's so much at stake now, you'll be blown away the first time you stick out your head. They'll destroy your DNA. They'll do anything they can to stop you. To tell you the truth, you don't have much of a legacy in this town. Is there anyone you know that has a secret only you know? We could try the twenty-questions route."

The comment intrigued Sam. Intimacy was not one of his better traits. With all the *schmoozing*, and all the campaigns he'd been in, no one had ever confided in him, told him their secrets, shared their vulnerability with him. Not like at the orphanage, where secrets were shared on a regular basis. The orphans were each other's family. And that's the way it was.

"On second thought, I don't think that would be a good idea, Mr. President. The opposition would have too much time to destroy your credibility. We have to surprise Congress at once. Startle them. And pray no one can get close to your DNA. Ironically, Shelby's people need your finger to confirm your death — I get sick thinking about it — I think we should wait until then."

"I don't know if we could last that long, Ruth. I'm the President. Congress will have to listen."

"Right now, Mr. President, you're a homeless person without a shred of evidence that you're the President. Who's going to take the time to even examine your DNA?"

"There are people I know, Ruth. All I have to do is talk to them."

"Your face is different and your wired jaw has changed your voice. Until that DNA becomes official, you're going to have less of a chance to prove yourself, Mr. President."

Now Sam was getting angry. Why can't the President of the United States just walk into the Attorney General's office without being thrown out? Or worse, getting killed. It just seemed unbelievable.

"Wait for Shelby to make his move on your finger and then come forward, that's my best plan, Mr. President."

"I'll consider it, Ruth. Where are we going anyway?"

"A place that is kind of the last place you'd expect any President to be at, Mr. President—at least I hope so."

After nearly a two-hour drive along the coast of Virginia they pulled up to a high wooden picket fence surrounding a beach area not far from the North Carolina border.

"My mother was a nudist, Mr. President. My earliest moments as a human were spent looking at the private parts of other people until I didn't notice them anymore. There are resorts that are more conducive to open sex, but this is not one of them. I'm sorry I have to do this to you, but it's the safest place we can be right now. We're sharing a cottage as father and daughter. I'm paying in cash."

Sam didn't know what to think. He turned to Ruth. "You know that feeling you get when you dive into water and it takes your breath away? That's how I feel now."

Ruth smiled. "They know me here as Ruth Baker, so you're Mr. Baker. Anybody that goes after us will have to take off their clothes first."

On the other side of the high fence were rows of neat cottages that were separate from each other. Sam could hear the water and the sounds of giggling children.

There were mostly women and children. The air was fresh and salty.

"The men will be out on the weekend," said Ruth. Inside, the cottage was not unlike a motel room except for cooking facilities. The light was wonderful.

"We want to get out on the beach as soon as possible," said Ruth. "We don't want to cast any suspicions."

"Ruth, I —"

"You don't have any clothes anyway. This wasn't a bad solution, was it? And we have twin beds."

"Would a father-daughter, share the same room?" asked Sam, still uncertain.

"It's not a problem Mr. President. And one other thing. Don't worry if you get an erection, nobody is going to say anything. You'll get one if you think you can't get one. And we just don't use towels to dry off around here. Carry one with you at all times, and use it to sit down on anything."

Sam could feel the blood rush to his face. "I don't know about this Ruth."

"Mr. President, you have to. Believe me there isn't anything you have that the nearest 3-year old hasn't seen."

This is crazy, he thought. He wanted to tell her that in repose his penis appeared somewhat small, but when erect it was much larger than most men. He had learned that from the whores in Saigon.

Ruth read his mind. "We know when it's not hard it isn't your real size, Mr. President."

Sam sat on the bed facing the beach. "There's not even a phone. Can we really stay here, Ruth?"

"Until Shelby makes his move — yes, Mr. President. And if they manage to destroy your DNA you'll never see the Presidency again. That's what I believe."

Okay, be sensible, thought Sam. *You've been through a lot. This girl has saved your hide more than once. Go with it.* But he couldn't.

"I'm just going to sit here, Ruth. Remember, I'm the President of the United States."

"You're just another body on the beach, Mr. President. To tell you the truth you'll feel a lot better if you take off your clothes. I'll be outside."

She undressed in the bathroom and came parading out as if she was wearing the latest fashion. Sam watched her go out the door, her pear-shaped behind not unlike a nude painted by an impressionist.

He had some coins. *Why not?* he asked himself.

The woman at the reception desk gave him a cold look as he dialed 1-800 COLLECT.

When the operator came on, Sam said, "I want to place a call to Representative Jack Finny." He then gave the number to Finny's Congressional office on Capitol Hill. It was one of the few numbers he knew. When given the number as President, he was assured that someone would answer the phone as the number was unlisted. Finny was the House Democratic Leader.

"And who's calling again sir?" asked the operator.

"Sam Wainwright."

He could hear the operator tell one of Finny's people that Sam Wainwright was calling collect. He also heard the party hang up.

"Your party said Sam Wainwright is dead," said the operator in a bemused sort of way.

It's not going to be easy, is it? Sam thought. Then turning to the woman at the reception desk. "Is taking your clothes off to make a call a problem for any of your guests. I always seem to have a problem with it."

* * *

"I don't judge," said the woman in a German accent. "Guests like to wear clothes when they're on the phone, I don't know why."

"Good, then it's not just me," said Sam. "You know, I can't wait to get out there on the beach."

"I know," she replied in an all-knowing way.

In his suburban Maryland home, Dr. Richard Levine listened to the music of Clifford Brown, just like his father Buzzy used to. Buzzy had been a hell of a bass player, but gave up his professional gig to bring up his two sons.

'You don't play like that from lessons,' Buzzy would say. 'They're playing off each other, looking into each other's face,' he would tell his son, his eyes blazing with respect. 'Trying to find out the truth about each other,' he always added. Placing the music in a category that nobody at the time was doing; knowing it would never get any better.

Buzzy wasn't around anymore, but Richard felt like he was when he played Clifford Brown, and his father's other favorite, Stan Getz. Both now upgraded to CD's.

Levine's wife and children were away for the summer, and he missed them terribly, even more so since the homeless man had convinced him that he was the President of the United States. He got a terrible feeling when that happened, it was as if nothing would ever be the same again.

Kennedy Cristiana, Jr. didn't bother to knock but just walked in the door.

Levine looked at Kennedy, not knowing he was in front of a celebrity, the grandson of one of the men who killed Kennedy, a real star in his trade.

"I knew it was trouble," said Levine, knowing this was it, that this time there was nothing he could do to talk himself out of trouble like he did as a boy in the schoolyard, where 'Jew boys' were always the target for shakedown artists.

"Sorry, Doc," said Kennedy, "but you fucked everything up. You must be really good at what you do."

"I am," said Levine.

Kennedy looked at him for a moment and then fired six, 9mm rounds into Buzzy's son.

And just like that, as if all his studying and degrees were supposed to stop a bullet, Richard Levine's body was now a soulless form staining the sofa with the blood of one of the original tribes of Israel.

"I'm glad your family wasn't here," said Kennedy to the dead man. "I don't like killing women and kids."

The President was on a cross-country trip to Los Angeles. The press on Air Force One was buzzing with a rumor that conclusive DNA had been discovered at the White House bomb site.

Luther Donald, of course, had ordered his staff to start the rumor.

The President insisted that Shelby Mannix sit beside him for the one-day turn around. One of those dues-paying trips that President's always had to make.

"I'm starting to feel that things are turning around Shelby," said the President. The rumor will keep them off my back for a few days."

"I'm glad about that, Mr. President."

The President leaned over and whispered. "I don't know how you managed to get your hands on Wainwright's DNA, and I'm not going to ask, but when is it going to make its appearance."

Shelby paused. He had to be careful. "I thought about it ,Mr. President It will take a few more weeks of analyzing the last batch of samples brought from the ground. The sample will be included in this latest batch. Just the cells mind you, we'll need some time with a larger piece of his body."

"You tell that Air Force processing team to get their asses moving. I want discovery *within* three days from now. And keep whatever else you got in the ground to rot for all I care — not that I know why — but get me some DNA for the 6:30 news."

"I'm doing everything I can, Mr. President," replied Shelby, although he knew he had been just given his marching orders.

Donald slid open the door to his suite in the sky to see who was in the pressroom, one compartment beyond his staff, then slid it shut again. "Whomever you're working with, you keep those people in line, Shelby," said Luther Donald.

"I wouldn't do anything to jeopardize your credibility, Mr. President. "Sometimes it gets complicated, though."

The President pulled a sourball from his pants pocket and popped it into his mouth. "That's the burden of being a Mannix. Isn't that right, Shelby?"

Shelby wanted to say, 'Sam Wainwright is still alive,' desperately wanted to tell that to the hard-boiled politician in front of him, bearing down on him with his intense hazel eyes.

"I'm afraid it is, Mr. President," said Shelby, scared now that Wainwright might slip through the cracks, but then reassuring himself that the New

Orleans people, and the extremist wing of his party, had the same interests, in many cases sitting in the same board rooms. No, Wainwright would not escape. They would get Wainwright because that's the way it was inside the beltway.

They think they're screwin' with amateurs? thought Kennedy Cristiana, Jr. looking at Ruth Hoffman's file. He was in a first class D.C. hotel room, sitting in his underwear. His new partner, Dennis, was out getting a pizza. Kennedy had a personal thing with this bitch. Real personal. She would hide where you would least expect it, that was his takeaway. *Goombas* always got caught when they ran because they couldn't break old habits, but this Hoffman was smart. She would do the opposite. If she were a money manager on the run, she was the type to go to Iceland instead of Paris. To think that she worked for that Mannix guy. He had to be careful about that though. It had to look like that was all he could do. He would bring them both down this time. But his curiosity had been aroused. Who the fuck was this Eddie O'Hara? New Orleans got a piece of the finger he knew. They had told him not to worry about that part of the hit now.

Whoever this Eddie O'Hara is, he's fast on his feet, thought Kennedy. Telling that President story to look like he was whacko was brilliant — fuckin' brilliant. Well, the bastard had gotten away again on Kennedy Cristiana's watch. That had never happened before and was not about to happen again. But who was he? Anyway he had Ruth Hoffman's file in front of him. He couldn't explain it, but they were running together now. He could sense it. Something in her file would slip her up. He always got them this way — always. There would be something that would just pop out; almost in an unnatural way.

It was understood that he would have to read Ruth Hoffman's file over and over, again and again, until he became her. And then he would know where they were.

Sam Wainwright sat in a deep-cloth beach chair — the kind the French love — that pretty much kept his private parts private. Ruth, lay next to him on a blanket, her body hiding no secrets.

The breaking waves relaxed Sam for the moment.

"There are parts of my body that have never seen the sun, Ruth."

"There's always a first time, Mr. President."

"I tried to call someone."

"I figured you would."

"I didn't think there would be a trace here."

Ruth turned over. "There wouldn't."

"I gave my name. They hung up."

"You had to find out for yourself, Mr. President. For most people you're dead, although your party has been giving the opposition a hard time." She explained about Billy Louis from Harlem. Sam could see what a political animal she was.

"How do I look under the 25th Amendment, Ruth?"

"Donald's opposition to your pick for Vice President and no formal letter from you saying you couldn't run the country, complicates matters for him. The Chief Justice was not all that sure himself when he swore in Luther Donald. At least that's the rumor."

Sam sighed. "I feel I won't live to see myself out of this mess, Ruth. The evil that the power of the Presidency can bring out is awesome."

Ruth smiled. "Awesome. The word doesn't seem to fit you, Mr. President."

He looked down at his crotch. "What does these days? You really think they're going to use my pinkie for DNA proof?"

"They have to, Mr. President. They'll just take a few cells for DNA testing and try to rot the rest of your finger as fast as they can. Make it look like it's been in the ground longer." She laughed sarcastically. "To think the Presidency of the United States rests on the pinkie of a former President. You couldn't make that up."

Sam watched the waves for a few seconds. "I was a terrible President. I know that now. Had my head up my you-know-what. I've never had a lot of self-esteem you know — odd that I became President at all. It was so unintentional. Now I see what an opportunity I've wasted. Luther Donald will probably do a better job than I did."

"The trouble is, Mr. President, the right of the right controls Luther Donald. It becomes seamless, the politics I mean."

"Seamless? I don't understand, Ruth."

"A stew of profiteers, lobbyists, and right-wing radicals, that are hard to tell apart. They only have one interest — themselves. They go way beyond what the Republican party stands for. In the House they destroyed anyone who got in Luther Donald's way. The double whammy: holding back on campaign contributions and dishing out the dirt in little cuts that bled the opposition to death. No one that's been impacted by this process, ever talks about it. The word is, if they do, things will get worse."

175

"I wasn't aware of this, Ruth."

"You're not the only one, Mr. President. Your party, which is my party, doesn't know diddly about what's going on. They think their daily sell-outs to the lobbyists and big donors are where it stops. They're just being prepped for the next stage — downright corruption. I'm ashamed to say we don't have a government of checks and balances anymore, Mr. President. The power brokers have their own form of government now run by lobbyists, and God knows what."

Sam said, "You know, as a Congressman I proposed a number of bills for campaign reform."

"You handled it like patty cake, Mr. President. Campaign reform is just the tip of the iceberg. Like they say, the road to hell is paved with good intentions. They come to Washington like the Jimmy Stewart movie, but they don't return to their communities. Even our best politicians become shrills for the lobbyists until looking the other way is a natural reflex. And that's when the big boys hook them. They have to keep looking the other way more and more until their heads can't turn anymore to where the truth is."

Sam watched two nude children building a sand castle. "How did this happen, Ruth?"

"Politicians like you with their head in the sand, if you don't mind me saying, Mr. President."

Sam took a deep breath. "Based on what I'm hearing, there's more vested interest in having me *dead*. Is that what you're saying, Ruth?"

Ruth rolled over, just the cleavage of her breasts and the crack of her ass were showing. The President ignored her nudity.

"It goes even deeper than you, Mr. President, but yes. Like I've been saying, stick your head out at the wrong moment and it's sure to get chopped off."

The sun ducked in for a moment. It was a welcome relief for Sam who said, "Well, at least it's nice to know that a Congressman from Harlem is sticking up for me."

Ruth became cynical. "Representative Billy Louis is just screaming the loudest about you because he wants a deal. It's always the deal."

"Maybe we should call him, Ruth?"

"No, they would expect that; figure on you reaching out to your first ally."

"Why weren't you my Secretary of Defense. The one I had could barely count."

"But you guys nominated him and he got through Congress. See what I mean, Mr. President?"

Yes, he saw what she meant, but it was even harder facing the fact that he wasn't just up against a group of bad people, but Washington itself.

This was almost too much for Sam Wainwright to take in. He got up and walked to the water, not caring about his nudeness for the first time.

Ruth got him to smile, however. It was against the rules, he assumed, but she said softly as he walked away from her, "Nice buns."

As Sam stood on the edge of the wet sand, the water seemingly trying to suck him in. The sky downcast, he could sense that his pursuers were closing in. He not only didn't have anything to defend himself with, he didn't have any clothes on, either.

CHAPTER 45

"I nailed the bitch," screamed Kennedy scratching his scrotum in his red Jockey shorts as Dennis entered the room with a pizza.

Kennedy Cristiana, Jr. and his new partner were made for each other. Dennis was the intellectual of the two and understood the logic that Kennedy was applying to Ruth Hoffman's bio. Dennis was scheduled to move up faster in the organization than his partner, but Kennedy didn't mind. He would always be a button man; no one in the organization was better at it. Unfortunately, he didn't know whether he would be whacked by Dennis or not when the job was completed. He assumed New Orleans had already figured out who Eddie O'Hara was, and why someone wanted him dead. You never knew how far up these things went. The bigger the fish, or secret, the more of a chance he was taking. But now it was personal and he didn't want to think about the other bullshit.

Dennis said, "Something stood out, then?" placing the pizza on a glass-topped table. It was one of the Mayflower Hotel's best rooms.

"What do you think?" Kennedy pointed to a sentence in her biography.

"Very subtle, most guys would have let that go," said Dennis in admiration.

"Exactly," said Kennedy, slamming Ruth's bio down to his side.

"Her mother was known to be a nudist — and who was at her side when she was at the beach? Right. Her little daughter. That's where that bitch is hiding. Who would have thought? She and that O'Hara guy standing around balls-ass naked while we look in all the wrong places for them. We got them I know it."

Indicating respect with his tone, Dennis asked, "How do we nail them?"

Kennedy opened the pizza-pie box. "I bet this freakin' crust isn't chewy enough. They never make it right in this town."

He looked up at Dennis with a slice in his hands. "We go to the Internet, we find out how many nudist beaches are in the vicinity, we make a few calls, and then we go in with our clothes on. I'll show you how."

"You're the best, Kennedy."

Kennedy smiled arrogantly and said, "Hey, don't I know that?"

That evening, as Air Force One returned to the Capital, Shelby Mannix tried to hide his in-flight discomfort by chatting with the President's Press Secretary, someone he detested. He dreaded the possibility of being called in to talk to the President again.

For Shelby, the trip in the morning from Washington had been torture. He had ended up sitting next to the President for the entire flight. Luther Donald had been feeling around, sensing something was not quite right, not really wanting to hear about it either, but trying to read between the lines. Shelby knew how Donald operated, but Shelby had already decided to plant the DNA sample in the ground when they got back to Washington.

It would be easy enough to do. Crews were now digging around the clock. He had to just make sure he planted the finger in the area assigned to the professionals from the Air Force. They had been digging for American bodies in Vietnam since the late eighties. They wouldn't miss it. He just had to make sure the good doctor only used the finger for DNA and no other tests.

It was Sam Wainwright still being alive that was the problem. He wanted to tell the President that Wainwright was still alive, but knew that would jeopardize the entire Presidency.

The best he could do now is not allow the President to hear something he didn't want to hear, Shelby decided.

"Shelby," ordered the President, sticking his head out of his suite.

It was what Shelby had feared. The President wasn't letting up.

Shelby feared Luther Donald would open his mind like a can opener.

When Shelby was settled in the President's suite again, even taking a sourball from the President, he said, "There's nothing you should know, Mr. President."

Luther Donald laughed without looking at Shelby. "You know me so well, don't you Shelby? Done all my garbage work for so many years. Kept the crazies who financed me into power happy."

"Yes, Mr. President."

"I'm afraid you would do anything for me, wouldn't you, Shelby?"

"Just about, Mr. President."

"But not because you admire me, but because I stand for something you believe in. The way this country should be run."

Shelby didn't answer.

"You know, Shelby, I want to be a great President, not just the President of Special Interests. But as it stands now, we're practically into my reelection on payback time. Maybe it's time to stop. Let things happen naturally. Maybe I've got to take my lumps and welsh on the favors. Somehow I'm beginning to suspect that I'll never get out from under if we continue on like this — that's why finding Wainwright's DNA is so important."

"That's the plan, Mr. President, nothing else."

"You know, Shelby. I stand in front of American's waving flags asking for help, and it's changing me. The Presidency is something I've always wanted and never thought I could have, but now I do. We know my shadow is longer than most. There's a lot of characters hiding in its darkness. Somehow I think I'm never going to get them off my back — they're not going to let me do my job, are they, Shelby?"

"What you've stood for, is what they want, Mr. President."

"Goddamn it, Shelby, I don't just stand for special interests and the right wing anymore. My supporters should understand that."

"They're helping you cement the Presidency, Mr. President."

Luther Donald popped a sourball into his mouth and looked out the window. "Half the Americans down there don't even know my name. I want them to know it, to respect it, to believe I'm their guy."

"Yes, Mr. President."

Donald turned to Shelby. His eyebrows thick and animated. "I appreciate all your help, Shelby, but for God's sake keep me honest, at least on paper."

"I will, Mr. President."

Luther Donald studied Shelby's face for a moment. "Good, now you'll have to excuse me, Shelby. I have to call the Vice President and get Billy Louis off my back."

Billy Louis lived in the same apartment building on Central Park West and 109th Street that Adam Clayton Powell and Duke Ellington had lived in on the edge of what was officially known as Manhattan Valley. It was still Harlem, but it was more than a few steps up from tenement housing and Central Park was across the street.

Billy Louis had attended Howard University and then went on to Harvard for his MBA. He had spent his entire career painting himself as someone who would go along with the program as long as there was something in it for him. He had studied powerful people, watched how they kept their cool, licked more than a few asses, but climbed steadily up until they were on top. Anwar el-Sadat was one of his favorites. They had called him *Nasser's Puppy* before he got into power. The rest, of course, is history.

Admittedly, Billy Louis told himself, he had started the Wainwright thing because he knew the Republican right didn't want any waves, but now he wasn't so sure. Maybe this was the place to make a stand. The fringe right had finally gotten control of the Presidency. The people behind Donald made Ronald Reagan look like Mario Cumo. *If it wasn't so real, it would be funny*, he thought.

Maybe he had to push this DNA thing some more even if the President came up with a few crumbs for his constituency. Maybe he had to stop thinking about Billy Louis for a change?

Billy was speed reading *Jet Magazine* when the phone rang. "The Vice President's on the phone, Billy."

"Yes, sir."

"This is Tuck Adams, Billy."

"I know."

"The President has asked me to call."

"Fine."

"It's caused a lot of angst among his close advisors, but the President is throwing a big one to your Congressional District, Billy. No Congressional bullshit. All done by Executive Order. The overview is a complex of low-rise federal buildings, 70% of which have to be built by minority contractors. Local hiring will be a priority. Low-interest loans will be given to locals who want to start businesses in the area. It's a two-hundred million dollar package, Congressman. Not including the purchase of land, we knew you would be sensitive to that."

"People on Park Avenue will profit nicely on that, won't they?" said Billy, trying to hide his contempt for the Vice President.

"No way we can put a stop to that," replied Adams.

"What kind of business is the Federal government going to be doing in those buildings, Mr. Vice President?"

There was a pause. "Every hand out program we have will have an office in that complex, including the Bureau of Indian Affairs. You have 18,000 Indians — Native Americans — in New York City alone."

Billy knew the Vice President was from a western state.

"Now that's the government I know and love," said Billy, facetiously. "That's what Harlem has been waiting for, the Bureau of Indian Affairs."

"If you don't mind me saying, Congressman, you're not seeing the forest for the trees."

"The offer sounds fine, I'll get back to you," said Billy resolutely.

Before the Vice President could speak again, Billy hung up the phone. There was no doubt in his mind now that he had gotten to the President. Few have ever been in a position to squeeze Luther Donald by the balls. So why wasn't he happy?

South of the White House Portico, Air Force Sergeant Joe Malone sifted the dirt like it contained gold. The site itself looked like an archeology dig.

Sergeant Malone had been digging in the jungles of Vietnam for two years looking for the remains of American bodies before getting assigned to the White House detail. He had problems, a lot of problems, not the least being the discovery by his wife that he had a Thai girlfriend. The Air Force team always gathered in Thailand before setting out for the latest area in Vietnam to search for American bodies.

It was a difficult assignment nonetheless. And had always been. When the search for American bodies first began, much of the information came from the refugee camps in the Philippines. Vietnamese boat people bartered in bodies with the US Government, hoping to get a reward if they identified a location that contained the remains of American servicemen. Most of Vietnam had been relocated so there was a huge problem. In essence, there were few villagers who would know where the American enemy was buried so long ago. However, Vietnamese Government cooperation was no guarantee either. Sometimes Sergeant Joe Malone would dig for weeks and only come up with animal bones.

Unlike Joe Malone, most of America didn't think of body parts, although Sam Wainwright's disappearance finally brought the issue up at the breakfast table. *Advertising Age*, a trade journal, reported a drop in breakfast cereal sales and concluded that the subject was more pervasive than originally assumed.

If only *he* could find some remains of the President, it would mean a bonus and maybe a fresh start with a new Thai wife, Malone dreamed. He knew his team had been given the most likely area to search and had the best chance, only the task at hand still seemed daunting. The blast was four times greater than the Oklahoma bombing, yet the White House was a smaller target. No, the only thing in the ground he would find were earth worms, he concluded.

Sam Wainwright spent the late afternoon going through the trash. He wanted just the right cans to string outside his cottage. Ruth was bemused at first, then incredulous. "They would never figure out where we are, Mr. President," she said standing over him.

"They're very bright, Ruth. They could probably be anything in life they wanted to be."

"No one knows I'm a nudist," she said, watching Sam Wainwright hanging cans on a rope held up by broom handles pounded into the ground.

"You would be surprised what is known about people these days, Ruth. Is anyone else in your family a nudist?"

"My mother was."

"That's down somewhere. I can assure you of that."

Ruth smiled. "You know you're still President of the United States in my eyes, Mr. President."

He looked up. "You don't have to remind me, Ruth. It's going to be a can of worms if I get out of this mess. The House Republican Leader rejected my Vice President, and then got the job himself — pretty convenient."

She sighed. "I always thought Shelby was capable of going over the line. That's what scared a lot of us in Washington. Luther Donald had some frightening people behind him."

"Who's his Vice President, Ruth?"

"A snake in the grass called Tuck Adams, former governor of Montana. The Presidency has become a loose cannonball I'm afraid. The House Democratic Leader seems to be having a field day with it, however."

"Jack Finny?"

"Yes, Mr. President."

"He wouldn't answer my collect call. Probably thought I was a nut."

"They're trying to kill you, Mr. President. There's nothing crazy about that."

Sam frowned, tied the last can on the rope, then shook it.

"We'll hear them if they're coming, Ruth."

"They just wouldn't know we're here, Mr. President. But if your tin-can warning system makes you sleep better, then I guess it's okay."

Sam stood up. Ruth was a small woman, but had a body that exploded in all the right places, he observed. "Thanks for your vote of confidence," he said. "The last single woman I slept in the same room with just asked for money."

Ruth smiled to let the President know she got the joke.

Sam took a last look at the beach. "If they're coming, that's where they'll do it from," he said, clearly nervous.

CHAPTER 46

Most Democrats did not give up their party's liberal heritage easily, but Jack Finny, House Democratic Leader, had no problem being a centrist whether he was between two opposing philosophies, or two hookers. The opportunity to embarrass the Republicans and put them on the defensive was apparent. The presidential transition had holes in it according to his view of the 25th Amendment, but then again the transition was for the good of the country. The country had been without a leader.

As House Leader for his party, Finny was squeezing out more legislative compromise from his Republican colleagues for reigning in his own people than at anytime in his career. The Republicans would pay later for Luther Donald, he rationalized. It was time for Billy Louis to keep his mouth shut.

Finny didn't like to wheel and deal in public places.

Billy Louis was not surprised at the dinner invitation to Finny's three-story row house on a fashionable Georgetown street.

After a catered meal, Finny's wife and daughter left the two members of the House alone in the living room. Finny was one of those types that tried not to get to the point too quickly. He kept blowing smoke rings from a Cuban cigar until Billy said, "Donald get to you, too?"

"You know we have a bunch of crazies in the White House, Billy. We're gaining points every day because of it."

Billy looked up at the crystal chandelier, scanned the room, and made eye contact again with Finny. *Could any home be more comfortable? He had it all*, thought Billy. *Swirling his brandy around, big fat Cuban cigar in his mouth. The fattest of the fat cats.*

"I know the President has asked you to calm things down a little, Billy. It doesn't seem unreasonable."

Billy stuck his tongue in his cheek. "For the good of the country?"

"Of course," said Finny.

Billy got up and looked out the bay windows. The lamplight spotlighted the cobblestone street.

Billy turned to face Finny. "I admit I had my agenda when I first started blowing smoke up Luther Donald's rightist ass, but the no show has always bothered me," he said, forcefully.

Finny drew his mouth in and let the smoke out slowly. "There's no trace of at least seventeen people at that dinner, Billy. I don't have to tell you it was the most powerful blast ever in the history of terrorism."

"They were low-level people, not center stage where the President was having dinner. They had enough parts of the Israel Ambassador to ship home, yet no trace of Sam Wainwright who was supposed to be sitting at the same table as the ambassador."

"Security could have been aware of the penetration — the President must have taken measures," said Finny defensively.

"That's my point. Where is the body? Or at least a few parts to really sound grotesque."

Finny frowned. He was famous for his frown. It telegraphed the intensity of his position. "Billy, the Democratic Policy Committee agrees that Donald is vulnerable, but his weakness is our strength. Anyway we're starting to look like we're picking on him. There's a piece of Sam Wainwright lying around in that yard and Donald will find it, no doubt."

Billy walked back to the leather chair that had been so comfortable, too comfortable. "My grandmother was the most instinctive person I ever met, sir. If she got a feeling about something that was it. She didn't let go no matter what the facts appeared to be. I don't ever remember her ever being wrong."

Finny put his drink down. "Damn it, Billy, we have to move ahead. You've got people joking about seeing Sam Wainwright as if he was Elvis. Damn if I didn't get a collect call the other day by some jerk claiming to be Sam Wainwright. Now this has got to stop, Billy. To get along you have to go along. You know that." Finny finished his drink. "You sure you don't want one?"

"No sir."

Finny fussed with the decanter for a few seconds. Billy expected the bomb.

Finny turned, his face full of confidence. "You want to act like an independent, you might have to run for reelection as one."

Billy Louis stood up. "My grandmother had a powerful influence on me, sir. Powerful."

Finny didn't respond. He knew a hot head when he saw one.

* * *

It was night. Shelby Mannix surveyed the White House grounds. He was confident that the experienced Air Force Team wouldn't miss where he buried the DNA sample, but in the unlikely event that they did, he would have to remember where he buried it. The Presidency was at stake, and no less.

Shelby wondered if the New Orleans people had figured it out yet. There would be compromises and Lord knows what else. Of that he was sure. The good news was that nobody had wanted Wainwright for President to begin with. He was a nobody who unbelievably wasn't too interested in the job in the first place. Yes, Shelby reasoned, Luther Donald's Presidency was made up of strange bedfellows, but it had powerful interests behind it that could get things done, whereas Wainwright's Presidency had been twisting in the wind.

Shelby observed the sifters. They worked in 12-hour shifts. From a distance, they looked like miners searching for emeralds. The 37-foot deep hole the blast created was not blocked off. Teams probed it just like the other areas, working the sharp angles of the blast hole with rock-climber equipment.

Shelby decided to wait until the shift changed at 11:45 and then plant the precious sample which would most likely be spotted in the morning. They were down to the small bits and pieces now. There would be no major body parts and that made it good. Each area was sifted and probed over and over.

As smooth as things seemed to be now going, Shelby was still deeply troubled. Sam Wainwright was still alive, moving about, with a face only a mother could love. It was a horrifying thought.

Sam marveled at Ruth's snoring. He wondered how she managed to sleep so well considering they were targets for killers.

Well, she's making up for me, he thought, because he could not sleep. There was that old feeling coming back from another time in his life when he was a Marine in Vietnam, and it would not go away.

No longer able to be comfortable in his present situation, Sam put his shirt and pants on and touched Ruth's shoulder.

"What?" she yawned.

"Ruth, I'm sorry we have a change of plans. And I don't want to explain myself. Is that clear?"

"Whatever my President orders," she grumbled.

CHAPTER 47

The Boston Whaler sneaked through the night like a water moccasin. Kennedy could feel Dennis watching him; they hadn't been able to spot Eddie O'Hara's car because it was inside the compound, but Kennedy knew they were there. All he had to do was call the front desk, describe Ruth and Sam, ask if they had arrived safely, and then ask what room he should send flowers to because they had secretly gotten married and probably not used their real name. He hit pay dirt on the fifth call.

"It's cottage 17," said Kennedy. "We'll whack them, take their bodies out in the water, and dump them, anchor and all. We should thank them for giving us such a convenient location."

"I don't like the water," said Dennis.

"Don't worry, I've been handling these suckers since I was a kid. I knew there would be a boat rental around here someplace. This is fishing country."

As Dennis scanned the shore with a high-beam flashlight, Kennedy deftly steered the Boston Whaler through the choppy waters. Occasionally, he would look at a coast guard map for buoys. He didn't want to end up on the rocks. He was close now. In a half-an-hour, he estimated, they'd be dumping the bodies overboard. This son-of-a-bitch Eddie O'Hara and the woman he was traveling with had given him enough trouble. Who would have believed that his partner would go down. He had to dump the partner's body as well, and he didn't like doing that. He hadn't liked calling his partner's wife and telling her that there wouldn't even be a body. No way did he like that.

He would wait a minute before pulling the trigger. Make the guy beg. They always begged if you asked them to.

"There it is, Starlight Cottages."

"Shhhhhh," said Kennedy, cutting the engine. "A regular D-Day landing," he whispered, as the engine died.

"I heard something," Ruth said. Both were lying on a bedspread on the eastern side of the beach. "Mr. President, what are we going to do?"

"Like we did in 'Nam, Ruth — keep quiet."

"Can't we run?" she whispered.

"No, keep down, Ruth. Flat as you can to the ground."

Sam could see them sneak onto the beach, their flashlight moving around in the darkness like it was suspended in air. "Quiet, Ruth, they're coming ashore."

Sam watched the flashlight move closer to the cottages. He estimated that Ruth and he were about sixty feet away, tucked in a corner of the beach.

Kennedy and Dennis walked right into Sam's first line of defense. He could hear them cursing at the clanging cans, then heard them kick down the cottage door. Suddenly the lights from the other cottages flashed on like lighthouse beacons.

"Ruth, don't move," ordered Sam.

His face was flat now against the ground, lips coated with sand.

He could hear the killers grumbling. Then a strong beam of light flashed across the beach as if it were the sky over Hanoi during a B-52 raid.

"We're going to get this son-of-a-bitch," was said loud enough by Kennedy to be heard by Sam and Ruth.

"It's the same voice of the man who attacked us when you had your other memory, Mr. President," Ruth said softly, the waves strong enough to drown out her voice.

"What's going on out there?" a man's voice cried from one of the cottages. "You kids get out of here."

Ruth lifted her head.

"Stay down Ruth, please," whispered Sam.

Suddenly a beam of light swarmed the beach, just edging near the blanket.

"He's here, I know it."

"We've got to go," Sam heard another voice say.

"We should search the area."

"We have to go. It's too risky."

"You're out there. I know it," screamed Kennedy

Sam heard the boat engine start up.

Would he be this lucky the next time? he wondered.

"We can't stop anywhere," Sam said, behind the wheel of Ruth's Saturn. "They'll check the 7-Elevens and any place that's open in this area. What was the name of that Congressman who's been raising a stink about me?"

"Billy Louis, Mr. President."

"Harlem's a big part of his district, isn't that right?"

"He could be there, or here, Mr. President. It's a holiday weekend."

"Here is no good Ruth. They can watch him too easily. New York might be another story and a bigger place to hide."

"It's about 450 miles, Mr. President."

"We have to take the chance, Ruth. Just give me a few directions. I haven't driven my own car in a long time. I'm sure Billy Louis has a local office in Harlem. We'll start from there."

"It's hard to believe, Mr. President."

"What's that, Ruth?"

"That the President of the United States is going to have to identify himself by his own DNA."

Sam didn't respond. Sometimes, when fatigue set in, he had a hard time himself believing he was President of the United States.

It was a rainy, gray morning, with some fog. Sergeant Malone drank his coffee from a thermos and tried to map out in his head how much ground he was going to cover. No one had to remind him how important his job was. The country seemed to be falling apart. America always prided itself on its orderly succession of presidential power, but the terrorist explosion had changed all that. Luther Donald had been Speaker of the House, not the Vice President.

Like many Americans, Joe Malone sensed a deep mistrust of the way the right of the Republican party had sneaked into office. In the same breath, he was as anxious as any American to find the remains of Sam Wainwright, to give legitimacy to the new President, and to get America moving again.

Malone's assignment was the southwest corner of the bomb crater. He supervised six men for that segment but did hands-on work as well. The computer projection had indicated the southwest corner as being the most likely place to find a smidgen of Sam Wainwright. Shelby Mannix had emphasized that over and over as well, which is why sifting in that area was done over and over.

Before finishing his coffee Malone looked down at his feet, and was startled. There it was at the edge of the crater. Decay had set in, but it clearly was a small finger. No need to get excited, he thought, a lot of hands and fingers had flown through the air, but most had been recovered, as were the blast victims except for the seventeen bodies that vaporized, ten of whom had been dining in the same area.

Using surgical gloves, Joe Malone picked up the finger and placed it into a container kept frozen by a separate compartment of dry ice.

He shouldn't be excited, but he was, he thought, as he clutched the container.

In her makeshift office on the grounds of the Naval Observatory, Dr. Lori Wells was troubled and excited at the same time. *What was that fox, Shelby up to?* she asked herself. The number of reporters outside the gate had increased ten fold in just 24 hours. How could he be so sure a sample of the President's DNA would be discovered, unless he was holding back? Had he somehow kept the sample from her until now? Let the President's enemies go out on the limb, then produce the evidence. It was the *way* he operated.

She wasn't going to think of how he got it, either. She knew he was doing stuff behind her back, testing samples all the time with an outside lab. She had never gained the confidence of the searchers.

Males were like pack rats in their intensity to be together.

Well, at least Shelby had not asked her to go to bed with him. Not yet anyway. But she wouldn't be surprised if he did. There was nothing that went on in Washington that surprised her. And like so many before her, Lori Wells knew she had to go along to get along. A small price to pay for being Surgeon General. And why not put closure to this matter? It was for the good of the country. She would not back off on the sample, however. It had to be from tissue, not blood — who knew how many samples of the President's blood were around?

In Lori Well's mind the President was dead, gone, and any tissue sample would be *prima facie* evidence that the President was indeed blown to smithereens. After, of course, base-sequence analysis determined that the tissue belonged to the former President.

Dr. Wells thoughts were disrupted by lots of voices coming from her laboratory. While only temporary, it was a state of the art operation incorporating every piece of equipment needed for Restricted Fragment Length Polymorphism Testing.

She opened the door. Sergeant Malone was holding a container as if it were full of precious jewels.

"You've already seen Shelby, I presume," she said with a chill in her voice.

Malone said, "We have something, Doc. The largest specimen in weeks, right where the computer projections said it might be. Funny though, we dug around that area for two weeks, found nothing and then it just appears. The ground is always doing things like that, pushing things to the surface that've been buried."

Without any sign of enthusiasm, Dr. Wells approached the container, opened it, looked in, closed it, and said, "My God, Malone, it looks good."

"Thank you, ma'am."

"If this turns out to be the brass ring, your life's going to be a lot easier from now on, Malone."

"Don't ask me why, ma'am, but I feel this has to be important. Mr. Mannix says he only wants DNA on this, no goddamn Sherlock Holmes stuff. This DNA business always has someone contradicting the evidence no matter how conclusive."

The President and Shelby had made it quite clear to her that they wanted the path of least resistance on any specimen discovered. If it passed the approved RFLP method for DNA then that was it. No further testing for anything else. And due to the high profile nature of the specimen, she agreed with the President and Shelby.

"It was right where the computer projection said it might be," said Luther Donald. "Took some digging though, didn't it?"

Shelby Mannix could not answer right away. All he could think about was Sam Wainwright getting away, and that one of his own people, Ruth Hoffman, was shielding him.

"I have a good feeling about this one, Mr. President," Shelby lied, trying to keep up a good front.

"You damn well better have a good feeling, Shelby. I knew you'd come up with something. The finger is brilliant, I can't imagine how you did it, and I'm not going to ask. I do know there are specimens of Wainwright all over the place from medical tests. I never knew about Wainwright's missing finger, though. Or maybe I have it all wrong, Shelby? Maybe the pinkie is from the blast, although I never knew you to play with a level deck."

"Why not just appreciate the discovery, Mr. President."

Luther Donald popped a sourball into his mouth, sucked on it for a few seconds, and said, "This goddamn better work, Shelby."

"It's foolproof, Mr. President."

"That Jewish princess we have on forensics is no slacker."

"The evidence is absolute, Mr. President."

Donald looked into Shelby's face, moving his own face a little as if he were scanning Shelby's face for clues. "You didn't find a blood relative of Sam Wainwright and chop his finger off, did you Shelby?"

"Our specimen is better than that, Mr. President."

"Something's not kosher with you, Shelby, I can tell. Want to come clean?"

Shelby laughed. "You wanted a sample, you got one, Mr. President."

"A goddamn finger? Where's the rest of the son-of-a-bitch? How come a finger and nothing else?"

"We're fortunate to have found that, Mr. President."

A hint of admiration appeared on Luther Donald's face. "You had the finger all along, didn't you Shelby? Tested it, knew it belonged to the former President, waited for our opponents to put themselves out on a limb? That's right, isn't it?"

"Very close, Mr. President."

Donald got up and walked to the window, each time expecting to see the Jefferson Memorial, and each time getting disappointed. His back to Shelby, Donald said, "It's a squeaker, Shelby. The country's just not happy with my succession. I don't know what would happen if Sam Wainwright turned up alive — the thought sends chills through me."

"I don't think that would ever happen, Mr. President."

Donald turned as if he heard a dog growling at him. "I keep feeling he's not dead, Shelby. That there's somehow an explanation for that finger, that's he's lying in some hospital like a vegetable — it's *spooky*. You're sure he's dead, then?"

"Yes, Mr. President."

Donald slumped back in his chair, his moment of triumph gone for the moment. "You let me wait on that DNA sample, didn't you? For sure it belongs to Sam Wainwright. You know that already don't you?"

"It belongs to him, Mr. President."

"There are reasons you couldn't tell me about it sooner?"

"Yes, Mr. President."

"Okay, enough. The DNA will come in and we'll move on. I'm going to do something for this country, Shelby. Make it come alive again. Make Americans feel like it's their country again. Who would have dreamed that Luther Donald would lead this charge."

By now, Shelby was only thinking of Sam Wainwright and the destruction to the country he would cause if he was discovered alive.

CHAPTER 48

She's a clever woman, thought Sam, as he watched Ruth pay for the gas in dollars. They were just outside of Manhattan, the dawn ready to explode. It had rained most of the way, but the stops for gas and food had given Sam new nourishment.

He couldn't remember what had happened to him as Eddie O'Hara, but in talking to everyday Americans at truck stops he realized just how decent Americans really were. And what an opportunity he had thrown away as President to help them.

"You think Billy Louis will be able to help us?" he asked Ruth getting into the Saturn.

"He might be paid a lot to look the other way. I don't know Mr. President."

As they approached the Lincoln Tunnel, Sam tried to recall past conversations with Representative Louis. Except for two brief calls from the White House, he could not remember any instance when they had been alone together. Was it possible that any individual, much less a politician, would believe him when he told him he was Sam Wainwright? Right now, he guessed, Shelby Mannix was getting his hands on all his fingerprint files; that was not hard to do when the White House was involved. The FBI Director worked directly for the Attorney General who in turn reported to the President. Shelby was probably having a field day with his records. It would get harder and harder to identify himself the longer his situation dragged out. He had to find a way to reach Billy Louis, get the ball rolling again, and get some protection. Was that possible?

The wipers on Ruth's Saturn seemed to say, *Yes. No. Yes. No.* as they swished back and forth.

The New Orleans people decided that Eddie O'Hara had stayed alive too long. He, and the woman Eddie was traveling with were now an open contract. Ruth Hoffman's license number would be faxed to all interested parties including a select group of New York City policemen and detectives who freelanced for New Orleans.

After all, it was nothing personal. Eddie and Ruth were dead meat anyway. Why not be the first to make a few hundred grand would be the reasoning. There would be no investigation. The organization in New Orleans was too powerful. It was common knowledge that these hits were worry-free. Almost an unspoken law in fact.

'The word is' were usually the first words to preface the person to be whacked. Whenever interested parties heard 'The word is,' they knew there was an opportunity to get in on a big payday.

Kennedy, and his partner, Dennis, knew about the open contract and were not too happy about it, but what could they do? They were not looking good at the moment. JFK had been an open contract as well, but Kennedy's grandfather had delivered the goods. That was the way to look at it, both thought.

Billy Louis stood naked next to his third-floor window and looked out at Central Park. The early morning fog was an apt metaphor for how his head felt. The young lady in his bed moved suggestively, which caused him to smile. The booze and the women would never be a substitute for his ex-wife, he thought. God, what he wouldn't do to have her back.

"Billy," she purred.

"What precious?"

"Keep me company."

"I'm about to put my political ass on the line, baby. I got to think this out."

"No wonder Dorothy left you. You're probably thinking politics even when you're doing me."

"It's what I do."

The young lady stuck her bottom lip out as if she were pouting and dove under the covers.

Billy laughed, but only for a moment, and then thought about his plan to be the finger in the dike, the one voice in the wilderness that cried out for some goddamn proof that Sam Wainwright wasn't alive somewhere. The conservatives had screwed over his people enough, he had to stop them, or at least slow them down.

In Billy's mind, the dumb terrorists didn't care who was in office. Fucking idiots. Well, it was the perfect opportunity to go after Luther Donald. He couldn't back down now, not even for concessions that would help his district.

Damn, what's wrong with me? he thought. *When did I become a man of conscience?*

He considered that Dorothy, his ex-wife, had finally gotten through to him, although much delayed, then dismissed the notion.

Luther Donald was just a front man as far as Billy Louis was concerned. Lately, it seemed to Billy, that Donald had softened considerably, but the power brokers were always lurking in the background, putting a cold chill on anything that got in their way, including Presidents.

The annoying buzz of the lobby intercom interrupted Billy's thoughts.

"What is it, Mike?"

"Two people here want to see you, sir?"

"You know my policy Have them go to my office on Amsterdam Avenue."

"They said they were there."

"Who are they, Mike?"

"They're white."

"White?"

"Yes sir, young lady and older man."

"They want to see me?"

"They say it's an emergency, something to do with Sam Wainwright."

Billy turned to the bed. "Get dressed, baby. I have company"

CHAPTER 49

Sam and Ruth were now in Billy's living room. Billy wore a silk robe, and fancy slippers. Sam could see that Louis was incredulous at what Ruth had just told him.

"And you work for Shelby Mannix?" Billy asked

"Yes Congressman, I do."

He turned to Sam, who was wearing a wrinkled shirt and dirty jeans. "And you introduced yourself as 'Mr. O'Hara for now'— a strange introduction."

"You'll understand in a few minutes, Mr. Louis."

Billy lit a cigarette. Sam could sense how reluctant he was to do it.

"I stopped for three days, but you two being here is the straw that broke the camel's back," said Billy

Ruth looked at him. "I don't understand, sir."

"You mentioned Sam Wainwright's name. It's a name I've been thinking about a lot these days. Hearing the doorman say it, made me very nervous."

Ruth looked at Sam who turned to Billy and said, "We know you've done a great deal to support the former President, Congressman."

Billy leaned forward. "Until they can prove he's dead he's not the former anything as far as I'm concerned, but you said you had information on him."

Sam took a deep breath. "We have information that he's alive."

Billy took a huge drag of his cigarette and slowly exhaled it. "Alive?"

"Very alive," said Ruth looking at Sam.

Sam could feel Billy Louis switching his eyes back and forth, searching for some weakness in the faces of his surprise visitors.

"Naiomi, honey."

"Yes, Billy," said a voice from the bedroom.

"Are you dressed?"

"Yes."

"Could you leave please?"

197

"Bil — ly."

"Please, honey. I'll call."

Billy waited before speaking.

A stunning black woman with striking cleavage darted by Sam and slammed the front door behind her.

"If this is a shakedown, let me know now," said Billy.

Sam walked to the window that faced the park. It was wide and offered no shade. It felt like he could reach out and touch the early-morning joggers, they seemed so close. But something didn't feel right, only he couldn't figure out what was bothering him about the view.

"Why would we shake you down, Congressman?" Sam replied.

"Because Sam Wainwright being alive is the most outrageous statement I've ever heard. And when I hear things that don't make sense, I assume there's another reason behind the words, kind of a code thing. Your talking about one thing, but you mean another. See what I mean?"

Sam walked back to the sofa, sat down, and said, "Sam Wainwright being alive is something you could never believe, then? Is that right Congressman?"

Billy smiled. "I only believe there's no proof out there that he's dead, but the sucker is gone, has to be."

"Why is that Congressman?"

"Well, the only other reason he could be alive is he had a stand-in that night like the movie, *Dave*. Because when you look at the hole in the ground that used to be the White House, it sends a powerful message."

"Then why are you so adamant about proof?" asked Ruth.

"A chance to get back at those right-wing bastards. I don't like the way they've sneaked into the White House. I've decided to do everything I can to keep them on their toes."

"You're on the HMO subcommittee is that right, Congressman?" continued Ruth.

"Not a lot of people know that, but yes, I am."

"You could probably get a physician up here in minutes."

"One of the perks."

"You could probably have a DNA sample in 48 hours, is that right, Congressman?"

Billy Louis smiled. Sam knew how much even a little pull like that could be a turn on.

Ruth stood up. In a sweeping motion of her arm she said, "Congressman Louis, meet the President of the United States, Sam Wainwright, although I understand you have chatted on the phone a few times."

Billy furrowed his brow and jumped to his feet. "I want you hustlers to leave right now."

Sam, somehow feeling a new sense of confidence, said: "Will you let me tell you what happened, Congressman?"

In the next ten minutes, Sam Wainwright gave Billy Louis the *Reader's Digest* condensed version of what happened to him. Billy listened carefully, sometimes with an incredulous look, sometimes with a look of astonishment."

Finally Billy said, "You know I want to believe you which is what all con artists are good at."

"This is not a con, Billy. I'm Sam Wainwright. Get a sample of my DNA and test me. It looks like that shouldn't be too hard for you to do."

It was obvious to Sam that Congressman Billy Louis was stunned by the revelation, almost frozen. Sam guessed that he was the type of individual that didn't like having anyone else telling him how to solve a problem.

"I'm having a hard time digesting your story, Mr. President. Damn hard."

Ruth spoke softly: We're on the run, Congressman. We need safe shelter. You could coordinate this whole matter for us."

"That's another concern," said Billy. "I don't need a Congressional investigation to know that a major political figure can get killed for making too much noise in Washington. Sometimes it even looks like murder. Mostly it's a rock climbing accident or something like that.

Give me a minute to think about this."

They watched Billy go into the bedroom.

Sam turned to Ruth, "Well, what do you think?"

"He's a gambler He believes us."

Billy's phone, sitting on the table in front of Ruth and Sam, rang. Billy came charging out of the bedroom in jeans and a charcoal pullover. He pressed the speaker button as he finished tucking in his shirt.

"Yes."

"It's me, Billy."

"Naiomi?"

"Yes, Billy."

"Where are you, honey?" he said giving Ruth a bemused look.

"I'm across the street. You can see me from the window. I need help."

Billy laid down the phone.

"What's wrong?" asked Ruth

"Weird, something's happened to Naiomi — the lady that just left — she says she's across the street."

Ruth rushed to the window. Billy followed. Sam realized what was bothering him, the window with no shades, the park across the street.

"No, don't." Sam shouted, but it was too late.

The bullets that shattered the window, splayed the room, and shredded everything in their path. Ruth's body dangled in the air like a marionette for a few seconds.

Sam crawled to her side, but the bullets had taken off most of her head.

"I'm okay," said Billy.

"But she's not, Congressman," Sam cried bitterly.

"*Oh my God, Naiomi,*" Billy said.

"They have no reason to kill your friend, Congressman, but you'd better get on the phone to the police."

Both of them were on the floor like animals. Billy said, "Mr. President, if you are the President, you'd better get your tail out of here. You don't even have any identification, do you? You don't want to get locked up."

Sam looked at Ruth's body. One had to wonder at the power of the organization behind these killers when they no longer cared about killing a person in a Congressman's apartment.

He was alone again, Sam thought. For a moment he considered walking in front of the window and letting them finish the job. He hadn't known Ruth for long, but he knew she would have been a lifelong friend. And he had big plans for her in the back of his mind.

Billy was already on the phone to the police. He was a cool character, observed Sam. While Billy was talking to the police he wrote something down on the back of a business card and handed it to Sam.

Sam knew he couldn't be in the apartment when the police arrived. That's what they wanted. That's why they didn't care about just getting Ruth. If their attack was a message to Congressman Billy Louis, he didn't seem to get it.

Sam went down the back stairs to the basement and entered the street through an alley. Congressman Louis's girlfriend was crying hysterically as a crowd gathered around her. Sam still had the keys to Ruth's car but decided that taking her car might not be wise.

He walked east. The residents of tenement buildings sitting on stoops looked at him suspiciously. It was another kind of trouble, he thought. He was white and unwelcome, and he understood why.

Sam saw a mail carrier about to enter a building. He stuck out the business card Billy Louis had given him and said: "Can you tell me where this is?"

"Three blocks over, six blocks up," she said. "But I wouldn't be walking around here," she added.

"I know," said Sam, turning around, wondering if the killers had spotted him.

CHAPTER 50

In his car, Kennedy Cristiana watched Sam scurry down the desolate street. It was only a matter of time now. In the background he could hear the police sirens arriving in front of the Congressman's apartment building. It was at times like these that the full power of his organization was evident. No one crossed into his world only separated from a crime scene by a few city blocks, but untouchable. It wasn't about money anymore. Whatever was going on, he knew it was bigger than money. And this O'Hara guy was the secret. Maybe the weird stuff O'Hara pulled inside the county jail, claiming he was the President was true? Wouldn't it be something if this O'Hara guy really *was* the President? But that would be too good to be true. On the other hand that might be bad news. They would want to plug holes fast. He wasn't sure about Dennis. Dennis was known as a trouble shooter. Nice as pie, and then you were part of a concrete foundation all of a sudden. Yeah, why *was* Dennis riding alongside of him, checking his pager every two minutes, cool as a Latin pimp.

When the former President of the United States reached East 115th Street, he saw a priest standing in front of a three-story rectory building waving his arm for Sam to hurry.

Sam didn't realize the address was a church.

"You were the only white person on the street you had to be who Billy sent over," the priest said, closing the door behind him, looking relieved. Sam recognized the priest at once.

He was Father John Tierney, a former Congressman from Massachusetts. They had served in the House at the same time.

Father Tierney said, "Billy's taking all the heat right now. The police want to know why he let you leave."

Sam didn't know what to say. They walked through a long hallway. At the end of the hallway, to Sam's right, was a kitchen. Sam had never had a kitchen as a boy. *It must have been wonderful to sit in a kitchen and eat,* he thought.

"Sit down, Eddie. I'll put the kettle on," said Father Tierney with a trace of an Irish accent.

"Is that the name Billy gave you? "Sam asked.

"He said you might have another," replied Father Tierney, heating up the kettle.

"You don't recognize me then John?"

"Why, should I?"

"Billy didn't tell you who I really was?"

"He says he's not sure who you really are, but he's convinced people are trying to kill you."

Sitting down, Sam placed his left hand, the one with the missing pinkie, under his right. "We served in the House together, John. You left to do missionary work, that was my understanding, anyway."

Father Tierney studied Sam for a moment. "Harlem has all the missionary work anyone could ask for, and who the be-Jesus are you? I don't have a clue."

Sam smiled before saying, "You were always eating potato chips. I remember that about you. Sitting there eating potato chips on the House floor."

Father Tierney looked at Sam suspiciously. Sam could feel his eyes probing his face for a clue.

Sam finally said, "I'm the President of the United States, John."

"Sam Wainwright?"

Father Tierney froze. Sam could see the confusion in the priest's eyes.

"My God, how could this happen? You don't even look like Sam Wainwright."

Over three cups of tea, Sam told Father Tierney his story.

There was a long silence before Father Tierney said, "Your story is a bit much, I don't know what to believe. And Ruth Hoffman is dead? I knew her very well."

"Yes," said Sam, his voice breaking.

Father Tierney said, "Your voice isn't the same either."

Sam pointed to his chin. "It's still wired."

The priest seemed dazed. "Then the killers could be at my door?"

"Yes, which is why I have to get out of here. I don't want any more lives lost because of me."

Father Tierney said, "No, give me a moment to think, Sam — Mr. President, whoever the hell you are."

Sam watched the priest leave the room. He looked around. The kitchen was dark, not bright and cheerful, not what he imagined a cozy kitchen should be. Sam could hear John Tierney faintly on the phone. Tierney was always someone he had admired from a distance. As the saying goes, tough but fair. The church had never liked one of their own being involved in politics, that was well known.

Father Tierney came back into the kitchen. "Billy is having a hell of a time with the police. They said you're wanted in Washington, D.C. as a material witness under the name Eddie O'Hara. I have more of a reason to believe in hell than your being *Sam Wainwright*, and I'm sorry for that."

Sam stood up.

"No, let me finish," said Father Tierney. "Billy believes in you, but he's tied up with what just happened. I'm going to have to figure out something and fast. I hope you don't feel too badly about me. I just can't find it in myself to believe you. I don't know why… it's troubling to me as well."

"Don't worry, John. I understand."

Father Tierney shook his head. "How could this happen? The President of the United States hunted like an animal?"

"DNA results will vindicate me," exclaimed Sam.

"Who but a handful of experts would know the difference? You can be sure if you're really Sam Wainwright you're going to have to get your hands on the proper DNA files. But right now it's best that we get you out of here safely no matter who you are."

Parked a few feet from the rectory, Kennedy Cristiana pondered his next move. Gunning down the woman should keep that Congressman Louis on his toes, but O'Hara or whoever the hell he was, was still alive. The doors of the rectory looked heavy and surely no one was going to open them, not right now. He would wait. Make sure you don't hit the priest he told himself. That might cause problems. The slum residents wouldn't care about O'Hara, though; another whitey down, so what.

If he had to, he was going in. The police weren't going to do dick. That's what power was all about. the captain of the precinct already knew a fat envelope was coming down. Those bastards could smell a political hit a mile off. It was business. Everything was business. They joked in New Orleans about lobbyists in Washington having the *right stuff* to be button men. The

US of A was going that way, Kennedy reminded himself as he watched six large African-Americans in bow ties approaching the rectory building of Saint Marks.

Kennedy turned to Dennis. "You see what those son-of-a-bitches are up to? They're going to walk out with him like he's some black student whose going to an all-white school for the first time. Can you believe it?"

Dennis didn't seem interested, he kept looking at his pager.

"What the hell you looking at that beeper all the time for? Numeric messages, up my ass, that's what I say."

Dennis continued to look at his pager.

Kennedy got out of the Toyota, walked to the trunk, took out a box that looked like it had Christmas tree balls in it, then entered the car again."

Kennedy reached in the box, took out a grenade, and smiled.

"Crude, but effective. Two or three of these should do very nicely. No way is that asshole walking away from this."

Dennis looked at the doorway to Saint Mark's rectory and then to his pager. His eyes darted back and forth several times from one to the other.

The next half an hour they just waited. Kennedy seemed transfixed, like a crazed jungle fighter about to charge a hill and get killed. Dennis now had his instructions.

"Oh no, look at that," said Kennedy, his face full of disappointment.

An armored vehicle, the kind that carried money, rumbled down the street, stopped in front of the rectory, and backed over the sidewalk curb until it reached the steps of the townhouse.

"I think I can still toss one," Kennedy said.

From his ankle holster, Dennis slowly slipped out his 9mm weapon already fitted with a silencer. He could see his partner was transfixed by the scene in front of him and oblivious to anything else.

Dennis placed the weapon six inches from his partner's head and fired three times.

Kennedy let out a sound like a baby gurgling and collapsed.

CHAPTER 51

When Luther Donald stood with his back to you, rocking back and forth on his heels, you were either going to get fired, or get the ass chewing of your life.

Shelby knew this when he walked into the temporary White House Office of the President.

His back to Shelby, Luther Donald turned like a snake coiling itself for a strike. "The good news is the DNA is a match, I understand?"

"Yes, Mr. President, it is."

Donald sat down, his hands pressed on top of his desk, poised to rise again. "I always thought you had something going on this, Shelby. *Depended* on you to get something, in fact. Figured some of the President's tissue was stashed somewhere — they're always sticking so many needles in us for tests. Suspected you were getting help from people that weren't choir boys."

Donald cleared his throat and continued. "That's what I figured, Shelby, because I couldn't imagine any other scenario. Who could?"

"I'd like to explain, Mr. President."

"Now I know you've been in contact with the people who seem to be the fourth form of government in this town. Say something you don't like and the chill comes — damn if I know how they do it — but they had the balls to have a message delivered to me — by my Ambassador to the UN no less — it was sealed, but it was clear. They wanted me to know they were taking care of a major problem for me. It took me less than instantly to figure it out."

"It was my sacrifice for you, Mr. President," muttered Shelby.

"Your sacrifice?"

"I knew the hit would have a life of its own once they found out who this person was. I never expected them to contact you. I expected to end up with all the mess."

"Ruth Hoffman is dead. Did you know that?"

"Yes, sir."

"Tell me it's not true that Sam Wainwright is alive?"

Shelby answered with silence.

"Jesus, good God, what is going on? No, don't tell me. Don't tell me anymore. Goddamn it Shelby, how did this happen?"

Shelby waited for a clarification. Did the President want to know or didn't he? But there was none. Donald was feeling his way, tossing it back and forth, skilled politician that he was.

Luther Donald drummed his fingers on his Reagan desk, popped a sour ball in his mouth, and said, "These things do have a life of their own, don't they Shelby?"

"Yes, Mr. President."

"You and I know the worst thing that could happen to this great country of ours is having Sam Wainwright come back from the dead, claim his right to the Presidency. It would rip this country apart."

"It would, sir."

Luther Donald leaned forward like a wolf who knew his victim could not fight back.

Shelby trembled.

"I hope this country never has to go through something like that, Shelby."

The cancer has spread, thought Shelby.

Sitting in his underwear in his Georgetown row house the House Democratic leader was incredulous. "What are you pulling, Billy? Sam Wainwright was vaporized, or damn near it."

"He's alive, sir. I spoke to him."

"Did he look like him?"

"No sir."

"Did he sound like him?"

"No sir."

They were on the phone. Billy watched the cleaning woman scrub Ruth Hoffman's blood out of his carpet.

"Have you been drinking Thunderbird or something like that Billy. That's what I hear your constituents like to have."

"Insult me all you want, sir."

"It's the worst thing that could happen to this country right now, Billy. You know that, and it's just not true. I know it."

Billy, like any good politician had not revealed everything up front. He told Finny about Ruth Hoffman.

"While this may sound callous, Billy. That woman's mouth was sure to get her blown away. And shootings in your neck of the woods are not uncommon."

Billy continued with the story Sam Wainwright had told him.

There was silence, and then, "It's just impossible, Billy — and who is trying to kill him?"

"Who would you think?"

"That's slander, Billy. I know everyone behind the President and not a single one of them would have the balls to do something like this. Maybe Shelby, but I have my doubts."

"Let me bring the man claiming to be Sam Wainwright before Congress, sir. A special session just for them."

"Damn it, Billy, even if he was alive, which is highly unlikely, he's not the President, anymore."

Billy, like many in Congress, was well aware that the transition of Luther Donald to the office of the Presidency was shaky. Billy said, "No one in Wainwright's office has ever delivered correspondence to Congress saying President Wainwright was not capable of serving—even if he wasn't around. What's more, Wainwright's nomination for Vice President was blocked by the man who eventually assumed the Presidency. Think about that. And if someone in Donald's office knew that Wainwright was alive, as we now suspect — well, the whole thing is negated according to what I read. Want me to go on?"

"Damn it, Billy, do you want to destroy this country?"

"I want a special session, sir. I want the man claiming to be Sam Wainwright to appear before the entire body. Let them take all the tests they want. I know this man is Sam Wainwright."

Billy could almost hear Jim Finny's wheels turning.

"Get him to me in one piece and he can appear before the Subcommittee on the Death of President Sam Wainwright. We'll do it in an off hour, no press. Just the twelve members of the committee including you. The Republicans run things you know. I'm just co-chairman."

"You got them licking your milk, sir."

"I'm not sure I know what you mean."

"They're playing ball because they know we can raise a stink about the 25th Amendment. And you've been making it easy for them on just about everything else."

"To go along you have to get along, Billy."

"So they tell me—when can we meet, sir?"

Finny looked at his watch as if he already knew the answer. "Let's say about 38 hours from now."

Billy took a few seconds to figure it out. "That's about 5:30 in the morning, sir."

"No press that way."

"What are you afraid of?"

"Damn it, Billy, I know what you're up to. You got this charlatan to stir things up, but it's not going to work. When we're finished with him he won't be able to get a job at Burger King. Goodnight."

As the heavy metal doors of the armored vehicle closed, Sam Wainwright, sitting on a bench, waved good-bye to Father Tierney.

Four African-Americans sat on a bench opposite Sam. So neat looking in their bow ties, well-pressed suits, and close-cropped hair. Black Muslim's, he suspected. *Father Tierney has some strange allies,* Sam thought, but he was grateful. Had he ever given Black Muslims a thought when he was President? Probably not, there was so much he hadn't plugged into that was America. He wasn't even sure if they called themselves Black Muslims anymore.

There was little chance he ever would be President again, but if that happened by some fluke, he wouldn't blow it this time, he promised himself.

Riding in the back of the armored car brought back memories of 'Nam, but Sam squelched them. He didn't want to think of anything but the present. Right now he didn't have the luxury of reliving the past, he told himself.

Sam discovered that his protectors were members of a religious organization called the Servants of Allah.

They rode for about an hour, then stopped.

The Servants of Allah got out first, stood in a circle, then signaled for Sam to come out. It was still daylight. The building they stopped in front of looked like a housing project. They entered a recreation room located on the first floor.

As soon as Sam sat down, one of Sam's bodyguards handed Sam a cell phone.

"You okay, Mr. President?"

"Billy?"

"Yes."

"They're taking good care of me, Billy. I feel like the Secret Service is back with me."

"Luther Donald should know by now. There's no tellin' what will happen," said Billy.

"Luther Donald is an ambitious man, Billy, but not a killer."

Billy said, "They found your finger on the White House grounds. That was before anyone knew you were alive. They're going to have to do something and everything points to their acting impulsively. I have something arranged, Mr. President, but I'm not going to talk about it now. Your safety for the next day-and-a-half is all I'm concerned about. We'll talk in a few hours."

Sam handed the phone back to the Servant of Allah bodyguard. "Thanks for helping me."

The huge African-American moved his head as if to say 'did I hear right?'

"We're doing this for Billy," Sam's bodyguard said.

"I understand," Sam replied, suddenly troubled by Billy's distrust of Luther Donald.

I'm holding the office held by Washington, Jefferson, and Lincoln, Luther Donald thought, as his Ambassador to the United Nations sat down before him.

Donald could feel his anger building as he said, "I would have never thought, Nathan."

"Ten years ago my son got into a lot of trouble. They got him out. They never asked for anything, Mr. President."

"Until now."

"Yes, I'm embarrassed to say…sir."

"You don't know what the message said that you delivered?"

"No, Mr. President."

"They want to get me out of a lot of trouble as well."

"I can't imagine what, Mr. President."

Luther Donald scoffed. "I only wish I could tell you so you would know what a filthy thing you've done."

The Ambassador looked down.

Luther Donald continued. "I know, Nathan. You're just a messenger. You hold one of the most important positions in our government, but you've been reduced to a messenger, just like I will be if I cooperate. But they will get their way one way or another, won't they, Nathan?"

"There are people in this country who can't be touched, yes sir. Lyndon Johnson always complained about it in private. He's the one that came up with the Cold-Chill metaphor, I believe."

"Cold-Chill my ass. It's the goddamn military industrial complex, big business, and white collar mobsters with the same agenda, and the intelligence community at their beck and call. Not to mention the lobbyists who would have promoted the sale of barbed wire in Hitler's time if they had the opportunity. Yes, we goddamn well know who's running this country, and it's not me."

Luther Donald took out a folded paper from a valise on his desk.

"You know, Nathan, the intelligence people knew there was going to be a major terrorist attack somewhere in this country. They goddamn knew it and they looked the other way. They didn't like Wainwright. They knew it would hurt him and his ability to lead — oh, they won't tell you that. They couldn't figure him out like they can me. They know what I want on my bread. I talk to the FBI Director he tells me, 'it slipped through the cracks.' I talk to the CIA Director he tells me 'it slipped through the cracks.' It was a duplicate operation they tell me. The same operation set up in two different parts of the world. It slipped through the cracks. Bullshit."

The Ambassador looked at the President, sheepishly.

Donald said, "What I have to do to save this country, Nathan. It's the most awful thing anyone should have to do, but I genuinely believe if I don't do it this country is going to go into a tail spin that it will never be able to get out of. Your friends, of course, know the person who's handling this delicate situation for me. They know they shouldn't be going over his head. But to make sure, you tell them never to do that again, that's what I want you to tell them."

"Yes, Mr. President."

"And one other thing, Nathan."

"Yes, Mr. President."

"Find an excuse to resign in the next three months."

Luther Donald watched his Ambassador to the United Nations leave his office meekly. The President's mind wandered to his future election. If he didn't get a reelected,, he would accomplish nothing. The special interests already had him tied up for his first term. Sam Wainwright's reappearance, however, would create incredible havoc. Of that he was sure.

"Get it over with, and let's move on," Donald mumbled under his breath.

Dennis watched them take Kennedy's body away. There was always less trouble at home if the body was available to be buried. That way the death could be viewed as a screw up on the job.

Poor bastard didn't realize how much he fucked up, Dennis thought. *They never do. Spraying a Congressman's window had to be sheer lunacy.* Dennis knew he could have stopped Kennedy, but why do that? The operation was in his hands now, and from what he could figure out, the biggest thing that ever happened to him.

Dennis had long suspected that Eddie O'Hara was somebody very, very big who somehow wasn't in touch with his identity.

Dennis wanted the kill. Kennedy's grandfather had been an icon in New Orleans for what he had done. The grandson never had it; thought he did, but didn't. This was his kill now. If only it could be done personally. That was the way to fame and fortune where he came from. Whack the guy while he thinks you're there to help him. Trouble was the Muslims couldn't be bought. Anyway, the point was to get the job done. Here, in this crummy part of the Bronx where the old *goombahs* were just minutes away holding Fort Arthur Avenue like Texans defending the Alamo, they had become Americanized and couldn't be trusted. But the deed would be done.

Right now, Dennis knew, some junkie was being set up to drive a vehicle bulging with explosive into the housing project where they were hiding Eddie O'Hara. He also knew it wasn't easy asking a loser to either take a bullet in the head or drive a truck into a building.

You never knew what kind of an answer you would get.

It was early evening. Luther Donald was flying to Minnesota for a fund raiser. He requested Shelby's presence for the short chopper ride to Andrews Air Force base. It was the last thing Shelby wanted to do. He knew the cat was out of the bag.

"Don't get out enough on the stomp, Shelby. Sometimes it seems like I'm frozen in place like an ice statue. Now what about that meeting of the subcommittee with the staff excluded? There's already a buzz about it. What the hell is going on?"

"We lost contact, sir?"

"He's actually scheduled to testify?"

"Yes, but there are things in our favor." Shelby explained about Eddie O'Hara's plastic surgery.

Donald relaxed. "Then he doesn't *look or sound* like Sam Wainwright? Am I correct?"

"Yes, sir."

"Then why should anyone believe him?"

"They won't unless he can come up with his DNA."

"Goddamn trap. We get our hands on his deoxyribonucleic acid profile, release it to the world to show we found his tissue in the blast, and then this living specimen walks into our lives again."

"I failed you, Mr. President."

"You failed the country, Shelby. Your *friends* went over your head. Came right to me — can you imagine?"

"I knew they would if they figured it out, sir."

Luther Donald turned and gave Shelby a cold look. "You gambled with my Presidency?"

"I truly believed if Wainwright appeared it would create havoc for your Presidency and the country, Mr. President."

Donald popped a sourball into his mouth, sucked on it longer than he usually did before biting into it, and said "We agree on that, but the problem hasn't been solved."

"We blew it. No excuses, sir."

"How much does Wainwright know of your involvement?"

"As Eddie O'Hara he would have no memory of me, but he was with Hoffman. I'm sure she rounded everything out for him. I really don't know when his memory returned. When I met him, he was Eddie O'Hara."

Luther Donald said, "Nobody is making a big deal about Hoffman. Apparently there are random shootings all the time in that neck of the woods. The building has been sprayed with gunfire more than once."

"Billy Louis isn't talking to the press. He'll unload when we least expect it, Mr. President."

"Then you're vulnerable, Shelby?"

"I'm afraid so, Mr. President."

"But you're a Mannix. You'll have no trouble getting us out of this, right?"

Shelby smiled slightly. "A Mannix always finds a way, sir."

"Well, you'll have some help. There isn't a Republican on that committee that's going to let his nonsense go any further, and we can thank God for that."

Luther Donald patted Shelby on the knee. "Thank you for being candid, Shelby. I have complete confidence that you'll be able to come up with a solution that will bring closure to this matter once and for all. Is that statement clear, Shelby?"

"Yes, sir." Shelby knew there was no way to tell what Donald was really thinking. When he returned to Washington, Shelby drove to the Watergate, took out a picture of his wife and two girls pressed a revolver barrel against his temple, but couldn't pull the trigger.

I will not die a failure, he thought. He still had one trump card left if all else failed.

CHAPTER 52

After a sleepless night on a cot, Sam Wainwright decided he didn't like the setup. "What if we were followed?" he asked.

"No one is getting through these brothers," was the reply from the only Servant of Allah who spoke to Sam, a very large man with a soft voice who introduced himself as Khalil.

Sam said, "I appreciate what you're doing for me, Khalil, but I don't like being in one spot too long."

"I can sympathize with that, sir."

"It's something I used to feel in 'Nam. I can't explain."

"You were there, then?"

"Yes."

Khalil studied Sam. "You're supposed to be an important man. I'm wondering who?"

"Some have called me, *Mr. President*."

The bodyguard smiled. "I've never seen you before."

Sam moved his face slowly to show where the reconstructive surgery had been done. In a good light you could still see traces of the road map that led to his new face.

"Blown up then."

"Yes."

"No one recognizes you?"

"That's what happened."

"And the powers in Washington trying to kill you?"

"That's what it looks like."

Khalil appeared to soften. "It's hard to believe you're President of the United States. On the other hand, it's not hard to believe that they're trying to kill you because you are. That should say something for this country."

215

"Do you remember me at all?" asked Sam, seeing an opportunity to be personal.

The big black man shook his head. "One President comes in, one goes out. It's all the same when you're black, or African-American, or whatever is politically correct these days. You Presidents would rather spend $57,000 a year to keep us locked up in prison instead of spending a few thousand on us when we're younger. That money could help us to get a decent education and try to straighten out any problems we have before we become adults. I don't look to you for leadership. I look to Allah."

Sam looked into the eyes of Khalil and said, "If I make it, this time I'm going to do the best I can to help all Americans."

"Makin' it might not be so easy. We're only three blocks from Arthur Avenue," said Khalil.

"I miss the point," said Sam, leaning forward on a worn out sofa.

"Well, the restaurants are great, and the locals are very friendly, but if it's a syndicate thing they're going to regroup there whether the locals like it or not. No tellin' what they'll throw at us."

"Then we should get the hell out of here."

"Billy is trying to work it out, sir."

"Thank you," said Sam, thinking he might be better off on his own.

Fat Frankie was a skeleton. As a junkie he was an embarrassment to his all-Italian Arthur Avenue neighborhood. Frankie owed a lot of money. When New Orleans asked for a driver who would not return, the local syndicate reluctantly agreed to Frankie, knowing this was probably the only way he would ever be of any use to them.

They found Frankie shooting up on the grounds of a nearby hospital for the terminally ill.

Frankie was now tied to a chair in a garage just off of Third Avenue, near 183rd Street. Frankie watched them prepare his death vehicle. *I have to think, not panic,* he thought. He had gotten out of a million tight situations before, but these guys, they were the elite, real pros. Why in the world they wanted to drive a Ford Explorer into a building like a terrorist would, was beyond him. But that's what it looked like they were doing — stuffing all kinds of plastic explosive into the vehicle, setting up all kinds of switches.

The garage they were in was owned by a local *goombah*. This was a sanctioned hit. *My time has come,* thought Frankie. *Well, fuck them, they think they got Fat Frankie this time, but they don't.*

Frankie whined, cried, begged, all the time knowing he was distracting his captors just a tiny bit. Maybe even enough to wiggle out of his situation, he prayed.

It was late afternoon, and raining. It had taken all day for Dennis and his crew to prepare the Ford Explorer while Fat Frankie whimpered like a little boy who just fell in the school yard. The plan was for the Explorer to jump the curb, go up on the sidewalk past the columns holding the building up, and crash into the bottom-floor recreation room. Fat Frankie would be tied down and told the truck was going to blow anyway, and the best thing he could do for himself was to do something right with his life.

If he stayed on course they would give his mother $50,000 and pay for his burial if there was anything left of him, which would be doubtful. If he tried anything, he would go up anyway, so it didn't make any sense to deprive his mother of $50,000.

"Please. Please. I want to talk to my mother," moaned Fat Frankie as he watched them prepare the vehicle.

"Your mother can't help you, Frankie," said one of the Arthur Avenue locals who had been sent over as coordinator.

The local looked at Dennis. "This guy you're hitting must be pretty important."

"Maybe, maybe not."

"Frankie won't do it," said the local.

Dennis scowled. "He has no choice. He either gets blown up with his mother getting 50 grand, or without. Either way we get our man, one way is just a little more professional than the other."

The local said, "Frankie will figure a way out. He owes some of the most important people around here, and he's still here. The guy is a survivor."

Dennis looked incredulous. "Are you his press agent or something?"

The local stepped on a cigarette he had been smoking. "We're just making this a matter of record so nobody's nose goes out of joint. The human bomb stuff is not what we do very well around here, nor the way we like to see things happen."

"Frankie will be fine," Dennis replied. "We're giving him an honorable way out. His debt to his creditors is paid off. His mother gets 50 big ones. And Fat Frankie gets to be part of folklore."

The local grimaced. "Whacking a bunch of people? I don't know about that." He looked over at Frankie, who gave him a pleading look.

"I'm supposed to ask where the target is."

Dennis gave the local a disparaging look.

The local moved his chin as if he was adjusting his neck. Dennis knew all the nervous ticks. Button men always did stuff like that.

"There's a lot of *jigaboos* around here," said the local

"*Jigaboos?*" said Dennis inspecting the Ford Explorer checking to see if it was rigged right.

"Blacks."

"No shit? I didn't know the South Bronx had any blacks."

The local backed off. It was known that these were the big boys.

And even the mob hierarchy of Arthur Avenue—what was left of them—knew better than to interfere.

The local looked at Frankie again. "You don't embarrass us, Frankie, you hear. Be a fucking man for a change."

"Please, I want to call my mother," moaned Frankie.

"We're going in ten minutes," said Dennis. "Strap him in."

They covered Fat Frankie's mouth with tape and dragged him out to the Ford Explorer.

The housing project stood between Lafontaine and Arthur Avenues. The traffic light was just far enough away for the Ford Explorer not to be conspicuous. In that part of the Bronx it would have been unusual to see an SUV at that hour.

Fat Frankie was dragged over to the driver's seat and strapped in. It was then that he concluded they were going to time the explosion. No way would they have rigged up an impact device as well, he reasoned.

He ran it over in his mind. They had to travel five blocks just to get to the traffic light. Any unusual movement would set off an impact device. It would take a skilled terrorist to set up an impact mechanism properly, Frankie guessed. Although he was bundled tightly, he had a little movement with his hands and feet.

"Right where that light is," said Dennis pointing toward the housing project. "There's guys in front. You'll see them."

"I can't do it," Frankie sobbed.

Dennis placed a revolver in Frankie's temple. "Do it."

Frankie continued to sob. He stepped on the accelerator, slowly moving forward, then, suddenly, pressed on the brake and threw the Ford Explorer in reverse. He knew his captors had a choice, blow him up and reveal the whole operation, or go after him.

As the Explorer lurched backwards it jumped the sidewalk and backed into the high, thick stone wall of a hospital which had once been a last stop for contagious diseases. The Explorer went up like a mini-nuclear blast, crushing sixty-feet of wall and sending boulders every which way, killing three of the New Orleans people and wounding Dennis slightly.

A few minutes later Dennis received a phone call inquiring whether the task had been completed successfully.

He said there were complications.

Sam's bodyguards looked in wonderment at that blast; for a moment frozen, then dropping to their knees and praying to Allah for sparing them. Moments later a taxi drove up and Sam was pushed into the back seat.

The taxi, Sam realized, had been waiting around for just such an emergency.

Khalil piled into the taxi right after Sam.

"Allah is on our side, Mr. President. I believe you must be the President."

"Thank you, Khalil, for believing me. Where the hell are we going?"

"To see Billy, Mr. President."

The taxi carrying Sam stopped in front of the Apollo Theater which looked empty. Surrounded by Servants of Allah, Sam entered the lobby then walked into the theater where Congressman Billy Louis was waiting on the stage.

Billy looked nervous. Sam assumed he already knew about the bombing attempt.

"The Republicans on the subcommittee are already saying you're the biggest phony anyone ever pulled out of a hat, Mr. President."

"Tell that to Ruth Hoffman's family," replied Sam, still shaken from the Bronx explosion.

"The Democrats aren't that enthusiastic either. It's just too unbelievable for them as well."

"What do you think?" Sam said, standing on the stage with Billy.

"You know what I think, but you have to live to prove I'm right."

"I'm doing the best I can in that department, Billy."

Billy told Sam about the meeting of the subcommittee at 5:30 in the morning.

"It's going to be fireworks," added Billy. "We just have to get you there in one piece."

Sam held up his hand to protest.

"I'm making this plan, Billy. Let me have some of your men and leave it to me."

"But, Mr. President…"

"It's my ass, Billy."

"Your bodyguards are my responsibility," said Billy.

"Then I'll see you in Washington, Billy?"

Sam turned to walk away.

"Mr. President, please, we'll do it your way."

Sam had already decided that no matter which way he got to Washington, his pursuers would have it covered, but at least he was the only one who knew at the moment. Maybe that would give him enough time, he hoped.

The Majority Whips for the House and Senate, along with the new Speaker of the House, and the Senate Majority Leader, watched the President pace in his office.

"Well, what do you think?" Luther Donald finally said.

The new Speaker of the House said, "It sounds plausible, Mr. President. They could be trying to put a ringer before the committee. It sure would create a lot of controversy, but if his DNA matched, what could we say?"

Practically stepping on the Speaker's words, the House Whip, the toughest politician in the room said, "You could say 'tough shit, Mr. Wainwright ,you *were* the President'."

The Senate Whip for the Republican Party was greatly troubled that a man claiming to be President Wainwright was going to testify at all.

"I'm worried about the transition, Mr. President. You can see in the films that the Chief Justice was clearly disturbed about swearing in the Speaker of the House. The whole process is shaky and open to challenge. There was no Vice President as Acting President thanks to partisan politics. And no communication by the President to the Pro Tempore of the Senate indicating that he was unable to discharge the powers and duties of his office."

"He was blown to smithereens," said the House Whip.

The Senate Whip replied, "But no one from Wainwright's staff who survived transmitted a written declaration that Sam Wainwright was unable to discharge the powers and duties of his office, and there was no Vice President to act as Acting President if they had done so.

If anyone in President Donald's office had any knowledge that Sam Wainwright was alive, everything would be negated anyway. And if the *unbelievable* did happen, and Sam Wainwright was alive, and he submitted a written declaration to the President Pro Tempore of the Senate, and you Mr. Speaker, that no inability exists for him to serve as President — well, I just don't know."

"The Chief Justice swore me in," cried Luther Donald as if he was going to be cheated out of something.

The Senate Whip said, "He may have overstepped his duties and infringed on Congressional authority — it's tricky."

"Goddamn it," bellowed the President. "There is no Sam Wainwright no matter how convincing this character is, and I'm not moving from this office."

"Nor does our party want you to," said the Senate Whip. "But you may not be able to govern if Sam Wainwright shows up. It could paralyze the government."

The House Whip stood up. "I'm tired of standing in a room with a bunch of pussies. This President is all we have and nothing can remove him, nothing, but his own death."

"And I'll outlive all you sons-of-bitches," said Donald, puffing himself up.

The Senator Whip said, "And then there's the death of Ruth Hoffman in Billy Louis' apartment."

"Certainly, it looks odd," said the Senate Majority Leader, who hadn't spoken yet. "I can understand someone taking a shot at that big mouth Louis, but Ruth Hoffman? It's puzzling."

The President's face revealed his disgust with the conversation. "We have DNA that says Wainwright was in the blast," he fumed. "Whoever testifies before the committee is a fraud. This is meant to embarrass the right wing of the party — nothing else."

"Maybe he lost that tissue and survived," added the Majority Leader, a disciplined man known for being steady at the controls.

Luther Donald glanced at the Aaron Burr-Alexander Hamilton dueling pistols. *Now that was a way to settle a dispute*, he thought, envious of not having that opportunity.

CHAPTER 53

Statistically, it's much harder to kill a man who expects it, Dennis had learned from experience. The pressure was on now. He was officially informed by New Orleans that Eddie O'Hara had been confirmed as Sam Wainwright, and sources revealed that Wainwright was on his way to Washington, guarded by a contingent of black men supplied by Billy Louis.

The bad news was, no one knew what means of transportation Wainwright was using. The good news was there was a tap on Billy Louis's five phones. New Orleans would know soon enough what Wainwright was up to.

Dennis didn't have to be told, but New Orleans emphasized that under no circumstances was Wainwright to make it to the Capital alive. There would be a chopper on hold at the West Side Pier to make up for lost time as soon as Wainwright was pinpointed.

Dennis hoped Wainwright would go by car — that would be the easiest, but he was ready to bring down a jet if he had to. One word from New Orleans could make it possible. The cargo-loading system at Kennedy and LaGuardia always had more than a few working at those airports who owed their souls to the mob.

Finally, he would be the man to bring a President down. *You couldn't do better than that*, he told himself, knowing he had to succeed, and somewhat nervous for the first time in his life.

At 9:45 that evening, one of Wainwright's Muslim guards called Billy Louis from Penn Station.

Within minutes Dennis was informed that Wainwright was taking the Congressional Limited at 10:10 that evening. Too late to make it, but no problem if he took a limo to the West Side Heliport, then hopped a helicopter to Trenton where he would be met at the Amtrak station by backup.

Dennis would then board the Congressional Limited to Washington with his backup. He already knew Wainwright would be difficult to reach, but he had a plan nonetheless.

* * *

It wasn't much of a gym, but Luther Donald enjoyed his evening workouts, particularly the punching bag. He was going at it full force, when Shelby Mannix walked in.

"There's talk that if we knew Wainwright was alive, *my Presidency* could be in jeopardy," Donald said throwing an uppercut.

"Eddie O'Hara didn't surface until long after you were in office, Mr. President."

"But then *you knew* he was alive?"

"I failed you, Mr. President."

"We've gone over that, already," said Donald punishing the bag with a left hook right-hand combination. "I'm afraid to ask how we got the DNA sample."

"There was a lot of bungling on the part of our friend*s*, Mr. President."

Luther Donald slipped a right over the hook of his imaginary opponent. "This goddamn thing makes Watergate look like a nursery rhyme — and they're your *friends*, Shelby. They'll never be *my friends*."

Shelby could feel the pressure, as well as the pain, of the President, but he also knew that if Wainwright didn't make it to Washington alive, there would be nothing but speculation and doubt and not much more. Luther Donald would be able to live with that.

"Wainwright is not mentally competent to serve, sir, in fact there's no telling what he'll do to himself in the next 24 hours."

"We'll let's hope he does it before he reaches the committee, Shelby. I'd prefer to win this by default."

"That would seem like the most likely scenario, sir."

The President threw a vicious left hook and then grabbed the bag. "Wainwright should never have been in office, and based on his injuries, shouldn't be in office now."

"That goes without saying, Mr. President."

"That Hoffman woman was on to you, wasn't she, Shelby?"

"She figured it out, yes sir."

"She'd always make a face when I offered her a sourball. She hated us."

"I didn't hate her enough to want her dead, Mr. President."

"I know that, Shelby," said Donald, crouching for a new assault on the bag," but if Wainwright makes an impression on even one House Member, I don't know what's going to happen."

"As I said, Mr. President, I think his appearance is highly unlikely."

Donald turned to Shelby with a look of menace. "I'd like to duel with that son-of-a-bitch. That would be a way to settle it."

Shelby suspected the President was not kidding.

"If Wainwright agreed, why not?"

"It could be just between the two of us."

Shelby chose his words carefully. "I don't think the opportunity will present itself. Honestly, I don't, Mr. President."

Donald walloped the bag viciously. "They're not taking the Presidency away from me, Shelby."

Shelby moved a little closer to the President. "I would never let them sir — never. You have my word."

The President turned toward his target and threw punches at the *Everlast* bag until both arms dropped from fatigue, but the bad feeling would not go away. He had gone too far this time with his ambition, he suspected.

The Congressional Limited left Penn Station one-minute late. The four Servants of Allah tried to make themselves inconspicuous, but they surrounded Sam nonetheless and were obvious.

Sam decided at the last minute to choose the club car. It was best choice because of its seating, swivel chairs that were spread out to take in a view of everyone in the car.

Billy Louis had laid out the cash not knowing what Sam was going to do with it, but snickered when he told Sam the entire cost would have to be refunded after Sam testified, and wasn't that great?

Maybe, but Sam wanted to get his life back, and he wanted to be responsible for it as well. He was beginning to have second thoughts about the club car. It was the last car on the train. They could be mowed down no matter how many Servants of Allah there were. It was that old feeling of being boxed in. He signaled to Khalil.

"Yes, Mr. President."

"I'm feeling uncomfortable in this section, Khalil."

"But we can jump if we have to, I think it's the best choice, sir."

Sam looked at Khalil. This man was willing to risk his life for someone he didn't even know. He hadn't spoken to Khalil very much but had learned that Khalil had spent most of his boyhood defending a grassy knoll in front of his housing project that led to a number of gang shootings. Remarkably, Khalil had gone on to change his life. Now Khalil was carrying a gun again because of Sam Wainwright. Sam didn't feel good about that.

An hour later the Congressional Limited pulled into the Trenton station.

After boarding the Congressional Limited in Trenton, Dennis knew all the stops had to be pulled out. At the same time the hit had to have a certain amount of discretion. The point was to get Wainwright to cooperate, get him off the train, and make sure he's never found again.

Dennis calculated that he had one hour and forty minutes between Trenton and Baltimore to complete his task. Just after Philadelphia would probably be best, but cut down his time. He used the time between Trenton and Philadelphia to finalize his plan.

After it's Philadelphia stop, Dennis waited for the big wheels of the Congressional Limited to start chugging again into the familiar rhythm of a diesel electric pulling hundreds of people.

Once the 4400 horsepower engine reached full speed, Dennis entered the baggage car. The conductor was sneaking a smoke.

"Hey, wrong way," the conductor said to Dennis.

"I don't think so."

"You don't think so?"

"Well, I think so."

Dennis pulled out his revolver. His plan was not to kill any innocent bystanders, but what could he do? The conductor, seeing the revolver and noticing the three men accompanying Dennis, tried to dart into the engineer's compartment. Dennis fired four bullets into the conductor's back, stepped over him, and entered the engine room.

There were a few moments of silence then, "Is that you, Charley?" The door to the engineer's compartment was partially closed.

Dennis was startled to hear the voice of a woman.

"No, it isn't," he replied.

"If it isn't you Charley, who is it?"

Dennis opened the door.

"What? —"

"Don't look at me, lady. Preserve your life. Now this is what I want you to do. Stop the train."

"I couldn't do that."

"You have stalled trains all the time in this corridor. I've been on a couple."

"I can't. It's too dangerous —it's night time."

"Stop the train," said Dennis, sticking the cold barrel into the back of the engineer's neck. *She smells good*, he thought.

"Why?" she moaned.

"Because this thing in the back of your neck says so."

Dennis was vague in his knowledge of the 'dead-man's-position.' Somehow he knew if he whacked her, something she was either stepping on, or pulling, would automatically set off a mechanism to stop the train. So be it. As he was about to pull the trigger, the engineer relented and slowed the Limited to a crawl, then to a stop. Dennis ordered her to get up without looking at him and walk into the baggage car. There, without saying anything, two of his men blindfolded her, and tied her up.

Dennis expected great confusion in the other cars, in fact planned on it. That was the whole idea for stopping the train. He was certain it would flush out the amateurs guarding Sam Wainwright.

Two more conductors entered the baggage car on their way to the engineer's compartment. They were blindfolded and tied up as well. Space was being utilized at a rapid pace. Dennis opened the door to the baggage car and kicked out some of the baggage.

He then peeked between cars to make sure his other two men, disguised as business travelers doing spreadsheets on their laptops, were alert.

At least one of the three men guarding Wainwright would be along in no time, Dennis estimated. After that, his trap would be set.

When the Congressional Limited crawled to a stop, Sam looked at Khalil for some sort of reaction, but there was none. Sam was troubled nonetheless and hoped the stalled train had nothing to do with him, but the old gut reaction was churning inside, warning him that trouble was coming.

Sam was alarmed as well for the other business people in the car, snoozing as if they had fallen asleep in the barber's chair. They could easily be harmed by indiscriminate gunfire.

Khalil sent two of his men to check on the sudden stop. One stayed behind.

The minutes went by slowly.

How long is this going to take? Sam thought.

Khalil finally looked concerned. He leaned on Sam's swivel chair. "What do you think, sir?"

"I don't know what to think, Khalil. I hear a lot of nervous chatter in the next car and that's about it."

"The boys could be having a problem."

"If they don't come back, we have a problem."

"If they don't come back, whoever's responsible has a problem," countered Khalil.

Sam was already studying the car. It would be in his pursuer's interest to get him off the train. The DNA from his finger would be enough to satisfy Donald's critics. His body however would be a problem. They wouldn't want it around, not after Billy Louis' intervention. They would try and take him alive and that was an advantage for him.

He stood up and looked at Khalil. "It's them. I feel it."

"They're not going to get near you, Mr. President."

"There's too many people around, Khalil. They want me to run. They can't have a shoot out here."

"That occurred to me, too, sir."

Sam got out of his chair calmly. "Let's go to the men's room, Khalil."

Khalil looked confused. Then signaled for his one remaining guard to watch the door.

CHAPTER 54

There was a roar of disapproval from the business people in the club car as the lights went out.

"Come to me baby," Dennis whispered in the sticky summer night. There was a feeling when you *knew* you had the guy and Dennis was getting it now. Grab him, then pop him. That's what you had to do in this case.

There was nothing that matched the feeling Dennis was getting waiting for the most important hit of his life to walk into his hands. Nothing.

A large figure opened the exit door to the last car on the train, paused for a moment, then jumped, his feet crunching on the ground. Then crouching low he moved silently like a soldier was trained to do.

Dennis could hear his own breathing as he threw a light on Wainwright, then watched Wainwright roll on the ground to the cover of a nearby bush.

"Sir, if you'll just come out from behind those bushes," Dennis said. "Or there's going to be a problem."

"Try it white trash," replied Khalil.

Dennis had imagined that his dead partner, Kennedy, had just not been up to it. Links to Kennedy's failure to finish the assignment had to be cut, and he was only too willing to do it. It was at this moment of deception by his target that he realized that he too had been outflanked by a smarter man.

He didn't like to think of who Eddie O'Hara was, but in the same breath he now understood why Sam Wainwright was still alive — a combination of luck, cunning intelligence, a raw instinct for survival.

Two people must have jumped off the train Dennis now realized. He had been watching for one person. He felt degraded and vengeful.

"Your man is still alive in the baggage car. Let's talk." Dennis cried.

"I suspect he is," Khalil replied. "He had a backup who should be taking care of your people right now."

Knowing he had failed entirely, Dennis fired. Khalil could do nothing but return the gunfire and defend himself. The amateur vs. the professional. But often, the greatest tool of the professional is surprise, and Dennis had no surprises left.

Sam moved quickly along the scrubby brush that lined the train track, grateful to Khalil for understanding the situation, knowing that Khalil would not only face anger from his superiors for letting Sam Wainwright leave his guard, but also face great danger as well.

As for himself, Sam was grateful that he had not allowed himself to be a victim of circumstance. That part of him had disappeared after Vietnam; it had been put in the closet like an old suit, but was now functioning again to Sam's approval.

In the near distance Sam could see the highway and hurried to reach it.

Luther Donald very well understood what Shelby Mannix told him on the phone in the code style of conspiratorial talk. "Mr. President, our friend has decided to come to Washington and appear before the board," said Shelby, the nervousness of failure clearly in his voice.

"Yes, thank you, Shelby," said Donald hanging up, then looking directly at his dueling pistols.

It's my Presidency, Donald told himself over and over, but he was not that sure. He had been briefed by some of the top constitutional lawyers in Washington. There was enough room for doubt to leave his Presidency crippled, whatever the outcome, as long as Sam Wainwright remained alive.

Maybe Wainwright would agree to a duel? Donald thought in one wild moment. Why not? This was the way to settle the matter once and for all. Let the better man survive. Congress had screwed up again with that 25th Amendment, so neat and tidy. Well, the world didn't operate neat and tidy. Wainwright would certainly prove his point, and then what? A run off vote by the electoral college? It was a possibility, and he would never win that one if they really thought Sam Wainwright was alive.

Of course, Wainwright would have to convince a skeptical group of politicians. In fact, the DNA profile of tissue found would be pretty damn conclusive that he was dead. An impostor could easily remove a pinkie, that's how the subcommittee would see it.

Donald, however, had not felt like the President since becoming President. There were reasons of course. He wasn't in the Oval Office, the Cabinet was a compromise he detested, and Sam Wainwright was breathing down his neck.

CHAPTER 55

Sam Wainwright, the 43rd President of the United States, stuck out his thumb. There was a slight fog and light drizzle as he edged along the highway.

A late model 4 x 4 pulled alongside of him.

"Need a ride, buddy?"

"Yes, I do."

"If you suck my cock." There was cackling laughter; the SUV took off as if the laughter was propelling it.

Sam shook his head. In some ways he blamed himself for his lack of moral leadership which America, it now seemed to him, needed so badly.

The traffic was light. Sam wondered how many hours it would take to make it to Washington, D.C. For the moment he didn't think of revenge, or even becoming President again, all he could think about were the people who had helped him. The poor and middle-class alike. The folks who kept American moving and somehow always knew when to do the right thing. He owed them so much, and he had let them down as President. He realized that as well as he knew the names of the men under him who had died in Vietnam.

The rain grew heavier. Sam was uncomfortably wet. The traffic, mostly SUVs, paid no attention to him as he did his best to flag a car down, yet at the same time he was fearful of the consequences.

About 30 minutes later, Sam heard a car slowing down. He turned to see a late-model Acura crawling just behind him. For a moment he didn't know what to think. Should he run? He hadn't stuck out his thumb for the last five minutes.

The car sped up to reach Sam.

Sam hesitated, confused now.

The window came down. "Mr. President," shouted Khalil, "I wasn't sure it was you."

There was relief in Sam's voice. "Khalil, it's you — where did you get the car?"

"I stole it."

Once in the stolen Acura, the President turned to Khalil: "The men on the train?"

"We left them for dead. If they're alive, it's not my fault, sir."

They are killers, yes I know that, Sam thought. But Khalil's coldness bothered him.

Sam said, "We'll have to return the car when we get to Washington, Khalil. You outfoxed them."

"No, *you* outfoxed them, Mr. President. It was a brilliant deduction."

"Lives have been lost, however."

"They killed the conductor. He had three kids the engineer said."

Sam closed his eyes. "I'm so sorry for what has happened, Khalil. Sorry that you got involved as well. It must have been terrible for you to hold a gun in your hand again and use it."

"All I know, Mr. President, is you would be dead now if we hadn't acted like we did. I didn't want that to happen. Only Allah knows why things happen. God is Great."

"Thank you, Khalil," replied Sam, looking at the windshield wipers swishing back and forth. He feel they were a good analogy for his life these past few months: First one way then the other way, one way, the other way. One way. The other way.

The Subcommittee Investigating the Death of President Sam Wainwright was not considered a very important committee inside the beltway. In fact it was considered a public relations ploy. It was obvious how Sam Wainwright died: he had been blown to bits.

As members of the subcommittee climbed the steps of the Capitol, they were familiar with the rumor that Sam Wainwright was still alive, but determined not to be influenced by anything but facts.

All the members of the subcommittee were familiar with the story of Anastasia — the woman who claimed to be the daughter of the last Czar of Russia and they all knew how that ended after her body was exhumed, DNA evidence proved that her story was false.

There were seven Republicans and five Democrats. Each tired and grumpy, climbing the Capitol steps before dawn to determine if a drifter was really the 43rd President of the United States.

* * *

Except for Khalil, Sam's guards had stayed behind to brief the authorities.

Billy Louis and four fresh Servant of Allah guards met Sam's car just as it pulled up near the steps of the Capitol building.

A few reporters had heard the Sam Wainwright rumor and were mingling about like pilot fish on a humpback whale.

Billy Louis seemed cocky which made Sam feel uncomfortable. It was as if Ruth Hoffman's death was already forgotten. Well *he* would never forget her death. She had saved his life.

Billy directed the four Servant of Allah guards to circle Sam as he got out of the car.

It was odd to be the center of attention again, Sam thought. Everyone looking at him, trying to think about what he was thinking, and wondering if he really was the 43rd President of the United States or just another Anastasia.

Billy was still beaming when he said, "Your White House Council was also lost in the attack, Mr. President. I've retained counsel for you. I hope you don't mind."

Sam nodded his head and continued to climb the Capitol steps. Moments later he was deluged by dozens of flash bulbs going off at the same time.

Where will this all lead? he thought.

The First Lady was in New York on a shopping trip. Luther Donald was reading in bed when Shelby Mannix knocked on the President's door and sheepishly entered the room.

"You wanted to see me, Mr. President?"

Donald said, "The Attorney General called me just an hour ago. He wants to know what's going on with this memory thing."

Shelby still wasn't sure how much the President wanted to know.

Luther Donald was not pleased with the pregnant pause. "For God's sake, Shelby, tell me."

"Sam Wainwright has no memory of being Eddie O'Hara — his initial cover identity. It's what caused all the problems to begin with, Mr. President. He didn't know he was President."

"You took a sample from him while he was alive, didn't you Shelby?"

"I was responsible, yes."

"Did you have a temporary loss of sanity?"

"At the time it seemed like the best thing to do, Mr. President. He didn't know who he was anyway. There is no trail to me if that's what you mean."

"We handled this matter very badly, Shelby."

"You knew nothing, sir."

"Wainwright has his memory back, I understand."

"It was bound to happen, but he doesn't have a clue what happened to him as Eddie O'Hara."

"My Presidency may be lost, Shelby."

Shelby lowered his head.

"I'll be direct this time. When did you know Sam Wainwright was alive?"

"A few weeks after you took office, Mr. President."

"Yes, you did say that."

Shelby could see that the President was trying to get his ducks in order, not sure himself what he should know, and not know.

"So there's no conspiracy?"

"Not at all, sir."

"And you'll testify that you did everything on your own volition?"

"If need be — anything — in fact, to save your Presidency, Mr. President."

"We may go down the shit-shoot on this one, Shelby, do you understand?"

"He will never become President again, Mr. President. Never, I can assure you of that."

Luther Donald studied Shelby for a moment. "I'm inviting Sam Wainwright over for breakfast after he testifies. It's the least I can do. It will show I'm not concerned about my job. "

Shelby blanched. "Whatever you do, Mr. President, please don't acknowledge his identity in a formal setting. They may never come up with conclusive proof — I've seen to that."

Luther Donald looked at Shelby, skeptically.

"He's alive, Shelby. That's the problem."

"We underestimated him, sir."

"Maybe it's for the best."

Shelby stood mute.

In a dismissive tone, Luther Donald said, "Goodnight, Shelby. Or should I say good morning?"

Shelby gave Luther Donald one final look before leaving. The pain and disorientation of Sam Wainwright appearing before Congress was obvious in the President's face. He felt that he had put a gun to the President's head and pulled the trigger. It was an awful feeling.

CHAPTER 56

Instead of returning to his Watergate apartment, Shelby went to his cramped office space in the temporary White House and pondered his next move. There really was no way out, he determined. The damage had been done and there would be more problems, perhaps enough to drive Luther Donald from office.

It really was a question of honor to even consider what he was thinking. It wasn't as if he would benefit in any way. Perhaps only a person like himself could end Sam Wainwright's life. Certainly the New Orleans people didn't understand a man like Wainwright. He was not a good politician and that's what made him so dangerous. His immediate elimination, while there was so much doubt about him, would create a gray area, a not-so-sure area, cloud his existence really, no matter how convincing his testimony to the subcommittee was, Shelby concluded. Certainly, the Republican Party would remain unconvinced — at least for the public record. It was that damn 25th Amendment. It hadn't covered all the bases.

Shelby Mannix turned his swivel chair in a circle like a child would, got up, and walked in the corridor until he was in front of the President's temporary office. He thought about the President having Wainwright over for breakfast. Giving Wainwright the benefit of the doubt would look good in the press and keep that 25th Amendment business in tow. Luther Donald was no fool that was for sure.

Shelby looked around. At this hour of the morning the White House was empty of staff including the Secret Service who were upstairs near the President but not conspicuous. The grounds, after all, were heavily guarded by the Navy.

Shelby opened the door to the President's office. No matter what they did with it, it would never look presidential. Luther Donald had gotten the short stick.

Shelby looked at the replicas of the Aaron Burr and Alexander Hamilton dueling pistols on the wall. Few but himself knew that these replicas were capable of firing real bullets. What's more, they were loaded just in case of an emergency. Luther Donald wanted it that way. All Presidents, he suspected, had some sort of escape plan in mind that they never bothered to tell anyone about, particularly the Secret Service. Eisenhower, he remembered being told, always had a parachute on Air Force One although he was told it would be useless at the height he was flying.

Shelby had to stand on the chair to reach the weapons. *The Burr replica will do nicely,* he thought.

The number of spectators around Sam Wainwright seemed to increase as he was led down the halls of the Capitol building. Finally, in a room that seemed as far away from the House Chamber as you could get, he was led into a cramped hearing room that appeared to have little official use. The front of the room was elevated as if it had served as a small stage at one time. The twelve members of the subcommittee peered down at Sam's table. An African-American lawyer introduced himself. "Lawrence White, Mr. President, I'm here to plead your case. Billy Louis has filled me in on everything."

"Have you appeared before Congress much, Lawrence?"

"First time, Mr. President."

"Can we prove who I am?"

"Billy has done a good job for you, Mr. President. I even have the temperature of your stool samples."

"DNA profile?"

"We're working on that one, Mr. President. So far no luck. It's one of our *bones of contention*, so to speak. What the hell happened to your samples at the National Naval Medical Center in Bethesda, Maryland, anyway? But Billy's on it. We'll get something. Looks like they're ready to begin."

The twelve House members peered down at Sam who was dressed in jeans, work boots, and a denim shirt. He could see most of the Congressmen were incredulous, even two members of his party whom he was acquainted with did not recognize him. Billy was at the far end of the dais, pensive but determined looking. The air conditioning was unusually loud.

Shelby Mannix, carrying a brief case and well-known to the Capitol guards, slipped into the room without being searched.

The Chairman, a Republican from Oregon, was obviously in a foul mood.

"This was supposed to be an informal hearing, but I can see that the vultures are perched on their high wires already," he growled, throwing a hard glance at a pool of reporters, then banging his gavel, his face showing distaste for the whole proceeding.

"The subcommittee will come to order. We convene today at this ungodly hour to hear evidence that supposedly contradicts what we have been previously led to believe. I understand there is a person in this room claiming to be Sam Wainwright, the 43rd President of the United States. He is, I'm informed, being represented by Lawrence White."

Despite the hour, the room was crowded with Congressional staff members making sure they were noticed by their bosses on the dais.

"Who the hell is Lawrence White?" Sam heard one of the Congressmen mumble.

However, to Sam's surprise, White had been well-briefed by Billy Louis. White spoke for nearly an hour on behalf of Sam Wainwright, going over each point of his argument like a farmer familiar with every inch of land that was ripe for cultivation.

White saved Sam's finger for last, but was careful not to implicate anyone at this point, particularly the sitting President.

Sam could hear the murmur in the hearing room. They hadn't expected to hear such a logical argument on behalf of a man who looked like he belonged in a homeless shelter. Sam could see that by the puzzled looks on their faces.

Finally, Lawrence White walked over to Sam, and placed his hand on Sam's shoulder. "Mr. President, if you'll hold up your left hand."

Sam did. The missing pinkie was apparent.

There was a gasp unlike Sam had ever heard inside the beltway.

The Chairman banged the gavel a number of times. Sam could sense the Congressman had convinced himself not to be convinced by any testimony.

"A remarkable tale, Mr. White. Is there factual evidence to support what you've just said. I look out and I see a man who claims to be the 43rd President of the United States, and I see someone I do not recognize."

The Congressman gave Sam a hard look. "Can you speak, sir? Or are you mute as well?"

"I can," said Sam. "Well enough to say that everything that Mr. White has stated about me is true."

"Yet your face, and now your voice, are unrecognizable to me."

"The face for obvious reasons, Mr. Chairman. The voice because of the wiring in my jaw."

"And your DNA profile for comparison?"

"Coming," interjected White.

One of the Republicans on the committee, a man who owed his power in the House to Luther Donald, said, "Sir, if you are Sam Wainwright as you claim to be, you are only the former President of the United States."

Billy Louis shot out, "My distinguished colleagues damn well know why we're here. If the man seated before us is Sam Wainwright, then the Presidency of Luther Donald is null and void in that we have evidence that his office knew Sam Wainwright was alive and did not inform the Congress. We can argue the technical points all day, but the Presidency was assumed under a lie — that is what prevails."

"He had no memory of being President," shouted a Republican from the far end of the dais.

From that moment on it was like cats and dogs. Sam could see the Republicans had let Billy take the first salvo so they could have an excuse to disrupt things.

Shelby Mannix could feel the shame rush into his face as the Chairman pounded the gavel for order and finally called an end to the hearing.

Not now, Shelby thought, *not in front of all these people. I can't do it here, but I must do it.*

CHAPTER 57

Seated in a bright, almost cheerful dining room, Luther Donald had little doubt that the man sitting down in front of him was Sam Wainwright, even if he looked like a mechanic. Thirty-five years of sizing up people had served Donald well.

They were sharing a breakfast of orange juice, bagels, and coffee. Donald said to Sam, "I've always felt that you were unfinished business, Mr. President. My party will be upset with my seeing you — I know this — but it's the right thing to do. I can assure you, Mr. President, I had no knowledge that you were alive, much less subjected to the awful things your lawyer had testified to. Nor do I have any knowledge of your medical records disappearing. I have to assume, however, that someone around me has not served me well."

Sam had always disliked Luther Donald, but he tried to remain calm. It seemed in this temporary White House, and in this temporary dining area, Luther Donald also seemed very temporary, but he was well acquainted with the fact that Luther Donald always had an agenda.

"But to be frank, Mr. President, you don't stand a chance of ever assuming this office again. My question is why would you want it anyway; my understanding is you thought the job sucked."

Sam reflected on Luther Donald's words for a moment. "I was wrong. I see how much has to be done, how much an honest man can do."

Sam could see by Donald's face that he didn't like his response.

"Then I'm forced to play hardball, President Wainwright. The mere fact that you couldn't perform your duties as President after the attack puts you out of the picture. Your own leader of the House, Jim Finny, is behind me on this as well."

Sam had expected as much. He looked into Donald's eyes and said, "Mr. President, Ruth Hoffman, who worked for Shelby Mannix, and is now dead, believed that Shelby was trying to have me killed. So do I. On a legal note, if he had knowledge of my being alive while you were serving as President, I believe that would create a serious problem for you."

Sam could see the veins forming on Donald's face.

"I had no knowledge. That's what's important."

"My understanding is, it doesn't work that way, Mr. President. It's a *prima facie* case. You have to prove you didn't know."

Sam studied Donald's face. He could see the defeat in it, concealed, but evident.

Sam continued, "The matter has to go back to Congress. That's my understanding, President Donald."

Sam now suspected that Luther Donald had known about Eddie O'Hara almost from the beginning.

He watched Luther Donald get to his feet and walk to his window appearing to be interested in his uneventful view.

"The process will destroy the country, Sam. I don't want that, and I believe you don't want that either."

Sam got up and walked to the window as well. Placing his arm around Donald, he said, "If that begins to happen, I'll back off."

Donald, with a look of surprise said, "You mean that, Sam?"

"Yes, Mr. President, I do."

"You're a better man than I," said Donald, his face relaxed for the first time that morning.

As aides who've worked in the White House will tell you, there are no hard and fast rules on how many times a trusted aide can approach the President before being above suspicion. It's plainly clear to every Secret Service detail who the President feels comfortable with, and who he doesn't feel comfortable with. Frisking trusted aides at the entrance to the Oval Office is not desired by the President, or the Secret Service. Which is why Shelby, still carrying his briefcase, waved to the Secret Service detail as he entered the dining area. Shelby Mannix, of course, was above suspicion.

Both Presidents, still at the window, were surprised to see Shelby, and suddenly uncomfortable as well. An orderly was clearing the table. Shelby waited patiently for the orderly to leave, then said, "I've thought about it Mr. President. There's really only one way to settle matters. It's plain to me now."

"You can relax, Shelby. I think Sam and I have a good understanding now."

"I don't think so, sir. You're losing the Presidency because of me. That's what those liberals will do. They'll pull your Presidency right out from under you like a rug. Their heart is only in politics, not what's best for this country — I got this from your office, Mr. President."

Shelby pulled out the Burr replica from his case.

"As the President of the United States I'm ordering you to put that weapon down," said Donald hoping the Secret Service would hear him, but suspecting they wouldn't. He had already told them that discussions with his breakfast visitor were going to be highly sensitive and to give him some room.

Sam knew he had to make a move, but Shelby was watching him closely.

Shelby, holding the *Burr* replica close to his body so no one could see it, said, "You can get a pretty accurate round from this replica. Did you know that, Mr. President? Yes, you did. You always have the last laugh. My military training at the Citadel will finally pay off. Ironic, isn't it?"

Shelby turned the weapon towards Sam Wainwright and aimed.

"Shelby don't," said Luther Donald.

Sam had not expected it, would never have guessed it, and was startled when it happened, but Luther Donald jumped in front of him and took the bullet.

Later some cynics would say that Luther Donald had no faith in the replica being accurate and had been grandstanding.

By the time Luther Donald fell to the ground, mortally wounded, Shelby Mannix was being torn to shreds by Secret Service gunfire.

CHAPTER 58

Luther Donald's body was still warm when Lawrence White, Sam's lawyer, submitted a written declaration signed by Sam Wainwright to the President Pro tempore of the Senate and the Speaker of the House. It stated that no inability existed for Sam Wainwright to serve as President of the United States.

This clearly blocked the Vice President's nomination to even Acting President and kicked into action the clause in the 25th Amendment that said, "Congress shall decide the issue."

Twenty-one days later, Luther Donald's appointment as President of the United States was vacated.

Sam Wainwright, in an exchange of power that could only happen in America, walked into the former office of the Vice President and assumed his role again as President without even being sworn in.

Three weeks later, right hand on his heart, Sam Wainwright stood at attention at the ground-breaking ceremony for the new White House. He knew that America deserved a better man than he had been. And this time they would get him.

This time there really would be a new President in the White House.

Printed in the United States
25821LVS00004B/220

9 781413 719581